A₂

THE SEARCH FOR LOVE

THE SEARCH FOR LOVE

Claire Lorrimer

CHIVERS
THORNDIKE

This Large Print book is published by BBC Audiobooks Ltd, Bath, England and by Thorndike Press®, Waterville, Maine, USA.

Published in 2004 in the U.K. by arrangement with the author.

Published in 2004 in the U.S. by arrangement with Claire Lorrimer.

U.K. Hardcover   ISBN 0–7540–9927–X (Chivers Large Print)
U.K. Softcover   ISBN 0–7540–9928–8 (Camden Large Print)
U.S. Softcover   ISBN 0–7862–6494–2 (General)

Originally published 1959 in Great Britain as *Lonely Quest* by Patricia Robins.

The sonnet 'The Penalty of Love' by Sidney Lysaght is reproduced by kind permission of Macmillan and Company Limited.

The text of this Large Print edition is unabridged.
Other aspects of the book may vary from the original edition.

Set in 16 pt. New Times Roman.

Printed in Great Britain on acid-free paper.

British Library Cataloguing in Publication Data available

Library of Congress Control Number: 2004101137

CHAPTER ONE

1955

Beverly replaced the tin of talcum powder on the bathroom shelf and had already half turned on her heel to hurry downstairs when she caught sight of her reflection in the mirror above the basin. She frowned and suddenly looked at herself with more than the usual glance. What she saw shocked her and added quickly to the day's growing depression.

I look a sight! she thought, touching the tip of her shiny *retroussé* nose, then trying ineffectually to tidy the mop of dark hair that seemed to be straggling rather than curling over her forehead. Her mouth gave her no encouragement either. Over large, it looked its best brightly outlined with lipstick and with her lips smiling and upturned at the corners. But now it grimaced at her from the looking-glass and her eyes lifted swiftly away from this feature to stare directly into themselves. Green eyes, beautiful eyes, Jonnie called them, fringed with dark curling lashes, but now red-rimmed from a bad night's sleep and ringed with violet shadows and tiny lines of fatigue.

Her expression became defiant.

'It's not my fault! When have I time to get

my hair done? See to my make-up? My clothes?'

She looked away from the mirror and down at her none-too-clean tweed slacks and slightly too tight twin-set. The slacks needed pressing and she needed a new jersey—three new jerseys, come to that. But there wasn't time or money to cope with these things.

It's not my fault! she repeated silently, but it was to her mother she was really speaking in her mind. Only last weekend Mummy had torn strips off her for going around looking the way she did.

'It's so *unlike* you, Beverly! You were always the fastidious one, the most fussy, most clothes-conscious, of my two daughters. And look at yourself! I can't think how you can bear to have Jonnie see you this way!'

'Oh, he doesn't notice,' Beverly had replied vaguely. 'And, anyway, I haven't time nowadays. Nor would you if you had five young children to care for and no money!'

Of course, that had been Mrs Bampton's cue to restart the old argument about Beverly and Jonnie taking a small allowance from her. She could well afford it, as they both knew. But Jonnie was proud. He hadn't forgotten that Beverly's mother had tried to prevent their marrying. 'Far too young,' she had said, 'and Jonnie hasn't sufficient money to support you the way you've been used to, Beverly.'

'Seventeen isn't young these days, Mummy.

And, besides, Jonnie's boss has promised him a rise next year. You just haven't any faith in Jonnie or in me. Because you've always given me everything, you think I can't do without it. Well, I'd rather have Jonnie and do without the so-called luxuries.'

In the end Beverly and Jonnie had won over Mrs Bampton, and, although she still maintained they were too young, once she had given in she had been very nice about everything, giving them the house as a wedding present and Beverly a magnificent and sensible trousseau. Really, Beverly hadn't had any new clothes since then, and it had turned out to be just as well she'd had such a large trousseau, for they couldn't afford luxuries like new clothes on their budget. With the ever-rising cost of living, even Jonnie's payrise hadn't helped, except to keep them out of debt. And Jonnie wouldn't accept a shilling-piece from his mother-in-law. Deep inside her, Beverly agreed. It was a question of pride, hers as well as Jonnie's. They'd said they would manage and they would! All the same, it was a terrible struggle and seeing herself now in the glass Beverly realized for the first time just how badly that struggle was showing.

It wasn't just herself—it was all over the house. They couldn't afford to have the sitting-room carpet cleaned this year and it looked spotty and shabby. They hadn't been able to buy new bathroom curtains; the children's clothes were patched and darned and nothing matched. It was the same with the china . . . all odds and ends because they no longer had a full set of anything.

They might have managed pretty well if it hadn't been for the children. Beverly could admit this to herself, though not to anyone else—least of all to her mother.

Nicky had been the first; they hadn't planned to have Nicky but he'd come along all the same exactly nine months after their honeymoon. She'd just had her eighteenth birthday when the baby was born. Although they had meant to wait a few years before they took on the responsibility of a family, they'd none the less been thrilled and happy about Nicky and with the very young's adaptability had reversed all their original ideas and decided to have the family first and a good time afterwards.

Jonnie had agreed whole-heartedly after the first surprise and delight in finding himself a father. Nicky had been such a good baby and they'd hardly noticed the extra expense at first. One of Beverly's aunts had given them a pram, her elder sister, Pam, a cot and baby bath and most of the larger items like a playpen which her own two children had outgrown.

'Let's have another, soon!' Jonnie had said. 'It's nice to have two boys growing up near to each other in age.'

So eighteen months later Philip had been

born—the brother they had wanted for Nick.

The second baby had somehow seemed to affect their finances more than the first. Maybe because they'd worked out on paper that he wouldn't cost anything. In theory he should not have done. He had all Nick's things to grow into. Yet in practice they began to find themselves really hard up.

'I hope that's an end to it!' Mrs Bampton had said firmly.

Beverly eyed her mother stubbornly. Privately, she thought they wouldn't have any more children—not yet awhile anyway. But Mrs Bampton's remark somehow seemed like a challenge, a doubting of hers and Jonnie's capabilities.

'Why not, Mummy? Jonnie and I would both like a daughter.' Her mother's shocked reply strengthened Beverly's belief that a daughter was now the most desirable thing in the world to have.

'Besides,' she argued, 'it wouldn't be fair to have one child all by itself, say, in five years' time. It would be almost as bad for it as being an only child.'

Twelve months after Philip, Julia completed the family. This time, Mrs Bampton knew better than to discuss any possibility of adding to the numbers. She didn't need to. Beverly had her hands full with three children under four and even an outsider could see how precarious were the young couple's finances.

Mrs Bampton was a widow, still young and extremely smart in her appearance. She needed to be for she was quite a personality in the fashion world where she had gone into business on the death of her husband ten years previously. Mr Bampton had left her very well provided for, but with her two daughters away at boarding school, she felt the need for some occupation and with her good dress sense, her social contacts and natural head for business matters, she had quickly risen to a position of authority in the fashion house who had given her a job.

Now she was by way of being very well off. Both her daughters were married and she had only her smart little London flat to keep up. There was more than sufficient money for her to have given Jonnie and Beverly a helping hand in the way of a regular allowance. But they wouldn't take it. Secretly, she admired them both for their spirit of independence, but she could not see that it *could* continue. Granted Beverly was nearly twenty-one and would come into an income from her father's legacy of a hundred and fifty pounds a year. Jonnie had eight hundred a year which was pretty good for a boy of twenty-three. All the same, they were five in the family now and neither Jonnie nor Beverly were really *trained* to manage economically. Jonnie had never considered giving up his Aston Martin sports car, nor his membership at the golf club—not that the latter cost him so much, but naturally he had to spend a bit of money at the club, rounds of drinks in return to those who treated him. And they liked to entertain, to offer their friends gin, whisky, sherry. It was important, too, for Jonnie to look smart at his work, and he had a new suit every year, tailored for him. No wonder they were poor! And Beverly might blame her appearance on her lack of time to see to herself, but the fact remained that more money could have bought Beverly a little domestic help and more time; not to mention clothes.

Then it had happened! Not intentionally—even Mrs Bampton had no doubt that they'd meant to confine their family to three children. But all the same, Beverly had found she was going to have another baby, and even her bravado had been finally shaken when later on an X-ray confirmed that 'it' would be 'they'—she was to have twins!

It was plain bad luck, Mrs Bampton said, but Beverly, after the first shock, had refused ever to allow her mother to call her two new babies 'bad luck'. She loved them, even while she resented deep down inside her the hopeless mess they were slowly but surely making of her life. She loved all five of her children when she had time and wasn't too worn out with the domestic chores to even think of them as individuals.

I look worn out! she told herself now,

turning away from the glass with tears of self-pity filling her eyes and spilling down her cheeks. And no wonder! Just look what my days are like!

She was up at six every morning, feeding the twins, then getting the other three children dressed and breakfasted with Jonnie so that he could be away by eight. By the time he'd left the house, she felt she'd done a day's work already! But the day had only started. There was the twins' mid-morning bath and feed to interrupt the mountain of washing and the housework. There was lunch to get, to be washed up, the twins to be fed again at two while the other children rested. Then ironing, or mending, tea, and the bedtime rush and scramble with the twins' evening feed and then Jonnie's supper. Granted, Jonnie helped all he could; he did shopping in his lunch hour, and as soon as he was home he took over the washing-up, the fires, the wood cutting, the coke and coal hauling. He even gave the twins their late-night feed.

But he wasn't home all the time. He had the supreme advantage of being able to get away from it five days a week for eight hours a day, and he had his golf every Sunday morning.

How she resented that golf.

'But, darling, I must have a few hours off in a week,' he had answered her request to him to give it up.

'And when do I get any rest?'

'Well, you can put your feet up every Sunday afternoon,' he'd suggested. 'I'll mind the kids.'

But of course it didn't work. How could she go to her bed and lie down and enjoy an hour or two with a book, knowing how hard she would have to work to make up for all the jobs not done while she had her rest? After the first try she'd given it up.

The continual round, day in, day out, had begun to tell on her nerves. Jonnie had suffered, for her temper became short and irritable. After their first, blazing quarrel, she had lain in their big double bed, sobbing in his arms.

'Look, darling, the trouble obviously is that you don't have enough fun. Neither do I, come to that. Do you realize we haven't been out dancing for a whole year? From now on we're going to go out once a week, without fail. We'll shut the door behind us and go out and enjoy ourselves.'

'But we can't afford it!' Beverly wailed.

'Yes we can. We must! We won't go anywhere expensive. Leave it to me.'

The first time had been wonderful. Until six o'clock next morning when Beverly realized that a late night, several drinks when you're not used to them, and four hours' dancing are not a good prelude to a heavy day's work beginning at six in the morning.

The night out had become fortnightly, then

9

monthly, and finally ceased altogether. Slowly but surely, the days, weeks, months went by, and now, suddenly, Beverly realized that she looked more like a woman of forty than of twenty-five. She was shocked, depressed, and suddenly wildly angry with Jonnie . . . with life. Between them they had cheated her out of all the fun a young girl should have had. It wasn't even as if she and Jonnie were madly in love any more.

This, really, was the key to her discontent. Whilst they loved one another, all the hard work, the economizing, the doing-without, had been worth while. Now, quite suddenly, overnight, it wasn't worth while any more.

But I do still love Jonnie, I *do*! Beverly argued with herself. But in her heart, she was forced to admit that love seemed to have flown out of the window. Granted, she and Jonnie still shared the big double bed, but they no longer slept in each other's arms. Only occasionally did Jonnie's arms reach out for her, and recently she had steeled herself against her natural inclination to be loved by him. Resentment stopped her. Jonnie couldn't expect to have it all ways. If he couldn't be bothered any more to kiss her when he came home at night or when he went off in the morning; if he never had time to pay her a compliment or bring her some little surprise, then he had no right to claim her body just because he suddenly felt in the mood.

Gradually, even that had stopped and they lived like strangers who happened to share the same bed, the same house, the same children and nothing else.

Downstairs, Beverly could hear one of the children crying. It sounded like Philip. He cried easily and noisily but it was never for long. Julia, once she started, could go on for hours, but at least she sobbed quietly, to herself.

Let him yell! Beverly thought rebelliously. It's just what I feel like doing.

As she went into the kitchen to put the kettle on for one of her never-ending pots of tea, she knew that at long last she was beginning to weaken. Hitherto, she had been heart and soul with Jonnie about accepting financial help from her mother. But the moment came, she told herself, when the camel's back was broken, and that was how she felt this morning. A pound or two a week would give Beverly some domestic help, and her mother had said a thousand times that *she* wouldn't miss it. After all, why should she go on wearing herself literally to the point of a breakdown just to bolster Jonnie's pride? He should see for himself that his wife had far, far too much to do. Every one of their friends seemed staggered to find she *could* cope, even though Nicky had started school. A daily help two or three hours a day. What an incredible difference it could make to her life! Jonnie ought to see that it wasn't fair to put his pride before her health. Tonight she would tell him so outright, to his face.

A little strengthened by the cup of tea and by her own new-found determination to remake her life, Beverly turned to the pile of washing. As she worked, her mind ran on, planning swiftly and with some of her old quick enthusiasm. With a daily help, she could get out to the hairdresser occasionally and have her hair done . . . it needed it so badly. She might even save up for a new dress. There would be time at last to sort out her things and give herself a few beauty treatments. Soon Jonnie would begin to notice the difference and he would fall in love with her all over again. It was his indifference that hurt so much.

Of course I do still love him, Beverly told herself by lunchtime. I'll always love Jonnie, all my life. It's just that we've grown apart . . . we are not the same two people who fell in love with each other. Jonnie's never fun the way he used to be. But we'll be able to get back to being ourselves.

By the time Jonnie came home, Beverly looked a very different girl from the wife who usually greeted him. She had found a moment to brush out her thick dark hair . . . to powder her nose and put on some fresh lipstick. She had even changed out of her slacks into a dress. Because her thoughts had carried her so far ahead of Jonnie in her planning of the future, she was totally unprepared for the fact that it was the same Jonnie who had left the house eight hours earlier. He glanced at her briefly and said:

'Oh lord, Beverly, we haven't got people coming in, have we? I wanted to go through my accounts tonight.'

Hurt by his tone as much as by his failure to kiss her, Beverly turned away from him and said coldly:

'No, no one is coming. Tonight is just the same as any other night.'

'Then why all the dressing-up?' Jonnie said, but without waiting for her answer: 'Supper ready? I'm hungry.'

Beverly controlled herself with an effort. Jonnie was always hungry and until he had eaten, it was best to let all she had to say to him wait. Silently, she dished up the supper and silently they sat opposite one another eating. Dutifully, Jonnie helped her with the dishes and then left her to make coffee. When she took the tray into the drawing-room, he was already buried in a mound of papers.

'Jonnie, I want to talk to you,' she began as she handed him his coffee. He didn't look up, but said:

'Not now, Bev. I'm busy.'

'Yes, now,' Beverly said, her voice suddenly sharp and angry. 'And you know I hate you calling me Bev. It sounds like that bottled coffee or whatever it is.'

Jonnie made no reply, and Beverly felt anger rising in her. How unfair Jonnie was— how rude to her these days. All he could think of was his work. A year or two ago he had come in about six and given her a hand with the children before supper. Now he was never in before seven and sometimes it was eight or nine. At least when he did get back he could pay her a little attention.

'Jonnie!' He looked up, his broad forehead creased in a frown of irritation. Beneath the forehead, the bright blue of his eyes stared at her with no love in them. There were lines beneath them that Beverly hadn't really noticed before—lines of worry and fatigue that maybe shouldn't be on the face of a man still in his twenties. Beverly's anger drained away as suddenly as it had come. Impulsively, she knelt down on the floor and leant her head on his knees.

'Darling, please listen,' she said, her voice now soft and appealing. 'It's something to do with us—with our life . . .'

'With us?' Jonnie's voice was sharp, questioning. She had his attention now—all of it.

'Yes! Jonnie, I've been thinking all day about—well—about the life I lead . . . you lead—both of us, and how everything seems to be a bit on top of us. It's true, and you can't deny it,' she added as she heard him draw in

14

his breath sharply as if he might have been going to contradict her. 'Jonnie, I want you to let me accept Mother's offer to help out a bit. I know how much you feel we *should* manage without, but it wouldn't be because of any failure on your side—it's me. I just can't cope. I get tired and irritable with the children, and I look a sight. Just a couple of pounds a week would make all the difference to all of us. You do see that, don't you?'

Jonnie let his breath out slowly. 'I suppose you really mean you want me to give up the club?'

Beverly turned her head so that she could look at him fully, but his eyes dropped and he did not hold her glance.

'No, Jonnie. I don't think that. I think you should have at least one pleasure outside your home. It isn't any reflection on you. It's just that it would make life easier and happier for me if you'll let me take something from Mother.'

Surprisingly, staggeringly, Jonnie said briefly: 'OK! If that's what you want. I don't mind.'

Beverly was too astonished to reply—even to thank him.

'Then . . . then you really don't mind?' she repeated.

'Not if it will make you happier.'

Beverly reached out her arms to fling them round her husband, but his lap was covered by files and letters and somehow he did not seem to notice the gesture. Slowly, her arms fell to her sides and Beverly felt a little of her triumph subside. She had been all prepared to talk Jonnie round and there wasn't any need. Maybe that was why she felt this anti-climax.

'Are you going to have to work long?' she asked.

'At least a couple of hours,' he replied briefly, already back in his books again.

'Then I'll do some ironing,' Beverly said, sensibly but without enthusiasm. 'Try and hurry up, darling. We might have half an hour's talk before bed.'

But he wasn't listening; she knew his attention had gone before she reached the door. Tiredness hit her with a sudden sharp ache in her back. It had been a long day and a wearisome one. Maybe after all she'd have a bath and go to bed early. It would do her good, and an early night might get rid of some of the shadows beneath her own eyes. Jonnie wasn't the only one to look worn out.

Uncertainly, Beverly walked slowly up the stairs and began to run her bath.

CHAPTER TWO

'It's no good, I can't, Elinor. You just don't understand.'

16

'But, Jonnie, darling, aren't we ever going to have more than a few kisses? Maybe it's enough for you, but I love you. I want more than a flirtation.'

Jonnie looked at the slim but voluptuous woman he held in his arms and abruptly moved away from her. The devil of it was, he too wanted more than a few kisses. Elinor attracted him in a way Beverly had never done. She was made for love and, Jonnie had no doubt, was thoroughly used to being loved. During these two months since he had met her he had known he could sleep with her just whenever he wished. Oh, he wanted to all right, but he hadn't. Loyalty to his wife prevented him.

I ought to stop seeing her, Jonnie thought for the thousandth time. It isn't fair to any of us, and least of all to poor Beverly.

But he couldn't make the break. Once or twice when he had tried, Elinor had quickly reopened the affair, ringing him up at the office, or managing to be at the club when she knew she would be bound to run into him on a Sunday after golf. It wasn't easy saying 'no' to a woman like Elinor. She took it for granted a man wanted her, and she was right to do so. Most of the chaps at the club—the unmarried ones—were after her. And why not? She was a young, rich and very, very attractive American widow. She knew her way around, especially with men. She was lonely and she wanted

Jonnie. It was as simple as that.

'Elinor, it's just no good our letting this flirtation develop. It can only end by hurting everyone . . . you, me and most of all Beverly. You must see that. I can't ever divorce Beverly.'

But she did not seem to understand even then.

'Why not? You say you aren't in love with her any more.'

'But I still love her in a way. I couldn't hurt her,' Jonnie said. 'Besides, even if there weren't Beverly, there are the children. I have five kids, Elinor . . . *five.* And I haven't a penny-piece to my name. I couldn't leave them and I couldn't afford a divorce.'

'OK, so you have five kids. What of it? That's no bar to divorce. We'd be in the dog-house, of course, but we could take that, and as to the money, well, I've got close on half a million dollars, my sweet.'

Jonnie had flinched. Of course, he didn't blame Elinor for feeling the way she did—it was flattering. But he couldn't see it that way. They'd just been brought up differently, that was all. Besides, he wasn't sure he wanted to leave Beverly anyway. Elinor seemed to take it for granted that because he had confessed to being in love with her, he must necessarily have stopped loving Beverly and the children.

'Honey, you can have your cake and eat it!' Elinor's voice broke in on his thoughts. Her arms were round his neck and he could smell her perfume, an exciting, provocative perfume that exactly suited her.

'Nobody can,' Jonnie said gloomily.

'Sure they can! You don't have to divorce your wife if you're so set against it. I'm not the one who suggested it—you brought it up. Why can't we just have fun together, you and I? You've every right to slip away for the odd weekend occasionally; your wife can't expect you to stay put all the time. What are you afraid of, Jonnie? It's so easy!'

'Is it?' Jonnie tried to steel himself against his mounting desire to stop fighting against her and comply with her demands. She might want him but he wanted her just as much. His desire for her was beginning to war with his own innate belief in what was right and wrong. 'Suppose Beverly finds out?'

'Why should she? It's easy enough to find an alibi—golf with a friend, or something. I'll rent a little house at the seaside somewhere and you can run down whenever you can get away. It'ud be such fun, honey . . . just you and me.'

They were in his car, parked in a side lane on the far side of the golf course. Jonnie was ostensibly working late, his unoriginal excuse to Beverly whenever he was stealing an hour or two after office hours with Elinor. Elinor had a small but very luxurious cottage a mile or two away and she wanted him to go back there with her, but he'd always refused. It was too dangerous. Beverly might get to hear of it, and how could he explain what he was doing in Elinor's house when he should have been at the office? Meeting Elinor anywhere was appallingly risky, but she just didn't seem to care. She cared about nothing except him. That was why it was so exciting to be with her. Once he'd meant everything to Beverly, but then the kids had come along and she had always been far too busy for his wants or his needs.

Come to think of it, Jonnie told himself morosely, he'd never really had much fun, getting married so young and with so many responsibilities always. It was enough to make any fellow feel a hundred years old. But with Elinor he felt like a new man. She was so tremendously exhilarating. She had enormous vitality and 'go', a zip which carried him along even when he, too, was tired.

Of course, when their relationship had first begun a few months ago, he'd never meant it to develop into anything serious. She'd caught his eye over a drink at the golf club bar and he'd smiled and she'd called 'Hi!' and suddenly they were talking to each other and finding they had lots of things in common. He'd kept an eye open for her next time he was in the club and, sure enough, she was watching out for him, too, and because his car had a flat tyre, she offered to run him home.

He'd never guessed she meant to stop on

the way. In fact, he'd even been a little shocked when she switched off the engine and turned to him, saying:

'Well, aren't you going to kiss me, Jonnie?'

It would have seemed boorish to refuse. Afterwards, he'd let her go reluctantly and somewhat shamefacedly confessed he was married. Again, Elinor surprised him.

'So what? We haven't committed any crime!'

It was Elinor's utter lack of guilt about their association that made it so difficult for him to sort himself out. One half wanted to stay completely faithful to Beverly, to his own beliefs in what marriage should mean. The other half saw himself through Elinor's eyes and he could see that to her he seemed bourgeois, narrow-minded, far too straight-laced for a man of his years.

Gradually, her influence became stronger as his own desire for her increased. He knew she wanted him to go back to her house and let their love-making go a step further, but somehow he still hadn't been able to do so. There was always Beverly and the children, and he almost hated them for their innocent hold on him. It just wasn't fair. There were plenty of men who had the odd affair on the quiet. Why shouldn't he? Beverly need never know. As Elinor said, there were ways of arranging these things . . . and it could be such fun!

They were back at the point of Elinor's last remark. It would be such fun. It never occurred to Jonnie that this was all Elinor wanted—the excitement of an illicit affair.

Elinor Wilmot was in her early thirties and smart and well groomed. She was essentially feminine and yet there was a hard core in her that paid little regard to the true attributes of femininity; gentleness, tenderness, unselfish love—these were totally absent from her make-up. Love to her meant sex, and sex was as necessary to her as food and drink. There had been plenty of young men before she married and she had not even been faithful to her husband. After he died she decided to make her home in Europe and although Jonnie did not know it, it was an affair with an older man which had first brought her down to this remote part of the country. When she tired of the man, she made up her mind to sell the lease of her cottage and get back to London, but just before she accepted a fairly reasonable offer for the place, she ran into Jonnie.

It hadn't meant much at first; she was attracted to him and she wanted him. But when weeks went by and she still had not been able to get him to do more than kiss her, her casual interest in him was fired into something more—a strong determination to make him put her before anything else. She told the estate agent she had decided not to move

22

anyway until the autumn, and settled down to firing all her guns in Jonnie's direction.

It wasn't difficult for Elinor, who had met Beverly once, to find little ways of running her down.

'She should take a little more trouble with her appearance, my sweet, if she wants to keep an attractive man like you. After all, there's no need to look forty when you're not yet thirty.'

'It isn't really her fault, she's too busy with the house and the children,' Jonnie had tried to defend his young wife. But when he thought about it later, he found himself agreeing with Elinor's point. A woman should always find time to look attractive if she wanted her husband to stay interested in her. Sometimes when he got home Beverly hadn't even bothered to put on any make-up at all. Not that she wasn't pretty in a way without it; she had beautiful eyes and naturally wavy hair. But somehow she wasn't as pretty as she had been when they were first married. He supposed it was make-up that made the all-important difference. He couldn't see that the loveliest eyes, red-rimmed and shadowed with tiredness, would not show their best; nor did wavy hair curl becomingly if it was limp and lifeless from lack of attention.

What has happened to Bev and me? Jonnie thought for the hundredth time. We used to be so crazy about each other. Beverly had been such a darling, so sweet and gentle and loving.

23

Had she really changed so much? Ought he not to try to put their marriage right somehow and not accept Elinor's view that once the gilt had worn off the gingerbread, it couldn't be put back? Once or twice he'd tried to get close to Bev again, tried to make love to her. His pride smarted still under her refusal.

It's her own fault! Jonnie thought bitterly. I wouldn't look twice at Elinor if Beverly really wanted me!

'Say, Jonnie, you haven't said a word in ten minutes. We're wasting all our precious time together, honey.'

Roughly, Jonnie leant across and pulled her back into his arms. He looked into the dark eyes and saw only desire in them . . . desire for him.

His hold on her tightened and his mouth came down on hers, bruising her.

'All right!' he said at last as he pulled away from her embrace. 'All right, but not now, Elinor; not here in a car. I want it to be quite perfect for both of us. We'll fix up something somehow, soon.'

'Soon!' Elinor echoed triumphantly, content to relinquish her immediate need in favour of certainty. To over-persuade Jonnie now might mean to lose him altogether. Tomorrow, she'd try to find a cottage away from this village. It was too near Jonnie's wife for his peace of mind. Once away from Beverly he'd be all hers and that was all she wanted.

CHAPTER THREE

'Well, of course you shall have an allowance, darling. I'm only too glad you've finally come to your senses. We'll see about finding you a good daily help right away.'

Beverly looked at her mother gratefully.

'I did think I might get a foreign girl to live in,' Beverly said hesitantly. She wasn't used to confiding in her mother and now that she wanted to, it didn't come easily.

When Beverly had married Jonnie, she had broken away completely and although Mrs Bampton visited them fairly frequently because she loved her five grandchildren dearly, Beverly had never imagined it was because of *her* her mother came.

She was, in fact, wrong. Mrs Bampton was primarily interested in her daughter's happiness. She did, of course, adore each of her five grandchildren, but it was Beverly she worried about. The eight years of her marriage had wrought a great change in her youngest daughter. She'd lost a stone in weight, had added years to her looks, and the sweet, sunny, gentle disposition was now slightly bitter, irritable, quick-tempered. The once pretty mouth was turned down at the corners and she was far too severe with the children, not to speak of 'short' with Jonnie.

Yet Mrs Bampton could understand why. Beverly had far, far too much to do. Her nerves were in shreds and small wonder. Secretly, Mrs Bampton admired Beverly's courage in having stood out so long against accepting help . . . help that had to come in the end. Maybe if the twins hadn't arrived, she might have managed. But come they had, and only Beverly's stubbornness and pride had prevented her from accepting an allowance before now.

'That's a splendid idea, darling. I know a woman in town with two children. She has a French girl. I think she only has to pay her thirty shillings a week. Her keep shouldn't come to very much since you have seven to feed already.'

Beverly leaned back in the arm-chair and just for a moment closed her eyes. She and her mother had just packed the last of the children into bed and now they were waiting for Jonnie to come home so they could have supper. How she hated cooking! Not that she had always disliked it. Once it had been fun, she and Jonnie doing it together. But since those days there seemed to have been a hundred years of meals to shop for, cook, dish up, eat and clear away. One interminable meal after another, in fact! But soon she would have someone at hand to do the vegetables, wash the dishes. What heaven it would be.

'I'm terribly grateful, Mum!' she said,

26

opening her eyes and smiling at her mother with genuine gratitude. 'I can't think why Jonnie and I didn't agree to it before.'

'Well, dear, it's always nice to be independent if you can, and I admire you both very much for the way you have managed—you especially, Beverly. I never in my wildest dreams imagined you could cope with one child, let alone five, the way you have. But I'm glad you're going to get a girl at last, you look so dreadfully worn out, darling!'

The unexpected and unaccustomed sympathy touched deep down inside some inner core of weakness. Unaccountably, Beverly found herself in tears. A moment later, she was sobbing uncontrollably in her mother's arms. For a few moments Mrs Bampton did not speak, but sensing that Beverly's crying was bordering on hysteria, she became brusque all at once and said:

'Pull yourself together, my poppet. Jonnie will be home soon, won't he, and you don't want him to see you like this!'

Beverly sniffed and then blew hard into the handkerchief her mother pressed into her hand.

'Perhaps it would do him good. I don't think he begins to understand how worn out I am. Oh, I know he works hard—too hard. It's been nothing but one late night at the office after another. All the same, he never thinks of me . . . never even looks at me now. Oh, Mummy, something's gone all wrong between us, and I don't know what it is!'

She hadn't meant to say it . . . to confess to her mother of all people, that she wasn't one hundred per cent happy with her lot. Yet she had to tell someone, and somehow in beginning a simple complaint about her own utter weariness, it had turned into a complaint against her marriage, too—against Jonnie.

Mrs Bampton appeared outwardly calm. Inwardly, she was appalled by what she was hearing. Beverly had always been so insistent about her happiness. Only last week she had waved her goodbye after just such an evening as this, saying brightly:

'I am lucky, aren't I, Mum, to have Jonnie and the kids!'

Personally, she thought Beverly's life was more an ordeal to be endured than to be enjoyed. But then she appreciated that two young people as much in love as Beverly and Jonnie could find happiness even under such circumstances. What had gone wrong, other than the first sweet flush of marriage wearing off? Or was that it?

'Eight years is quite a long while, darling. You can't expect Jonnie to behave the same way now as he did when you were first married. It just doesn't happen that way—with men, anyway. I'm sure Jonnie does understand how tired you are. Why, if he didn't, surely he would not have agreed to your letting me help you a little?'

Beverly sighed. Maybe her mother was right. She had been terribly surprised when Jonnie had said 'yes' to her request, and without even an argument. Perhaps he had noticed her after all. Poor Jonnie; he looked tired, too, and worried. Yet he'd sworn to her all was going well with his work. There was even chance of further promotion next year, and if he made the grade it would be a really good rise in pay.

'Of course, I've got to work for it,' he'd said vaguely. 'I—I might possibly be kept late fairly often at the office. I may not always be able to let you know about supper, I mean, or which train I'm on. Just shove mine in the oven if I'm not home by the usual train and go ahead and eat yours.'

He'd looked almost guilty as he said it, as if he expected her to jump down his throat. Well, maybe she deserved it. She very often did jump at him for nothing at all and he'd probably thought she wouldn't like him being home too late to help her at the children's bedtime. It was true she missed his help. By the end of the day they were all tired and the children could be difficult. Somehow with Jonnie, it was all laughter and fun; he made a game of it and they responded and were quite different with him. The more *she* tried to hurry them, the more maddeningly slow they were. All the same, it was worth it if Jonnie really did get a partnership. The extra two hundred a year would be a godsend.

'Maybe Jonnie and I need a holiday alone together,' Beverly said thoughtfully, remembering a magazine story which had sounded very much like her own life with Jonnie. In the end the couple had left their children with their grandmother and gone on a second honeymoon and fallen in love all over again. 'You know, Mummy, except for that one week at Selsey two years ago, we've never had a holiday since our honeymoon.'

'Well, dear, once you get your help settled in and are quite sure you can trust her, why don't you and Jonnie go off together for a few days? I think it's a splendid idea. In fact, I'd been wondering what to give you for your birthday next month. Suppose I give you a cheque instead of a present. It would help towards your expenses, wouldn't it?'

Beverly smiled. 'It's very generous of you, Mummy. And this time, I'm not going to refuse. I think Jonnie and I both need to get away. Of course, he won't like the thought that you're paying for it.'

'My dear, don't be so silly as to say where the money is coming from. There are some things best kept from one's husband, you know, and I think this is one little secret you and I could keep to ourselves.'

'But he knows I haven't any money of my own.'

'Well, say you have saved a little each week from your house-keeping—he won't question it; or that you've sold some of the children's old clothes.'

Beverly looked at her mother in astonishment. 'Mummy, *you* telling *me* to tell lies? I can't believe it!'

Mrs Bampton smiled. 'Not real lies, dear, just fibs. They're permissible to save Jonnie's face, for I know he is fearfully proud about taking help from me. I'm afraid that is my fault, too, for the way I once talked to him. Perhaps this way I can make amends. You see, if I hadn't been quite so scathing about the possibility of his supporting you when he asked my permission for you to be married, maybe you wouldn't have had to go so long without help, and then maybe you and Jonnie wouldn't have—well, grown a little apart. You know, dear, it stands to reason that love and poverty just don't go together; they never will. I'm not saying you have to be rich to be happy, far from it. But you must have enough to enable you to have a little time free for being together, for keeping your love fresh.'

'I think you're right,' Beverly said. 'All the same, I don't like the idea of leaving the children with a young girl. I'd never trust her, however capable she was.'

'But you'd trust me, and I'd come down and stay here the week you were away. I'd enjoy it. I haven't been able to suggest it before because I don't pretend I could do all you do and last even a day. But with the girl here to do the fetching and carrying, I'd manage the children quite well.'

'Mummy, you're an angel!' Beverly cried, flinging herself upon her mother and hugging her in a way she had not done since she was a young child. 'Oh, I do wish Jonnie would hurry up and come home so I can tell him!'

But although they waited another half-hour, Jonnie still had not arrived, so they had their own meal and put the casserole back in the oven.

CHAPTER FOUR

Spring had come, and with it Beverly had felt an increasing restlessness. She found she could no longer concentrate on the day-to-day routine and that her mind wandered away thinking and planning her week's holiday. Of course, she had a little more time for daydreaming since Annette had arrived. Annette was nineteen, French, and very pretty. Beverly had liked her enormously from the first moment they had met three months ago. Since then the young girl, inexperienced though she was, had become Beverly's right hand. She no longer knew how she had ever managed without her. Not the least of

Annette's assets was her wonderful way with the children. They all adored her, and they all behaved far better with her than with their own mother.

If Beverly had been a little more self-opinionated, she might even have felt jealous of Annette's endless qualities! No matter what she was asked to do, the young French girl did it, efficiently, coolly, calmly and with a smile.

'I don't know how you stay so calm!' Beverly had once said to her. Annette smiled, and in her very halting English, replied that this was her nature.

Questioned as to his feelings about their young 'help', Jonnie had been satisfactorily indifferent. 'She seems a nice kid,' he'd said briefly.

'Don't you think she's pretty, Jonnie?' It had been pure feminine jealousy that had prompted this question and Beverly waited a little anxiously for Jonnie's reply.

'Pretty? I suppose she is. I never really noticed. Not my type, though—too insipid!'

It was true, in a way, Beverly had to admit. There was nothing glowing or vital or exciting about Annette. She was pale-complexioned, fair-haired, her eyes a light misty blue. But perhaps this very 'paleness' detracted from her sex-appeal, at least, in Jonnie's eyes. None the less, Beverly thought her both pretty and sweet, and was doubly grateful for the fact that she wasn't Jonnie's type.

'Not that I'm the jealous kind, Mummy,' Beverly had related this episode to her mother. 'At least, I don't think so. But I did wonder rather if I'd been a bit silly having so pretty a girl living in the house right under Jonnie's nose.'

Mrs Bampton had smiled. 'Of course, you're jealous, darling. Anyone with any real depth of feeling is jealous. That doesn't mean they don't control their feelings. If you weren't jealous of Jonnie, I would really be worried about you both. Anyway, you needn't worry about Annette. I'm so pleased she is such a success. What about that holiday you and Jonnie are going to have?'

'I think I'll plan it all and then just tell him about it when it's all fixed,' Beverly said, musing.

'But suppose he can't get off work at the last moment?'

'I know he can get off in May,' Beverly replied triumphantly. 'He was talking about it the other night. He said he had a week's leave due and that he wished he could get off somewhere for a bit of golf. I thought I'd try to find some little hotel on the south coast near a golf course. I might even take my clubs and play, too. That's been the whole trouble with us, Mummy. We just haven't been able to do things together.'

Now it was all arranged, and Beverly was excited and happy anticipating the week away with Jonnie. She meant to tell him tonight . . . put the letter from the hotel finalizing their bookings in front of him and say:

'It's all arranged, darling. The first week in May.'

He'd have a whole month in which to fix his leave to coincide with her arrangements. Her mother had long since promised to be away from her work that week and Annette was more than capable of managing the children with her mother's assistance. Nothing could go wrong, unless Jonnie couldn't get away.

Staring out over the heads of the yellow daffodils bordering the lawn, Beverly suddenly shivered. Maybe she'd been wrong to spring this as a surprise. Suppose Jonnie had something special coming up at the office which would prevent him getting away?

Then she saw Annette come towards the house pushing the twins' pram, Julia running behind her, her rosy face alight with laughter. She was calling something to Annette but Beverly couldn't catch the words—only the happiness on this glorious April day. Her own spirits soared upwards again.

It was going to be all right. She and Jonnie would have their second honeymoon, just as she had dreamed and schemed and planned.

How like Jonnie Julia was growing. The same springy corn-coloured hair, the same eager eyes and firm set of the jaw. She could be very stubborn, but mostly she was an easy-going placid little girl with a great deal of charm; a child everyone loved. Philip was thinner, wirier, not unlike herself at the same age. Or so her mother kept saying. He was always right up or right down; he felt things keenly and his childish disappointments were tragedies just as his happiness at other times was pure golden joy. Yet he seemed popular enough with the other children at his nursery school. He was like her, in temperament, anyway. It seemed she was herself right up or right down and the pendulum could swing one way or the other in no more than a minute.

Well, at the moment, it was right up. She was happy . . . happy . . . happy! Glad to be alive on this lovely day, glad to be the mother of five such perfect children—all the more perfect now that she knew she could get away from them for a little while. And most of all, glad that she had married Jonnie. She felt suddenly terribly sad for Annette, who was nineteen and who, by her own admission, had never yet fallen in love. Why, at nineteen she had been married and twice a mother! Poor Annette, to be growing old without life's most wonderful experience.

Beverly laughed and ran downstairs to begin the lunch. The day passed in its usual routine manner but without its usual minor upsets. Nicky came home from school with two red stars for good behaviour. None of the children quarrelled during playtime after tea. The sponge cake Annette had made—her first under Beverly's instructions—turned out perfect.

Jonnie was home early for once, as if he, too, were trying to do his best to make this one of those days where everything sought to make her happy. Dinner was over, washed up, and Annette had gone upstairs to wash her hair.

Beverly handed Jonnie his coffee and sat down beside him on the worn sofa. Her hand trembled a little as she handed him the envelope containing the hotel's bookings. It was crumpled from the heat of her body for she had carried it around all day in her apron pocket.

'Jonnie, will you look at this?'

She watched his face as he took the letter from her and read it slowly. She watched the colour drain from his cheeks and something in his expression froze the smile on her lips.

'Darling, what's wrong? You *are* going to be able to get away, aren't you?'

He avoided her direct glance, looking down again at the letter in his hands.

'I . . . I'm not sure . . . I . . . I don't think so!'

'But, Jonnie, it's a whole month from now. Surely you can arrange it? You said you were due for some leave. You *must*; it's all arranged—just the two of us. Jonnie, you can't say no.'

He couldn't—he hadn't the heart or the stomach for wiping that look from her face. He hadn't been too blind to notice the change in her this evening. Not just her looks, but her whole person had radiated happiness and excitement. This explained it. How *could* he dash her hopes to the ground?

'Jonnie, you're not worrying about money? It's all fixed. You won't have to pay for anything but the petrol to get there.'

But he wasn't thinking of money. He was thinking of Elinor. He'd promised he'd wangle at least a long weekend in May so that they could go away together. Elinor was counting on it. Why, why had Beverly to spring this on him now? What had put such an idea into her head? Now of all times!

'What . . . what made you think this up?' he asked hesitantly.

Beverly looked at him in hurt surprise. 'You mean, you don't *want* to go? You don't think it's a good plan? I just don't understand, Jonnie. We haven't had a holiday alone together since Selsey. I've thought of little else for months. With Annette here and Mother to give her a hand, it means we can go at last, and now you ask me *why.*'

He heard the hurt and bewilderment in her tone and bit his lip in sudden remorse. How could he explain? How could he say, 'I do want a holiday, but I want it with Elinor—not with you.'

'Jonnie, you said you were due some leave, that's why I went ahead without asking you first. Is that what's worrying you? Because I didn't ask you first?'

Weakly, he nodded his head. Better let her believe this than the truth. Yet he hated lying to her. Dishonesty was foreign to his nature and he longed suddenly and quite desperately to say: 'I'm crazy about someone else; I can't get her out of my mind; the thought of her is tormenting me. She wants me and I want her, and I *have to* have her.' How many thousands of times had he gone over just such a longing to confess? How many times had he quelled that longing, believing that it was better to deceive her than to ease his own conscience at the cost of her happiness. What good could it do either of them? Beverly was hardly the kind of wife who'd say, 'All right, go ahead and have your fun, I'll turn a blind eye. I don't care.' She would care, he'd be forced to a decision he never wanted to make: to give Elinor up or to leave Beverly and his children. There would be rows, scenes, tears, recriminations, and for what? He didn't want a divorce, and to go on living with Beverly once she knew how he felt about Elinor would be to ruin all hope of happiness for either of them.

'I . . . I expect I can fix it,' he said helplessly. Beverly flung her arms round him and kissed him swiftly on the mouth. Some automatic instinct prompted him to return that kiss, but even as he did so, his mind swung back to Elinor. What would she say? Would she walk out on him when she knew he was throwing away their long weekend together? Would it mean he'd have to stop seeing her . . . knowing her, before their love affair had really started? Or was there still some way out? Perhaps at the last minute pressure of work might stop him going. But he couldn't do that. Beverly was flooding him with a hundred plans and hopes for their holiday and heaven alone knew, she deserved one.

He felt ashamed, and at the same time, angry with his wife who made him feel so. It was all so terribly unfair. And, anyway, how could such a holiday be a success when his own thoughts were concentrated on Elinor? Beverly was speaking now of 'a second honeymoon'. Well, he couldn't. It was Elinor he wanted now; Elinor with her exciting perfume, her violence, her experience. Instinct told him that it would be different with such a woman. She would lead and he would follow. With Beverly, he had been the master, he had done the teaching—and he had not wanted it any other way. But he hadn't known women like Elinor existed then.

'Jonnie, I don't believe you are listening to a word I'm saying. What *is* wrong? You are pleased, aren't you? Don't you see how important this is to us? For years now we've just taken each other and our love for granted. It . . . it's been bogged down amongst the daily routine. We'll have a chance to find each other

40

again.'

He looked at her blankly, not because he didn't understand but because he understood too well. Beverly, too, had begun to find their marriage dull and lacking in its essential needs. Well, that made two of them. But she wanted to try to fan the old embers into a new flame, whereas he was already afire with a longing for someone else.

Something of his inner bewilderment must have shown itself to her for she said softly:

'I didn't mean to hurt you by those last remarks, darling, but I think it's time we were honest with each other. Jonnie, don't turn your face away like that. How can we hope to know what we feel or want from each other when you try to hide yourself away from me? I know I'm not easy to live with; I know I've probably been perfectly beastly to you, but it's just because I was tired and nervy. I'm sorry, darling, and I want a chance to prove I still love you as much as when we were married. Say you understand.'

Guilt swept over him again, souring, hateful. To be honest with each other—how could he? You don't say to someone who has just told you they love you that you love someone else.

'It . . . it hasn't been your fault, Beverly; it's mine. I'm the one who should say I'm sorry and apologize.'

Beverly laid her cheek against his hand and said softly: 'It doesn't matter, Jonnie, just so

41

long as we do find each other again. I don't ever want to lose you. It's so lonely living by yourself.'

He reached out his other hand and gently stroked her hair. No one could be more generous than Beverly. One had only to offer her half an inch and she gave a yard in return. How could any man help but love her? That was one of the puzzling things about his feelings for Elinor. He was violently and quite madly *in love* with her so that he thought of little else, yet he would always love Beverly. His feelings for her were almost those of an elder brother—protective. They'd more or less grown up together. Maybe that was the root of the trouble, marrying too young. They'd neither of them really known what life was all about, and they'd just fumbled along its roads side by side, hoping for the best. Only it hadn't turned out for the best. If only he'd never met Elinor, never let her get under his skin. Beverly didn't want an elder brother, she wanted a husband, a lover. Yet he couldn't belong to two women.

'Oh, Beverly,' he whispered in an unconscious appeal for the understanding she could give him.

'Yes, darling? What is it?'

'Nothing, nothing. Just life, I suppose. It seems so strange, the way things work out.'

'We've been lucky, haven't we?' Beverly said, her voice rich with content. 'Do you realize, Jonnie, that there are probably thousands of men and women, sitting together like we are, but wishing desperately they could be together always and knowing they can't? Yet here we are, with our own home where we can shut ourselves away from the world and just be together, like this, whenever we want. And we have the children, too. Think of all the couples who *can't* have children—and we've got five lovely healthy kids. I'm so happy, Jonnie; so very glad I'm married to you.'

It should have ended differently. It was the first time in months that Beverly had spoken so openly and intimately about their relationship and their marriage. Had it not been for Elinor, maybe he could have shown her the response she must be hoping for; told her how glad he was to be a married man with five children. But he couldn't—not with every nerve longing for freedom and release from the very responsibilities he had taken on.

He tried to smile but felt that the result must be more a grimace. He felt beastly and treacherous, and hated himself. If only he could hate Beverly, too, instead of feeling this overwhelming pity for her. She was so innocent, so good, so sweet! How could he feel anything but love for her when she was like this? Yet he didn't want to feel tender towards her. It made everything he was thinking and feeling about Elinor so tawdry, so mean and deceitful.

'I . . . I think I'll go out for a walk!' he said, suddenly and abruptly. 'It's a lovely evening and I could do with some fresh air.'

Beverly jumped to her feet. This was like the old Jonnie, impulsive and unpredictable.

'What a good idea. I'll come with you. It's so nice to be able to say just that . . . I'll come with you. I just can't get used to the wonder of having Annette here. I'll go and get a coat.'

Jonnie slumped back in his chair, his face pale and taut. He'd wanted to be alone, to escape from Beverly. He couldn't trust himself any longer—not under such circumstances. If Beverly went on being so enthusiastic and happy about their life, sooner or later he would blurt out the truth: that for him, their marriage had become a disaster . . . a failure. Yet that wasn't true. Nothing had failed—yet. If he could only keep some control of the situation, nothing need go wrong. But how could he keep control when the reins were out of his hands? On one side Beverly, planning to have a 'second honeymoon', and on the other, Elinor, planning a week-end on the quiet.

Blast Elinor! Jonnie thought, trying to hate the woman who had completely uprooted all that was sensible and secure and dependable in his life, and made him see the fun and excitement he was missing. Did every man reach this same feeling about his marriage? Or was Elinor right when she had said:

'Ours won't be just an *ordinary* affair . . . we

love each other. It's something we can't control—too strong for us. If it were just a casual interest, I don't believe you would have thought of being unfaithful, darling, you aren't the type. But this . . . well, you feel the same way, don't you, Jonnie? We're made for each other and we have to belong.'

Once he had been so sure that he and Beverly had been 'made for each other'. They'd been so terribly in love, but as Elinor had argued, he'd been only a boy then. What a boy demanded from life could be quite different from what a *man* needed from the woman at his side. Beverly hadn't 'grown up' the way he had. Elinor was right about that, too. She still looked like a rather untidy schoolgirl in spite of bearing five children. The children; there lay one of the most disturbing elements of this whole wretched affair. It was possible that Beverly might have found someone else. She was still young and pretty in an unsophisticated way. But there were the children—his children. He loved them all deeply; Nicky most of all perhaps. Now he was seven years old, he was becoming a real companion to Jonnie. He was getting on fine at school and in another year he'd be off to Jonnie's own prep school—as a day boy, of course. They couldn't afford boarding school fees, and in any case, Jonnie wanted him where he could keep in touch. He and Nicky had a lot of fun together, when there was time.

Just lately there hadn't been so much time. Weekends that he and the boy had spent mostly entirely in each other's company, Jonnie had lately spent more often in or around the golf club with Elinor. Nicky had been a bit hurt.

Of course, the boy couldn't understand *why* his father had suddenly decided he wasn't suitable to 'caddy' his clubs. Jonnie's excuse that he'd be better employed playing about the garden had sounded pretty feeble to both of them. After all, it had been Nicky's job for the last year now, to push the trolley round the course every Sunday morning.

Fortunately, Nick had suddenly become great friends with a lad who lived at the other end of the village. Jonnie didn't know much about him except that he was a year or two older than Nick, but they were now pretty continuously in each other's company and Nick no longer pestered Jonnie to give him some time.

Much better for the boy to have someone his own age to play around with, Jonnie told himself uneasily. But he wasn't quite happy about it. Nick seemed to have managed to get along without him so easily, it wasn't exactly flattering. He'd believed he was his son's idol.

'Darling, you aren't ready? Aren't you coming out after all?'

Jonnie jumped to his feet.

'Yes . . . yes, of course. I was just thinking

about Nick. Beverly, what is that boy's name, the one Nick's always playing with nowadays?'

'You mean Paul Marshel?'

'Yes, that's the one. What do his people do?'

'I'm not quite sure,' Beverly said, as they closed the front door behind them. 'I think his father is a lorry driver. I've never met him but the mother is very nice. She "does" for Sue Bates. I think she goes a couple of hours every day as they aren't very well off. Paul goes to the same school. He's a bit slow but that's probably why the boys get on so well. Nick's bright and that levels out the difference in their ages. Paul's ten, you see.'

'Slow?'

'I think he's just behind with lessons not in other ways. At least, I've always found him quite intelligent. He's always very polite when he calls for Nick. But shy. He never quite looks you straight in the eye.'

'Do you think it's all right Nick spending so much time with him?'

Beverly glanced up at Jonnie surprised. 'Why yes! Mrs Marshel is as nice as could be and Sue says as honest as the day is long. So I don't see why you are worrying about Paul.'

'No . . . but, well Nick seems to be changing a bit lately. Perhaps he's just growing up.'

It was on the tip of Beverly's tongue to tell Jonnie that he'd been neglecting Nick the last few months but she bit back the remark. With

47

this new-found happiness, she did not want to take any chances. It wasn't as if Jonnie meant to be selfish about his 'spare time'. He had a right to spend part of the weekends the way he wanted. Men needed physical exercise and golf was Jonnie's only sport now.

Just because he had to work late so many evenings in the week and *she* saw so much less of him, there was no valid reason to suggest he give up his one hobby. Maybe the answer was for her to take up golf again. She had played before they were married, in fact she'd been learning when she first met Jonnie. If it hadn't been for golf, they might never have met at all. It certainly wouldn't be reasonable to expect a young man with Jonnie's temperament to be tied to a household of young children all day long. But at one stage he had been so eager for Nick's company; unable to wait for him to grow up so that he could take his son out alone and teach him things—golf especially. Nick adored his father and had been his shadow. But when Jonnie rejected his company to be his caddy Nick had suddenly turned against his father and transferred his hero-worship to young Paul Marshel. Beverly had been pleased that Paul had turned up at the psychological moment, as for a week or two Nick had mooched around the house like a bear with a sore head. Paul had been the very companion Nick needed and now the two boys were always off on some jaunt together.

Once or twice, Beverly had been a bit anxious about them. Nick was on the young side to go roaming about the countryside. But he was a sensible little boy, and he was always home at the time Beverly stated; muddy, dishevelled, but content with some wild game they had been playing; and he glowed with health. Beverly had stopped worrying and given the two boys her blessing. If Nick had become a little less well-mannered, she did not really blame the new friendship for it. Nick was bound to go through a stage of 'showing off' and wanting to appear 'tough'. The use of an occasional 'blast' or 'damn' was what she would have expected of him. She thought that it was a thoroughly good thing that Nick should learn to mix at an early age.

'No, Nick's all right,' she said again. 'It's Philip I'm worried about. He's so dependent on Julia. We always meant him to be a companion to Nick, didn't we, but it just hasn't worked out that way. Nick and Phil are so different it doesn't seem as if they'll ever be really close companions. Phil is nervous and sensitive and thoughtful. I think that's why he attaches himself to Julia—she's never unexpected. But it can't be right for a boy of six to be so reliant on a girl only just five, yet Julia organizes him and bosses him as if he were a younger brother.'

Jonnie frowned. He'd never been able to make much headway with his second son. Phil

49

seemed neither like him nor Beverly. He didn't understand the boy the way Beverly seemed to, even though he wasn't like her either. He cried easily and Jonnie felt he was a bit of a sissy. Yet in some ways, Phil was sharper than Nick. When it came to games that demanded thought and observation, Phil soared on top despite the year's difference between his age and Nick's. He was doing well at school, too. Probably the child would turn out a brilliant scholar. Nick's brilliance was nearly all sporting.

To Jonnie's relief, discussion of their children occupied the remainder of their walk and continued even when they had gone to bed. Not only did it keep Beverly from becoming too personal, but it kept his own mind off Elinor. Nevertheless, once the light was out and he lay awake in the darkness, listening to Beverly's soft, regular breathing, his mind turned again to the fresh problem this evening had evinced. What would he say to Elinor? How could he tell her the weekend was off? How would she take it?

It was a long while before Jonnie fell asleep.

CHAPTER FIVE

Jonnie followed Elinor into the drawing-room of her cottage and looked around him with a mixture of curiosity and interest. He'd known Elinor nearly six months now and yet this was the first time he'd been to her home. Of course, it wasn't really hers, as she was pointing out to him now—only a rented cottage. But it had acquired her personality and her perfume. It unsettled him, reminding him why he was here.

He watched her go to a corner cupboard and find some bottles and two glasses. He did not take in what she was saying. He could think only of the line of her body as she lifted her arm to reach for a glass and stood for a moment, poised, slim, mysterious yet familiar.

He began to tremble and clenched his hands. He knew that it was only a matter of moments before he would have to take her in his arms. He wanted that moment to come, and yet he dreaded it. Until now, he had never made love to her fully and completely. Until today, he'd withstood the temptation to come back with her to the privacy of her house.

He'd argued against it nearly all afternoon as they had walked round the course together, not thinking about the game, but only about each other. He'd told her the week they'd planned together was off. He had expected a scene, or at least, for Elinor to argue violently against it. But she hadn't. Surprisingly she had not said a thing.

'Elinor, I'm terribly sorry. It—'

'You don't have to make excuses, Jonnie.

No woman likes to be given reasons why the man she loves doesn't want her.'

'Elinor, that isn't true; you know it isn't. Want you! Good heavens above, I can't sleep, eat, think for wanting you. You *know* that.'

'If you loved me, Jonnie, you'd have found a way to be with me. It's nothing but a thousand and one excuses from you—it always has been. Don't let's talk about it any more.'

'But we have to talk about it, darling. You've got to understand why—'

'I'm just not willing to discuss this here and now, Jonnie. If you'd like to come back to tea at my house, I'll listen to anything you have to say. But this is too big a thing to thrash out on a golf course. If I'm getting the brush-off, I'd rather have it in private.'

After that he hadn't had the face to make further excuses not to go to her cottage. As if reading his thoughts, she had said:

'And if you're afraid to come back to the cottage, I suggest you get over that one by being perfectly open about it. Come back and have tea—just that. Then you can tell anyone who might drop in, or your wife when you get home, that that is how you spent the hour between four and five. Having tea with me.'

So he had come, openly and without deceit. As Elinor pointed out, there was no law against him going back to tea with her. They'd played a round of golf together and it was quite natural she should ask him back. If it had been anyone else but Elinor, he would have gone without a second thought about the propriety of such an action.

Now he was here, really alone with her, and 'tea' was going to be champagne, it seemed.

'Cheer up, honey! We might as well drink to the end of a glorious friendship in style. Why so gloomy?'

But he couldn't laugh. Her own light-hearted tone of voice, slightly bantering, goaded him almost beyond bearing.

'How can you talk like that, Elinor? Doesn't it mean anything to you after all?'

'Doesn't what mean what and why? Drink up, my sweet.'

She clinked her glass against his own and drank, her eyes never leaving his.

'You know, you're even more attractive when you're scowling. You look like a cross old bear.'

'Elinor!'

She was in his arms now, her half-empty glass dropping unheeded to the floor, the contents spilling over the carpet making a stain neither of them saw.

He kissed her wildly and desperately, believing that this might indeed be the last time he held her in his arms. Her mouth was open and responsive, and then suddenly she broke away from him.

'No, Jonnie! It's silly to go on behaving like two school kids. Frankly, I've had enough of

53

it.'

Jonnie leant back against the wall, his breath coming in deep uneven gasps. How Elinor remained so cool and calm was beyond his understanding. She always seemed to be the complete master of her emotions. Yet she did not lack passion. Every line of her face and body breathed fire that he knew to be within her.

'You . . . you want this to be goodbye?' he asked, his voice hoarse and barely audible.

Elinor stooped and picked up her glass and went slowly across the room to refill it. She took a deep sip before she replied.

'It's *you* who want to end it all, Jonnie. *I* never said it's what *I* wanted.'

Jonnie looked at her in bewilderment.

'But—'

'There are no "buts", Jonnie,' she broke in, coming over to where he stood and leaning against him provocatively. 'It's quite simple to understand. I'm not mad at you because you can't make that weekend we were planning. I'm sure you've got a good reason for calling off. It's just that I can't go on any longer not being sure of the way you feel about me.'

'Not sure!' Jonnie echoed stupidly. His arms went round her and he tried to bring his lips to her mouth, but she half turned her head and said:

'No, I'm not sure, Jonnie. If you loved me, you'd have proved it to me by now. Even now you're hesitating. You don't need me the way I need you.'

White-faced, Jonnie caught her chin in his hand and forced her head round so he could look deep into her eyes. He knew now what she meant—that he had always avoided the actual act of unfaithfulness to Beverly. So long as he did not give way completely to his desires, he could still go on at home more or less as if nothing had happened. But now it couldn't go on like that any longer. No man ever needed anyone more than he needed Elinor. He had to have her. Beverly; the future; nothing mattered any more beside the terrible alternative of losing her completely.

'Jonnie, honey, I'm so crazy about you. I'm not ashamed of the way I feel. I'm a woman— all woman, and I want you just the way you want me. You do want me, don't you? It could be all that was ever meant to be, between us, Jonnie!'

Her soft voice was drumming in his ears and he knew he had reached the end of control. For too long he had tortured himself and her with kisses, embraces, words which were all just symbols of what they really wanted of each other. And Elinor was making it all seem so easy, so natural. It wasn't as if she expected him to break up his home, mess up his life, to do anything more than he wanted himself.

For nights upon nights he had lain awake, imagining this moment when he would make her his own. Now there could be no turning back. Already she had slipped off the thin cashmere cardigan she had worn for golf and the blouse beneath, of some transparent nylon, clearly revealed the creamy rounded shoulders, the long bare column of her neck, the tiny pointed breasts.

'Elinor!' he murmured before she turned, and smiling at him with a strange, savage triumph, wound her arms around his neck.

*   *   *

An hour later, he drove himself slowly towards his home. The mad, incredible emotions of the past hour seemed already like a strange unearthly dream. He wanted to forget, to put Elinor out of his mind; but tired and depressed though he was and apprehensive about his coming meeting with Beverly, he kept remembering snatches of time spent with Elinor as if he were seeing flashes of film. He'd never known a woman could be like Elinor. It was as if he had held a wild warm panther in his arms. She made no attempt to control the swift tide of passion that engulfed her and himself, too. The very force of her feelings was sufficient to arouse in him every nerve, every sense, but of the body rather than the mind. It was a mating of the senses rather than the spirit; swift, cruel, but intensely satisfying. The primitiveness of their behaviour only now in retrospect had the power to shock him a little. Was this how man and woman were meant to love? Had he and Beverly only touched on the delicate fringes of real emotion? Or was this thing that existed between himself and Elinor born of something greater that made them behave not as gentle, loving people, but as hungry insatiable creatures.

Love! Where had there been time or place for love in that mad hour? There had been only desire and now, the after-effects of guilt and shame. No shame for the way they had behaved for it seemed as if with Elinor there could be no other way, but shame for what Beverly would think if she knew.

Thank God she would never know. It was something he could never ever explain to her; something she could never hope to understand. For Beverly, the act of love had been an act of giving, and Jonnie had taken and given in return. But Elinor had not stopped to give—only to take and take and take again, and in her wild, uncontrolled need she had given herself with an abandon which Beverly would never understand.

Jonnie stopped the car, and was suddenly physically sick into the ditch by the roadside. The nervous and mental strain was beginning to take its toll of him.

When at last he reached home, Beverly took one look at him and said: 'Jonnie, what is the matter? You look ghastly. Are you ill?'

He could thank God now for the lack of need to lie. 'Must be something I ate or drank,' he said weakly. 'Just been terribly sick.'

'You go straight to bed,' Beverly ordered. 'I'll call Dr Massie.'

'No. No, don't, Beverly, please. I'm all right now. I'll go upstairs and lie down, but don't call the doctor. It's all over, anyway. If I ate anything to upset me, it's not inside me now.'

'Then I'll bring you up a hot-water bottle,' Beverly said anxiously. She was well aware how Jonnie hated being ill and to have the doctor was something he would always avoid until he was so ill he had to give way. There was a little more colour in his face now, but he'd looked really terrible as he came into the house, grey, tired, almost shocked.

A few minutes later, she went up to their room with two hot-water bottles. Jonnie had undressed and was lying between the sheets, his eyes closed. She slipped the bottles beneath the bedclothes and whispered:

'Sure you're all right, darling?'

He opened his eyes and looked at her, fully in the face, as if, Beverly thought afterwards, he were uncertain who she was. Then he said slowly:

'Yes, thanks . . . and . . . I'm sorry, Beverly.'

'Poor darling,' Beverly told Annette downstairs. 'He was half asleep but he still managed to apologize for being ill. As if it mattered. I suppose he was thinking of the supper being spoilt. Well, we'd better have ours and then I'll go up again and see how he is. If he isn't better in the morning, I'm going to call the doctor, whatever Jonnie says.'

Suddenly the phone rang. Beverly went to answer it, expecting her mother. Instead it was Elinor.

'Is that Mrs Colt? This is Elinor Wilmot speaking. I wonder could I speak with your husband a moment?'

'I'm afraid my husband isn't very well. He's gone to bed.' Beverly said, puzzled, 'Could I take a message for you?'

There was a brief pause, then Elinor said: 'I guess it isn't important. Your husband was kind enough to run me home after golf this afternoon and he left his cigarette-case in my house. I thought he might be worried, which is why I called. He can stop by and pick it up any time. Say, I hope he's not real sick?'

'Well, I don't think so. We think it's probably something he had to eat.'

'Say, we had a drink at my house but I guess it wasn't the champagne. I had the same myself and I'm OK. Well, I won't keep you talking. Please tell Jonnie "hullo" from me and say I hope he'll be OK tomorrow.'

'Thank you. It was good of you to call.'

'That's OK, Mrs Colt. You must come to tea one day so we can have a chance to get better acquainted.'

Beverly was pleased. 'I'd like that very much. I don't get out much. Do you and Jonnie often play golf together?'

'Oh, we make up a four when an odd man or girl's needed,' Elinor said casually. 'Your husband's got a better handicap than I have, but he gives me an occasional lesson when there's time. You don't play, Mrs Colt?'

'Well, I used to, but I'm just a beginner, and I've no time now,' Beverly said, laughing. 'Look, won't you come and have tea with me, Mrs Wilmot? Why not tomorrow?'

'Say, that's too sweet of you to ask me, but I can't tomorrow. I'll call you again and we'll arrange something soon.'

'She sounds fun!' Beverly thought as she went back to the kitchen to rejoin Annette for their evening meal. 'I must ask Jonnie about her. Funny he hasn't mentioned her before. She seems to know him quite well.'

A sudden swift pang of jealousy struck her. Suppose Jonnie and this woman . . . but how silly! Jonnie wasn't like that. Besides, in a village like Buckley, what possible hope was there of any man taking any girl anywhere without it being all over the place five minutes later. If Jonnie had been out with Mrs Wilmot, she would have been told about it long before now.

Yet although she dropped the idea almost as soon as it had come to her mind, somehow she could not quite forget the American voice on the telephone. She had hoped Jonnie might wake during the evening, but he slept on, as if exhausted, and did not even stir when she went to bed herself.

Unable to find sleep, Beverly let her mind wander. Would it matter so terribly if Jonnie were unfaithful to her? Would she divorce him if she found out or would she forgive him? Her vivid imagination invented a dramatic scene with a mythical American woman as her rival. For ten minutes, she faced Jonnie, white-faced, trembling, telling him that he must give up this woman or else.

Beverly relaxed and turned over on her other side, one arm resting on Jonnie's warm familiar body. How silly to think of such things. Better to lie and imagine happy thoughts such as their holiday together.

Smiling, warm and content, Beverly slowly drifted into sleep.

CHAPTER SIX

'Beverly, I can't make the holiday after all. I . . . I'm terribly sorry!'

Beverly looked up from her sewing, her face white with shock. '*Not go*? But, Jonnie, you said—'

'I know!' he interrupted swiftly, getting up and walking across to the window with his back towards her, so that she could not see his face while he destroyed the joy in hers with a lie. 'I thought I could, but now, well, a works study has come up during that week and I just have to be there.'

Beverly relaxed and drew a deep breath. 'Oh, darling, if that's all, you can come, you silly! Then the day you're needed you can catch a train to town. It wouldn't take more than an hour. For one awful moment I thought the whole week was off!'

Jonnie sighed.

'I don't see how I *can* get away. I know this will be rather a disappointment, but I can't help it. There'll be work to do before and after the day I'm needed in town. Couldn't we postpone the week and take it later on in the year?'

Beverly put down her sewing and swung round so that she could look at him. But he still stood with his back towards her. Her heart was beating double time, but she managed to keep her voice level and quiet as she said:

'What's the matter? Don't you want to come?'

'Don't be so childish, Beverly!' The words were out before he could stop them. He knew in his heart that his only method of defence against her shot in the dark was to attack. But was it just a shot in the dark? Had Elinor said something during that phone call? She couldn't have been so silly. Besides, Bev had shown no more than an idle curiosity about her.

'Childish!' Beverly's voice was higher pitched now and taut with the disappointment that welled up in her. 'Jonnie, don't you know what this week means to me? I've been looking forward to it for weeks on end . . . counting the days. Mother had planned to take time off especially from her work and it's all arranged. You *can't* back out now!'

'You can't blame me. I have my work to do and it must come first or I'll lose my job, you know that. I'm sorry about the holiday, but *you* can still go.'

Jonnie's voice was stiff and cold. It seemed as if one lie must inevitably lead to another and he hated himself at this moment more than he had ever done in his life before. Yet he couldn't go on this holiday; *he just could not go.* It would be a far worse tragedy to give in and then disappoint her when they were away together; because disappointment was certain. Beverly had not tried to hide her dreams from him. She meant them to become lovers again and he knew he could not pretend. It would be impossible to hold Beverly in his arms now, if ever again, since Elinor . . .

'I see! It doesn't seem to have struck you, Jonnie, that it wasn't because I wanted a holiday that I planned all this. It happens that I wanted to go away with *you*—be alone with you. Perhaps that is just what you are trying to

63

avoid?'

Another shot in the dark but how near the truth. Involuntarily, Jonnie shivered. One read in so many books about a woman's intuition. Did it really exist, this kind of sixth sense? Or was it he himself who was giving the show away by his behaviour?

'If you want a quarrel, Beverly, then I suggest you find someone else to quarrel with. I've told you the reason I can't go; now let's leave it at that.'

Beverly stared at her husband in silence. Her feelings were so strong that for a moment she was left speechless, unable to express the appalling disappointment, the fear, the anger, the surprise, all of which shook her in turn. It couldn't be Jonnie saying this! It was a bad dream and she would wake up. But she knew it *was* true. He did not intend coming with her. It was on the tip of her tongue to say to him bitterly, 'You know I wouldn't go without you,' but she bit back the words, pride suddenly surging uppermost in her emotions. She wouldn't let him see how desperately she had wanted this week with him. If he could say quite casually that it was all off, she could be equally casual. At least, he should not have the pleasure of knowing how much he had hurt her.

'All right. I'll go alone. I'm not going to have Mother's plans upset for nothing.'

She turned and walked out of the room, her

head held high, the tears that threatened carefully held in check until she reached the privacy of their bedroom. Then she flung herself on the bed and burst into tears . . . tears of frustration and disappointment.

But she did not cry for long. Soon Jonnie would be coming up to bed and she didn't want him to see her with her defences down. On a sudden impulse, she picked up her pillow and night-clothes and marched through to the tiny spare room where the bed lay made up for her mother's visit next week. She would sleep in here tonight. That would show Jonnie just how deeply she felt about all this.

Silently, unhappily, she undressed and climbed in between the cold sheets. She longed for a hot-water bottle, but it would mean going downstairs and she did not wish to speak to Jonnie again that night. After what seemed hours, she heard Jonnie come upstairs and go to their room. A moment later he called her name. She did not answer.

'Beverly?'

This time his voice was louder and she was afraid he might wake Annette or the children. She got out of bed and crossed the room.

'I'm sleeping in the spare room,' she said coldly, through the locked door. 'Good night, Jonnie.'

He had heard her for he stood for a moment on the other side of the door.

'Let him want to come in . . . let him try the

door!' Beverly prayed silently. 'Don't let him leave me here alone!'

But he neither called her again nor tried the door handle.

A moment later she heard his footsteps return to their bedroom and the door close behind him.

Beverly climbed back into bed shivering uncontrollably. What had she done? This was the first time in all the years of their marriage that they had slept apart. Far from making things better, her action had only made things worse. How could Jonnie leave her like this? Didn't he care any more? What had happened to their marriage?

Frightened, cold and utterly miserable, Beverly lay dry-eyed and tense. Not more than two hours ago, she had been perfectly happy, perfectly secure, certain of Jonnie's love and the difference that their holiday would make to them both. Now the ground had been swept from under her feet and she was no longer sure of anything. Had Jonnie ceased loving her? Months had passed since he had last made love to her, but then that may well have been her own fault, for before that she had rejected his attempts and in doing so might well have hurt his pride. Somewhere along the road their love had dwindled from a glowing, living flame, to a tiny spark. It was this spark she had counted on to build a fire once more . . . and Jonnie had simply and quietly put it out.

Tears came now, hot and salt, rolling down her cheeks and wetting the pillow. She felt bruised and hurt deep down inside herself. No matter whether Jonnie really had work to do to prevent him coming away, he still need not have shown how little he cared by leaving her alone like this! Any man who really loved his wife would have tried to break down the door, force his way in and take her in his arms and tell her not to be so silly!

Beverly choked on a sob and sat up straight in bed. She was shocked by her own train of thought. Where had it led her? To the conviction that Jonnie no longer loved her. It hadn't really anything to do with their holiday; that had just been the last straw. For months and months now Jonnie had had no time for her. He even tried to avoid her company, or so it seemed in retrospect. She hadn't worried because she was so certain in her own mind that this second honeymoon would put everything right. Now there wouldn't be this chance and what would happen to their marriage?

'I can't live with a man who doesn't love me,' Beverly whispered into the darkness. 'I'll go away and leave him.' Yet she knew it wasn't possible. She had five children, and she didn't *want* to go. She still loved Jonnie—if not in the same way she had once loved him, then in a different older way. But was it so different?

Remembering their early days together when she had still been uncertain whether Jonnie was going to propose or not, she could find a similarity to her present predicament. She'd taken Jonnie and his love for granted, and now suddenly she was without confidence.

'Perhaps I'm being silly,' Beverly reflected, trying to find hope. 'Just because Jonnie has called off this holiday is no reason to believe he has stopped loving me. If he really has work to do, he can't help not being able to go.' As to his calm acceptance of her removal to the spare room, it could be that he, too, had his pride and wasn't going to force himself on her when she'd shown so clearly she wanted to be alone.

For a moment Beverly toyed with the idea of complete capitulation. She would unlock her door and go along to their room and tell Jonnie she was sorry. He would put his arms round her and tell her to stop crying and not to be such an imaginative little goose. But the moment did not last. *Why should she?* It was not for her to make the first move, it was for Jonnie. He had been responsible for the rift. He must have known how much his cancellation of their holiday would mean to her.

'I hope he's as miserable as I am,' Beverly thought wretchedly, lying back on her pillow.

Jonnie was indeed as wretched if not more so. His relief at finding Beverly had moved into the spare room had been mixed with consternation. Could she have guessed at the real reason for his backing out of the holiday plan? If not, why should she take the symbolic action of leaving their shared bed? Never, even after the most serious of their arguments in the past, had they slept apart. Beverly must be feeling this very deeply to have made this gesture. Of course, he knew she was terribly upset that their joint holiday was off. But this departure to the spare room signified more than disappointment. It meant she had finally rejected the significance of their marriage.

He was torn by uncertainty. Privacy was what he had longed for, yet without Beverly's accustomed presence beside him he could not settle to sleep. Her absence was more effective than her presence could have been. If she had been here to argue or storm at him, he might have stayed on the crest of the wave of his irritation with her. Now he felt confused and deeply guilty. He had refused the holiday and now there might be repercussions that would permanently affect their marriage. Was this what he wanted? Did he want his marriage to alter in its meaning, if not to break up? Was this behind his reluctance to force his way into the spare room and make her come back? How was it possible that one hour alone with Elinor in his arms could make so much difference? She had sworn nothing need touch his marriage, that he could keep his liaison with her quite apart from his life with Beverly. Well, Elinor was wrong; he could not. He couldn't make love to Elinor one day of the week and to Beverly the next. The idea revolted him and he felt that Beverly, if she were to know the truth, would never have let him come near her.

He turned restlessly in bed. If he could only hate Elinor, he could put an end to an affair which was against his every principle. But he could not find anything but intense excitement in the thought of her ivory body twisting itself around and against his own. Her face, her eyes, her expression were but a dim haze; he could not even bring her features to mind . . . only the tempting, glowing, passionate body needing him as much as he needed it.

Jonnie bit his lip. Renewed desire for Elinor could only complicate matters further, and he did not want to think of her now. He wanted to think of Beverly, poor little kid. She didn't deserve this; yet in a way it had all begun because she had not wanted him the way he wanted her. It wasn't her fault. Maybe she was just less passionate by nature than Elinor.

He forgot that Beverly had once been wholly and completely everything he desired in a woman; forgot that for years they had been contented and happy lovers. He forgot that Beverly had borne him five children within almost as many years and that she must have been tired, physically very tired, and not always able to respond when *he* was in the mood. He remembered only her rejection of him and his own unsatisfied need . . . a need that had persisted until Elinor had come into his life. Their love-making had been catastrophic and overwhelming and completely and perfectly satisfying, even if he had been a little frightened, too. It was almost as if he had been placed under some primitive spell; as if Elinor possessed some black magic which gripped him even while his innermost beliefs still warred against her. He hadn't wanted it to happen, yet it had happened, and now there was no turning back. All week he had thought of her. He could not break it off now. He must see her again . . . *he must*, no matter what it cost. And he could not go back to living with Beverly as if nothing had changed. Everything had changed. He was somehow a different person and beyond Beverly's reach. To go away with his wife for a week now would be to court disaster, for he knew he could not be a real husband to her any longer.

Jonnie's mind closed sharply at the thought 'and never again'. Such thoughts were too dangerous. It was easier to think of Elinor. He heard her voice saying:

'This is only the beginning, honey. Next time will be even better, you'll see. I'll love you the way you've never been loved before, Jonnie . . . Jonnie . . .'

'Damn, damn, damn!' Jonnie swore aloud,

71

his fingers tearing at the bedclothes as he tried to still that voice, to stop his thoughts. Somewhere in the next room, one of the children cried out. He held his breath listening, and then relaxed as the house went quiet. How he hated himself! How could he look young Nick, for instance, in the face? Only yesterday he'd caught him out in a fib and given him a good ticking off, telling him that there was nothing so nasty as a lie. Yet here he was living a lie and without the slightest intention of trying to break away. His hatred for himself once again had its physical effect on him, and he had to get up hurriedly and go to the bathroom where he was very sick.

On the way back, he heard the spare room door open and saw Beverly's shadowed figure standing there, white-faced, looking at him.

'Was that you, Jonnie? Are you all right?'

For one desperate moment, he wanted to go to her, to feel her arms round him warm and comforting, to be able to tell her how very wrong life had become—and why! Beverly was so gentle and sweet and full of tenderness whenever he or the children were ill or distressed. She was really a born mother, and it was as a mother he needed her now. He wanted her to comfort him, to put things right. The relief of confession would be so enormous, yet he could not do it. He swallowed and stepped away from her.

'Quite all right, thank you,' he said coldly, and without looking back at her, returned quickly to their room.

Beverly nearly followed. She had been wide awake when Jonnie went to the bathroom and she had heard him—known he was being sick again. Twice in a week; he couldn't be well. No wonder Jonnie kept away from her. If she went to him now, she could tell him how sorry she was, make him admit he wasn't well; that he was overtired, overworked. He needed a holiday . . . the thought pulled her up sharply. Of course he needed a holiday, and this was the one thing he wouldn't take. So what use in going to him now? He would only believe she was trying to nag at him. If he got really ill, the doctor would tell him he had to go away.

Slowly, Beverly went back to the spare room. Now she was kept awake by a fresh wave of uncertainty. Should she go without him? If she called it off for the time being, maybe Jonnie would get away later on—would have to get away for his health's sake. He looked ill and was pale and tired and lined around the eyes. And he had no appetite. Maybe she would cancel all the arrangements and let Jonnie make the next move. Sooner or later he was going to crack up physically. No man could take his hours of work with no rest and not crack up. She could have a chat with Dr Massie and get him on her side.

Comforted at last, Beverly fell asleep, little

knowing that Jonnie's health, happiness and well-being no longer lay in her hands.

The morning brought a fresh crop of worries. It was Saturday, and soon after breakfast Nick appeared in the kitchen in jeans and a yellow polo-necked jersey, waiting for Paul Marshel. He seemed preoccupied and continually asked her the time as if he were incapable of seeing the clock for himself.

'What is the matter, Nick?' Beverly asked at last. 'Is Paul late or something? Where are you going, anyway?'

'None of your business,' was Nick's staggering reply.

White-faced, Beverly faced her small son. He'd never been so rude to her in his life before and this morning she was in no mood for making allowances. No matter what was bothering Nick, he had to learn he couldn't talk to her like that.

'Go up to your room, Nick. When Paul comes, I shall tell him you won't be going with him.'

Nick took a step forward and looked up at her aghast. 'But I am going . . . I promised!'

'Don't argue or I'll send you to bed as a further punishment. Now, upstairs, quick!'

For a full minute, the boy remained in front of her, looking straight at her defiantly. But slowly, his eyes fell and he half turned towards the door. 'If I say I'm sorry I was rude, can I go with Paul when he comes?'

'No, you can't!' Beverly said. 'You can spend the morning tidying your desk and drawers. I'll think about letting you go out this afternoon.'

Nick made no further effort to apologize but ran out of the room and upstairs, banging the bedroom door hard behind him.

Beverly sighed. This was a fine start to a new day! If Jonnie hadn't gone out to golf immediately after breakfast, *he* could have dealt with Nick. Maybe the boy wanted some heavy masculine discipline; he was getting a bit too much for her. Well, Jonnie could speak to him at lunchtime.

The morning wore on with its usual round of domestic activities. Annette took the four younger children for a walk, the twins in the pram, Philip and Julia walking beside her. They were going to pick wild flowers and they at least were happy.

At eleven o'clock, Beverly made herself a cup of tea and took a cup of cocoa up to Nick's room. But when she tried to open the door, she found it locked.

'Nick, open this door. You know I don't allow you to lock it.'

There was no reply. Angry, but not yet frightened, Beverly called again. 'If you don't unlock this door by the time I count three, you'll spend all day in bed and without a book!' she called.

Still no reply, and suddenly anxious, Beverly put down the cocoa and leant her ear against the keyhole. There was no sound at all. Nor could she see anything for the key on Nick's side of the door was in the lock.

Panicky, Beverly ran downstairs and picked up the wood chopper from the coke-hole floor. She ran back upstairs and tried to wedge open the door, using the chopper blade as a lever. After five minutes, the lock gave and the door swung inwards, Beverly fell in on her hands and knees, grazing her cheek against the chopper, which she still clenched in her hand.

The room was quite empty. The window was wide open, the curtains blowing gently in the breeze. Seeing them, Beverly rushed over and only then saw the old rope ladder Jonnie had used when he was making a tree-house with Nick last summer. Nick had attached it to the metal window frame and it dangled down almost to the ground outside. Nick had made his escape!

Relief that he had come to no harm flooded over Beverly, making her want to laugh and cry at the same time. All anger had gone and, deep inside her, she felt quite pleased with her young son at such daring. It was a good fifteen feet down to the garden below, but clearly he hadn't hesitated. He must have known he'd pay for it eventually, but whatever he and Paul Marshel were going to do today obviously was worth a punishment.

'Jonnie will have to give him a good talking to,' Beverly thought as she went downstairs again. 'He can do it when they both come in to lunch.'

But although lunch was late, neither Jonnie nor Nick appeared. Giving the other children their meal, Beverly glanced up at the clock every few minutes. She felt the first feeling of fear gnawing again at her heart. Where was Nick? Had he got up to some mischief? Perhaps Jonnie had been called somewhere to see to him? Perhaps he had had an accident and Jonnie had gone to the hospital? Yet how would anyone have known where to find Jonnie? The police would have come home first to find out where Jonnie was.

'Not to worry, Madame. Mr Colt he probably lunch at the club, no?' Annette suggested, seeing Beverly's anxiety.

'But he always rings, Annette! And where's Nick?'

'Perhaps Madame could telephone the club-house to find if Mr Colt stay there for his dinner?'

'Yes!' Beverly agreed, relieved. 'Then I can tell him Nick isn't back.'

But her fears only increased when the club secretary informed her that Jonnie had been on the course that morning but had left about midday in his car.

'It's one-thirty now and Jonnie knows we never lunch later than one. Where *can* he be?'

'Maybe that the car break down?' Annette suggested.

'Well then, where's Nick?'

Beverly sat down and tried to eat her own lunch. But nervous anxiety made it all but impossible. She pushed her plate away at last and told Annette to put the children down for their rest and wash up. Then she went to the telephone.

Sue Adams answered almost immediately but she could not help. Mrs Marshel had left at midday and wasn't on the phone. So Beverly could not find out if Paul had returned for his lunch. She was sure the boys were out together.

'If you're really worried, can't you run down in the car to the estate? It wouldn't take you five minutes, Beverly.'

'I haven't got the car,' Beverly said. 'Jonnie went out to golf this morning and *he* isn't back either.'

'Then he must be lunching at the club,' Sue said in an attempt to soothe her.

'He isn't. He left at twelve or thereabouts. It's so unlike Jonnie; he always telephones if he's going to be late or miss a meal. Oh, Sue, I really am worried.'

'Look, I'll get Pete to run you down in our car to Mrs Marshel's if it will help, Beverly. I can't go myself because I'm feeding Jane in two minutes. You know how she gets if she's late for her bottle. But Pete won't mind going.'

'I can walk, Sue. Thanks all the same,' Beverly said.

'Nonsense—it'll take you twenty minutes, and I know how long that can be when you're on tenterhooks. Pete's here beside me now. He says he'll be along in five minutes.'

Beverly thanked her lucky stars for these two good friends. Sue Adams was a little younger than herself and Jane was her first baby. They hadn't been in the village long but the two girls liked each other from the start and were rapidly becoming close to each other. Beverly saw more of Sue than of anyone else. Pete was nice, too. He was a year or two older than Jonnie and they sometimes played golf together.

When Pete arrived, Beverly climbed into the old Austin beside him and said, 'I suppose I'm making a lot of fuss about nothing, but I can't help feeling worried.' She told him how Nick had had to be sent to his room and how he climbed out of the window.

Pete laughed reassuringly. 'I expect he thinks he might as well be hung for a sheep as a lamb. He'll be back by bedtime, if not before. Boys will be boys, you know.'

Beverly smiled. 'I suppose so. I wish Jonnie was home to deal with him. You didn't play golf this morning, Pete?'

'Why, yes, and I saw Jonnie. He was playing with Mr and Mrs Ward and that American woman . . . can't remember her name now. They were on the eighth tee just as we finished the seventh, and we had to wait for them to get ahead of us.'

'You mean Elinor Wilmot,' Beverly said slowly. 'Pete, what is she like? Do you know her?'

'Only vaguely,' Pete replied as he turned down into the council house estate. 'Rather a striking woman. Bags of sex appeal, of course; very American. Not my type though. Too sophisticated. But she plays a good round of golf.'

Beverly felt suddenly and unreasonably jealous. Was it Elinor Wilmot's golf that attracted Jonnie—or something else?

But she forgot Jonnie as Pete stopped the car outside the Marshels' house. Mrs Marshel answered the door, asking Beverly to step into the spotless little hall of her home.

'I just came to ask if Paul was home,' Beverly said. 'I think he and my Nicholas were playing together this morning.'

'No, he's not home,' said Mrs Marshel, pushing the greying hair back from her forehead. 'Isn't your boy back neither?'

'No, he's not, Mrs Marshel, and I'm very worried. Nick's never missed a meal before . . . he knows he has to be home for meals. Did Paul say if he was coming to fetch Nick?'

'I left home afore John this morning,' Mrs Marshel replied. 'You see, I leave for Mrs Adams' house at eight-thirty and John hadn't got up, not by then, he hadn't. I know he's most often up at your place. It's very good of you to have him around so much.'

'Well, I don't see a great deal of him; the boys are usually off somewhere in the woods or fields. Does he often stay out all day?'

'He's got used to fending for himself, and I don't worry none about him, not Paul. He can take care of hisself. You see, I'm often as not not here myself. I do for another lady as well as Mrs Adams, and we don't bother much with lunch. We have our main meal come teatime.'

'I see!' Beverly said. 'Well, I'm sorry to have bothered you. At least it looks as if the boys are out together, so I'm not quite so worried. Paul would have told someone if anything had happened to Nick, I'm sure.'

'That he would. Paul's no fool. For all he can't do his school work, he's brighter than most boys of his age in other ways. Don't you worry about your boy, Mrs Colt. If my Paul comes home and he hasn't been with Nick and seen him home first, I'll send him along right away to tell you.'

'That's very good of you, Mrs Marshel. Thanks,' Beverly said.

Pete treated the matter much in the same way as Mrs Marshel. 'He's just showing you how independent he's become,' he said as he drove Beverly home. 'I know you will worry, but I'm sure there's no need, really. Would you like to come back for a bit and chew it over with Sue?'

Beverly shook her head. 'No, I'd rather be

home. Maybe Jonnie is back by now and he can take the responsibility. It's just that if he, Nick, I mean, hasn't turned up by dark, I really shall be frightened. But Jonnie will know what to do. He may go out in the car and have a look around for him. I expect you and Mrs Marshel are right and he's out with Paul somewhere.'

But there was no sign of their own car in the garage as Pete dropped her back at home, and by three o'clock Jonnie was still not back. Nor was Nick.

Beverly was by now nearly frantic, alone with an imperturbable Annette, who seemed not to be able to understand any of Beverly's fears for Nick's safety. Her very placidity only increased Beverly's powers of imagination. Suppose Nick had been run over . . . kidnapped . . . had fallen off a tree and broken a leg and was even now lying alone calling for help in some wood.

At last, unable to bear the waiting any longer, Beverly telephoned the golf club again. Jonnie had not reappeared.

'Annette, I'm going out to try to find Nick. If he comes home while I'm gone, or if Mr Colt comes, please tell them both not to go out again in any circumstances. Do you understand?'

Beverly hurried out of the house and along the lane that led to the woods. It was a lovely spring day, mild, sunny, agreeably drowsy except for the busy chatter of the birds in the hedgerows. Everywhere was green and fresh and full of growth. Great clumps of primroses clustered in the banks and occasionally she saw patches of mauve and white where the wild violets were growing beneath some tree.

Where *was* Nick? She'd be so relieved to see him it was doubtful if she'd even be cross if she caught sight of him now. Perhaps she was silly to fuss. Jonnie would probably have told her not to be so silly. Where was Jonnie, come to that?

'I beg your pardon!'

She had collided unseeingly with a tall rather large man who had been walking towards her. A moment later she recognized him; it was Mr Forbes, Nicky's schoolmaster.

'It's Mrs Colt, isn't it? I am so sorry.'

Beverly smiled. 'I am looking for Nicholas. I suppose you didn't happen to have seen him on your walk, Mr Forbes?'

'Nicholas? No, I can't remember meeting anybody. Is Nicholas lost?'

'I don't know,' Beverly said truthfully.

Suddenly, her companion laughed. Beverly looked at him in surprise. Allan Forbes had the reputation of being a very quiet, shy man, difficult to converse with. She had only met him once or twice at school gatherings and had not really paid much attention to him as an individual; merely interested in the man who was Nick's teacher, and in what he had had to say about the boy's progress at school.

But Nick seemed to like him, though he, too, said he was 'different' and that 'he never laughs, you know. He just sort of smiles.'

Well, he was laughing now, not stiltedly or nervously, but with a deep-throated kind laughter that seemed to make the nightmarish quality of the day no longer real.

'I suppose that did sound rather silly!' Beverly said, smiling. 'But I've been so worried I hardly know what I'm saying.'

'Then suppose you sit down here on this log, have a cigarette, and tell me all about it?'

Beverly looked at the man beside her, really seeing him now for the first time. He was older than Jonnie; nearing forty perhaps, with dark hair greying very slightly at the temples. He had a nice face with hazel-coloured eyes set wide apart, a long straight nose and a gentle, sensitive mouth still curved a little in laughter. Beneath, his jaw was square and firm.

'He's really very good-looking,' Beverly thought, as she accepted the cigarette and sat down obediently beside him. 'I never noticed it before.'

Allan Forbes was in turn studying the girl beside him. Perhaps he should have thought of her as a woman, but she looked so incredibly young with her dark hair curling carelessly over her head, her coat hanging loosely from her shoulders as if she'd flung it on in a hurry, her nose shining and, not least, a large dark smudge across one cheek. He wondered if she knew it was there and decided not.

'What are you staring at?' Beverly asked, seeing his glance and the amusement in his eyes.

'Well, it's rude to make personal remarks, but I think you probably ran out of the house in a great hurry, having just made up the boiler, brushed your hair back from your cheek and left a black streak on it in doing so.'

Beverly grinned, wrinkling up her nose in an unconscious gesture of self-disapproval. 'Oh lord . . . and I haven't got a hanky!'

'Then borrow mine.'

He offered her a clean white handkerchief, but when she scrubbed the wrong cheek, he took it gently from her and lightly rubbed away the mark.

'There; now you're perfect,' he said—and meant it. This was the way a woman should look—without artificial make-up, the colour in her cheeks and lips natural, and the light in her eyes as she began to laugh again, making them sparkle and shine. He liked the untidiness of her hair, too. The curls were just as the wind might have blown them. She looked like a wood nymph.

Beverly heard the compliment with some surprise. The words had been spoken so easily, so naturally, that it was somehow quite wrong to question them, yet they were curious words to come from a complete stranger. This whole crazy day had a strange and quite unnatural and unending quality that did not add up. To be sitting here on a log with Allan Forbes listening while he told her she was 'perfect' when she had set off from home in a panic to look for Nick.

'I have lost him,' she said suddenly and inconsequently. 'Nick, I mean. I shut him in his room after breakfast for being rude to me and he got out of the window by climbing down a rope ladder and he hasn't come back to lunch.'

The man beside her nodded his head as if she were recounting a perfectly normal episode in Nick's life.

'Of course I'm worried. I must find him!' she added less forcefully.

'I wouldn't try to find him. I'm sure it's just what he hoped you'd do when he set off. He was trying to scare you. If you go after him, you'll have done just what he wanted.'

'But suppose something has happened to him?' Beverly said anxiously. 'Suppose he and Paul went tree climbing and they fell off or something.'

'Paul?'

'Paul Marshel. Of course, he's older and I suppose he would come home and tell me or his mother if Nick had had an accident. But Nick's never missed a meal before . . .'

'It's my bet he won't have missed a meal today. Paul probably had some food with him and shared it with Nick. I don't suppose he even thought about lunch till he got hungry, and by that time he'd no doubt forgotten why he dashed off the way he did. He wouldn't want Paul to know and he wouldn't want to have to explain his reluctance to go home for lunch. I expect they just said, "Let's have lunch here", and had it.'

Beverly looked up at the calm face beside her and said: 'You don't seem to think I ought to be worried. But it's very naughty of Nick. I shall get Jonnie to give him a thoroughly good dressing down when he gets back.'

'Good! Now you're at least certain he'll be back. A moment ago you had the young rascal dead in a ditch. I expect Paul has put him up to this. He's not exactly a good influence, you know.'

'Paul Marshel? But his mother is such a nice woman.'

'Yes, I know,' the man said. 'I like her, too, but the father's a thoroughly bad lot. Drinks too much and is pretty unsavoury one way and another. Paul's a strange lad. It's my belief he could do a lot better at school if he wanted, but he doesn't want to, and he distracts your Nicholas. His marks are right down this term. As a matter of fact, I was coming along to have a talk with you about him sometime, but, well, I just haven't had time.'

'Oh dear!' Beverly said miserably. 'I wish I knew what to do. Nick and Paul are such good friends, and I've encouraged them to be. You see, my husband is away from home a lot and Nick needs someone . . . a companion. I thought Paul seemed a nice enough boy.'

'I'm not saying he's a *bad* child,' Allan Forbes said thoughtfully. 'All the same, I don't think he's the best companion for a boy like Nick. Nick's at an impressionable age, and liable to set far too much store by an older boy's example. He's quite all right in class until Paul starts a shindy, and then he follows suit and ends up the worst of the lot. I don't think he'd behave like that if it weren't for Paul.'

'Then you think I should try to break up their friendship?'

The man looked directly at her as he spoke. 'I don't like interfering with children's friendships,' he said carefully. 'It makes for complications if you do. But in this case, I think if Nick were my child, I would. He's a particularly nice little boy. I like him. I wouldn't want him growing up into a bully.'

'Nick—a bully! But he's always so gentle with the younger children.'

'At home, maybe, but not at school.'

'But why didn't you tell me before?' Beverly asked. 'I had no idea Nick wasn't behaving the way he should.'

The man beside her laid a restraining hand on her arm as if sensing her anxiety. 'Because so far nothing very serious has happened. It seemed to me to be just a phase he was going through, and in fact I'm sure that is all it is.

He's a very nice boy at heart. He's intelligent, too. I knew he was copying Paul and guessed he'd been a little too much impressed by an older boy's ideas of what was right and what was wrong. I did not know he was seeing a great deal of Paul out of school. I had hoped he might be an influence for the good on Paul.'

'Does Mrs Marshel know what you feel about her boy?' Beverly asked abruptly.

'Well, I have spoken to her once or twice, but, you know, it isn't always easy for a master to criticize a child to its parents. Parents have a way of being quite certain it isn't their child at fault.'

Beverly's face relaxed into a smile. 'Well, you can't accuse me of that. You are the one who has been trying to exonerate Nick. Goodness only knows what he's up to this minute, but I know Jonnie will give him a good telling off and a severe punishment to go with it when he gets back.'

'Not too tough,' Allan Forbes said quietly. 'After all, he's only a little boy yet. Besides, it's so easy to give vent to one's own feelings in that way and it doesn't always meet the bill . . . a thrashing, I mean.'

'Then you are against corporal punishment?' Beverly asked curiously.

'No, not really. But it should be applied in moderation, I think. Did you ever read that poem by Coventry Patmore called "The Toys"?'

'I don't think so,' Beverly admitted. 'Say it to me. I love poetry.'

Quietly, the man beside her began to speak. Beverly watched his face, seeing in the steady profile a sudden inexplicable sadness, hearing it in his voice, too. Then her mind became fixed on the words he was quoting.

'My little Son, who look'd from thoughtful
    eyes
And moved and spoke in quiet grown-up
    wise,
Having my law the seventh time disobey'd,
I struck him, and dismiss'd
With hard word and unkiss'd,
His Mother, who was patient, being dead.
Then, fearing lest his grief should hinder
    sleep,
I visited his bed,
But found him slumbering deep,
With darken'd eyelids, and their lashes yet
From his late sobbing wet.
And I, with moan,
Kissing away his tears, left others of my
    own;
For, on a table drawn beside his head,
He had put, within his reach,
A box of counters and a red-veined stone,
A piece of glass abraded by the beach,
And six or seven shells.
A bottle with bluebells,
And two French copper coins, ranged there

    with careful art,
To comfort his sad heart.
So when that night I pray'd
To God, I wept, and said:
Ah, when at last we lie with tranced breath,
Not vexing Thee in death,
And Thou rememberest of what toys
We made our joys,
How weakly understood
The great commanded good,
Then, fatherly not less
Than I whom Thou has moulded from the
    clay,
Thou'lt leave Thy wrath, and say,
"I will be sorry for their childishness." '

Both were silent for a moment or two when his voice stopped at the poem's finish. Beverly was moved and extremely curious about the man beside her. What a strange person he was—not a bit as she had imagined him to be; not a bit like the usual school-master in a village school. He was obviously very well educated, a man of sensitivity and perception.

'You're not married?' she asked suddenly.

'No. I was, once. But my wife and our small son were killed the last year of the war.'

So that was why that face was so full of sadness just now. He must have been thinking of the terrible tragedy of his own life.

'It seems so inadequate to say one is sorry . . .'

He turned and looked at her and smiled, a

91

quiet, gentle smile, as if he were comforting her. 'You mustn't be upset on my account. It happened eleven years ago and I've learned to accept it in that time. I don't very often talk about them, but there's something about you which reminds me a little of Louise. She must have been about your age when . . . when she died.'

'Do you live alone now?' Beverly asked curiously.

'I have a cottage just this side of Bartel village. It's tucked away under a hill, so I don't suppose you've ever noticed it. Sometime you might care to walk over with Nick and have tea with me.'

'Oh, I'd like to very much. I love walking; though I don't often have a lot of time nowadays. There's four more at home, you know, besides Nick.'

'Four? I knew there is Philip in the kindergarten class and a sister coming next September—I didn't know there were five.'

Beverly laughed.

'I'm afraid so; the twins are just toddlers. But I've more time now we have a French girl staying with us. If you really mean that invitation to tea, we'd love to come. How long would it take us?'

'From here? About half an hour if you go by the lanes. How about Wednesday week? It's half term so Nick and I will both be off from school. If you like, I'll walk over and meet you both here.'

Beverly nodded. Then suddenly remembered that she was supposed to be going on holiday. But she knew now that she wouldn't go alone. She'd wait till Jonnie could get away, too. Besides, from all accounts it sounded as if Nick was going to need some extra care and attention. It wasn't fair to leave her mother in charge if Nick was going to be troublesome.

The thought of her small son brought her to her feet.

'I really ought to find Nick,' she said. 'I wish I knew where to look though.'

Allan Forbes stood up and laughed. Beverly noticed inconsequently how much younger he looked when he smiled. He was attractive in a rugged, masculine way.

'If I were you, I'd go home and wait there for the young scamp. I'm sure you've no real cause to worry.'

'Well, if you really think that, perhaps I will go home. Look, if you're not doing anything, why not come home with me and let me give you some tea. Jonnie—my husband—may be home by now and I'd like you to meet him and the other children, too.'

'I'm sure you've enough to do without me there,' the man said hesitantly.

'But I'd like you to come,' Beverly insisted. 'That is, if you wouldn't be bored. Maybe you have enough of kids at school.'

Again he laughed. 'Well, fortunately I love

them all, or I wouldn't have picked on being a school-teacher. If you really mean it, I'd like to come.'

They began walking back along the lane towards Beverly's home, talking lightly and easily as if they were old friends. Beverly felt happier than she had done for days. She did not analyse her feelings, but the sudden lifting of her spirits was there, none the less, and she smiled often and her steps were light.

Mostly they talked of Nick and school. By the time they reached the house, the last of her fears for Nick's safety had vanished; what a reassuring man Allan Forbes was!

The children rushed to her as they heard her voice at the front door.

'Is Nick back?' Philip asked eagerly. 'Annette said he'd escaped. Has he run away? Will he get a bad punishment?'

'*I* think he's silly!' Julia remarked placidly. 'There's crumpets for tea and if he isn't back soon, we'll eat them all.' She turned her rosy-cheeked, chubby little face to the stranger. 'Who are you? Phil and I thought you might be Daddy, but I suppose he's still playing golf. Are you staying for tea? We're having crumpets.'

Beverly allowed them to lead Allan into the sitting-room and was glad of the chance to stop a moment and think. Jonnie wasn't back. Where had he got to? Should she ring the club again? Surely he couldn't stay out all day? Or was he trying to punish her in some way because of the way she'd behaved last night?

Her chin rose stubbornly.

If that was the way he wanted it to be, he could have it. The last thing she wanted was to let him think she cared whether he ever came home. At least, when he came back, he'd find her enjoying herself for a change. It might do him a power of good to see Allan Forbes entertaining his wife and children.

'I'll go and see if Annette has started tea,' she told Allan. 'Now, Julia, don't climb all over him.'

When she came back into the room Julia was curled up in Allan's lap, her head against his shoulder, Philip leaning against his knee, both silent and absorbed in the story he was telling them. Julia put a hand to her lips to show Beverly she must not interrupt.

'. . . and so Thumbelina found her Prince, married him and lived happily ever after.'

'Tell it again!' Julia said promptly. 'Please!'

Allan laughed and lifted her off his knee, dumping her fat little body down beside her brother's.

'Another time,' he said. Smiling at Beverly, he added, 'Can I do anything?'

'No, thank you. Tea is ready. We're having nursery tea, if you don't mind; the twins are far too young to eat in the drawing-room and, anyway, Julia and Philip are better behaved if they're sitting at table.'

He followed her into the dining-room where the twins, already in their high chairs, were stuffing small squares of bread and honey into their open mouths. Annette joined them and they sat down to a noisy meal, Julia and Philip talking incessantly to their visitor who seemed to know just the right way to converse with them.

Beverly looked at them happily. This was the way family meals should be; and how nice Nick's school-teacher had turned out to be. What a pity they hadn't met him long before this. He must be lonely living by himself; maybe this kind of home life was just what he needed. And she so badly needed a friend, especially now.

It was six o'clock and Allan Forbes was just about to depart when Nick, filthy from head to toe, burst in through the kitchen door. He made no attempt to conceal himself but went straight to Beverly, his face rosy and his eyes bright.

'Gosh, Mum, I've had a super day!' he said. 'Paul and me walked all the way to Bartel Wood and we nearly caught a squirrel, and, Mum, we pinched some potatoes from a farm and made a camp-fire and baked them, and they were super. For lunch, I mean. But I haven't had any tea yet—'

He broke off as he suddenly caught sight of his school-teacher. His young face suddenly stiffened as he remembered that this was no ordinary day. He was in dire disgrace and he was supposed to have spent the morning in his room. It had seemed such an enormous long time ago that he'd rushed into the house forgetting all about it. Mr Forbes and his mother, standing together, suddenly reminded him.

'Gosh!' he said flatly. 'Gosh!'

'You seem to have forgotten you weren't supposed to have gone out,' Beverly said. 'And I don't suppose you've stopped to think once how worried I've been.'

'Gosh!' was all Nick could find to say.

'Suppose I have a chat with Nick?' Allan said with a glance at Beverly's face. 'Alone!'

Beverly returned the glance with gratitude.

'Would you? Thanks. Nick, go into the dining-room, please. And take off those filthy boots first.'

'Seems to have had a good day,' Allan said with a grin which Beverly could not but imitate. 'Still, he's got to learn he can't do this kind of thing. Don't you worry. I'll deal with it.'

'But you won't—'

'Strike him and dismiss him with harsh words . . .?' the man quoted simply. 'No, I don't think it's necessary. See you in a minute.'

In the dining-room Nick stood with his back to the window facing his teacher with wariness. He had a very healthy respect for Mr Forbes, and he was impressed that his mother had

97

thought fit to call him in to deal with this crime. He must have done something pretty serious for her to do that.

'Well, Nicholas, I hate to spoil what has obviously been a thoroughly happy day, but, all the same, I think it's time you accepted a few responsibilities. You're quite old enough to know what you're doing. Your mother has been in a terrible state of fright about you. Is that what you wanted? Did you want to hurt her because she had had to punish you for being rude?'

Nick shifted on to another patch of carpet. 'No, I didn't want to hurt her. I just wanted to go out. It's silly to stay indoors on a super day like this morning. I don't see why I shouldn't go. She said yesterday I could. Besides, Paul was waiting for me. He'd have thought I was a sissy to stick in my room just because my mum said so.'

'What Paul might have thought isn't in the least important, Nick, not when you weigh it up against your mother's feelings. Paul is just a rather silly boy. Oh, I know you think he's clever and that he's a friend of yours, but he's not a bit clever really. If he were, he wouldn't be in a class for seven-year-olds when he's past ten.'

'Well, he's clever at other things!' Nick defended his friend loyally. 'Things like tying knots and carving your name on a tree and tracking squirrels and things. And he's jolly good at pinching potatoes. He had to go right into the yard and he crept in so quietly nobody saw.'

'I see! So you think it's clever to steal?'

Nick flushed. 'It wasn't stealing. We were just pinching a few for our lunch.'

'Pinching is stealing, Nicholas. The potatoes weren't yours and you weren't paying for them, so you stole them. I would have thought *you'd* know better. Escaping from your bedroom down a rope ladder was naughty but not bad. Stealing *is* bad, and I'm sure you do know that. Just the same as hurting someone who loves you is bad. If you had stopped once today to think about your mother, you must have known she would worry. Mothers always do, unless they know you are safe somewhere and what time you'll be home. Then they don't fuss.'

Nick grinned. 'Gosh, that's right! Mum doesn't really fuss much. Did she think I'd run away or something?'

'She didn't know what to think. Don't do it again, Nick; not if you love her, which I'm sure you do. And don't ever steal again either. You do know that was wrong, don't you?'

'Y-yes! I s'pose so. But it was jolly good fun!'

'There are plenty of ways of having fun without resorting to theft!' Allan said quietly. 'And you know, Nick, Paul is by no means the only person who can tie knots or track squirrels or bake potatoes. Why, although you're only seven, I could teach you all those tricks in one afternoon, and I dare say a good many more difficult knots than Paul can tie, too.'

'Gosh, would you?' Nick asked eagerly. 'Paul says he's got to be the leader because he can do things better'n me. But I could be leader if I knew more'n him, couldn't I?'

'Yes, you could. What's more, I think you *should* be leader if Paul's idea of leading means leading into mischief. But you'll need to pull up your socks, Nick, before you're captain of anyone else. Captains have to think before they act. What you did to your mother today you did without thinking first.'

'Well, I can think all right when I have to,' Nick said with conviction. 'I had to think about tying that rope ladder to my window to get out. I say, sir, do you think a granny knot would hold with my weight on the end? I'm sure it wasn't a proper reef knot I tied. It's right over left and then left over right, isn't it? Will you show me?'

'Not now, Nick. I want you to go and find your mother and tell her how sorry you are. You are sorry, aren't you? Deep down inside, I mean?'

'Gosh, yes!' Nick said. 'Mum's jolly nice really, and—well, I s'pose I was rude. I like her much better'n Daddy.'

Allan Forbes was shocked, not just by the

100

child's words but by the casual tone in which they were delivered. Why didn't Nick care for his father? What kind of man was he? Surely a decent enough fellow if a woman like Beverly Colt loved him. And he must be fond of kids or he would never have had five!

'I expect you just said that because it's usually your father who administers a little discipline,' he said lightly.

'You mean Daddy does the punishing? Not much,' Nick said scornfully. 'He's never here. He's always working.'

'I see. But at the weekends when he's home . . .'

'Oh, he's always playing golf. Silly game, golf! I'm not going to play golf when I grow up. I'm going to be a footballer like Stanley Matthews.'

'Yes, well, run along now and find your mother,' the man said quickly. The puzzle was beginning to fall into place. The boy's tone of voice when he spoke of his father was a pretty clear indication of how he felt about him— jealous and resentful. It was usually something of the sort that started a thoroughly decent kid like young Nicholas off on the wrong road. But how could he suggest to Beverly that her son needed a little more of his father's time and attention?

As if he were the devil whose name had just been spoken, a man's voice could be heard in the hall. Then Beverly's:

101

'But, Jonnie, where were you all afternoon? I was worried to death because Nick had disappeared and you chose the same time to do a disappearing act.'

'I was at the club, of course.'

'But, Jonnie, you weren't. I rang at lunchtime and they said you'd left.'

'All the same, I was there. Whoever spoke to you couldn't have looked very far for me.'

'Time I went,' Allan Forbes thought, suddenly tired and dispirited. A domestic quarrel was obviously about to ensue and he knew that he would not be able to feel impartial. He'd already taken a strong liking to Beverly Colt, and from what young Nick had just said, an equal dislike to his father.

He went out to the hall and held out his hand to Beverly.

'Thanks very much for giving me tea. I enjoyed my afternoon, and I don't think Nick will do anything like it again,' he said.

'Oh, Mr Forbes, this is my husband,' Beverly said quickly, nervously. 'Jonnie, this is Nick's teacher. I don't think you've met before. We met when I was out looking for Nick and he very kindly came back with me.'

'I've just given your young son a good "talking to",' Allan said, and could not refrain from adding, 'since you weren't here, and Mrs Colt felt a little masculine influence would be a good thing.'

Jonnie flushed. 'I see! What did the boy

do?'

'Not a great deal, but enough!' Allan said. 'He climbed out of his bedroom window and took a day off with Paul Marshel. I gather they stole some potatoes from a farmer and baked them over a camp-fire. I should say the biggest crime was worrying his mother, though I don't honestly think that occurred to him till I pointed it out. He's a good kid, Mr Colt, but I don't think Paul Marshel is any too good a companion for him.'

'Oh! Well, thanks for dealing with it. Won't you stay and have a drink?'

'No, I must get home,' Allan said quickly. He turned back to Beverly and noticed how pale and tired she looked. 'Don't worry!' he said. 'Nick's all right. I've told him if he likes to come over sometime to my place I'll teach him a few things he wants to learn. Thanks again for asking me here.'

Beverly stood watching him as he walked away down the garden path. She felt as if some strong support were being dragged away from beneath her. Now she had to face Jonnie and find out where he'd been all day.

Jonnie was in the sitting-room pouring himself a drink when she rejoined him. He avoided her eyes, and it was quite plain to Beverly that he was nervous.

'Where were you, Jonnie?'

'I told you . . . at the club. For goodness' sake don't start nagging, Beverly. I wasn't to know Nick had done a bunk, or even that you'd had to punish him this morning.'

'You weren't very likely to know since you weren't here,' Beverly said coldly, her hands clenched at her sides. 'It seems as if you prefer to be out of your own home than in it these days. The children and I rarely see you now except at the weekends, and if you're going to start spending Saturday as well as Sunday playing golf, you might as well stop away altogether.'

'I don't see what you've got to complain about. You said if you had Annette to help in the house, you'd be more than satisfied.'

Beverly flushed. 'I didn't engage Annette as a replacement for my husband's company, Jonnie, and I do expect a bit of help from you with your children. If you'd been here today none of this would have happened with Nick.'

'Just because the boy had the guts to climb out of his window and stay out the whole day—'

'Don't defend him, Jonnie. He was extremely rude to me after breakfast and he had to be punished. I wouldn't have kept him in his room all day. If you'd been here you could have dealt with him and then he wouldn't have had to be punished further.'

'So it's all my fault!' Jonnie said truculently.

'Yes, I think it is! And I think it's time we had a good long talk about our marriage, Jonnie. It's not just today, or Nick or the golf.

It's . . . it's everything!'

Nerves, tiredness, tension, all combined to bring Beverly to the point where she could no longer restrain the threatening tears. She sat down in the nearest arm-chair and for a moment or two sobbed uncontrollably.

Jonnie looked down at her, appalled. He'd never seen Beverly cry like this . . . not in all their years of married life. Was this what he had done to her?

'Bev, don't!' he said wretchedly. He took a step towards her, his hand held out to touch her bent head, but slowly he withdrew it. He was afraid to touch her, afraid of what might be said; afraid to face up to the mess he'd made of their life together.

He'd been with Elinor all afternoon. He'd gone back to lunch with her in a mood of defiance. Elinor, probing his mood while they played a round of golf during the morning, had lost no time in taking full advantage of the situation.

'If she moved out of your bed, honey, she must have stopped caring altogether. I don't know why you worry the way you do. Chances are she couldn't care less about us if she did know.'

'But you don't understand her, Elinor. She was dreadfully disappointed because I'd backed out of the holiday. I think she acted on impulse. It was her way of showing me how upset she was. She'd have come back if I'd asked her.'

'You mean she expected *you* to be the one to eat humble pie!' Gradually, Jonnie's feeling of guilt about last night had vanished and it had seemed as if it had all been Beverly's doing.

But now here alone with Beverly, he felt mean and deceitful and he hated himself. There was no excuse, and deep down inside he knew it and fought against it hard. Beverly had every right to complain and to demand an explanation, but there wasn't any explanation he could give her. He couldn't say: 'I spent the afternoon with Elinor Wilmot. I was making love to her. I was being unfaithful and because I'm so weak, I'll probably be unfaithful again. Elinor fascinates me. I can't leave her alone. When I'm with her, she bewitches me. It all seems so completely right. Now it seems wrong, but I can't give her up. I can't.'

'Beverly, please stop. There's nothing to cry about. Nick's safely home, and that chap Forbes seems to have dealt with him quite satisfactorily. I'm home and I'm not going out all tomorrow. Suppose we take the kids on a picnic if this nice weather holds?'

She looked up then, her face wet with tears. 'Jonnie, you mean that? It would be wonderful!'

' 'Course I mean it,' Jonnie said, feeling better now that he was offering something by way of compensation. 'Now, what about some supper?'

Beverly blew her nose and tried to straighten her hair. 'All right,' she said shakily. 'But before I go, will you tell me what you *were* doing this afternoon? I—I suppose it's silly of me, but I keep thinking . . . well, Jonnie, were you with Elinor Wilmot?'

Jonnie's whole body tautened at the name coming so unexpectedly, and without warning, from his wife's lips. A quick denial rose in his mind but he hesitated a moment, and in that moment, gave himself away.

Beverly's face was white as she said: 'So you *were* with her? Jonnie, why? What does she mean to you? Are you attracted to her?'

'I like her company,' Jonnie said stiffly. 'She's good company and amusing, and . . . well, fun to be with,' he finished lamely.

'And I suppose I haven't been amusing and fun to be with! All right, I'll accept that, though it isn't easy to be fun and amusing when you have five children to care for and a house to run and very little time alone with your husband. That's why I was counting on this holiday, Jonnie. Don't you see? It's because I've known in my heart that we were beginning to lose each other and perhaps a little of our love, that I knew we had to have time by ourselves to be the people we really are. Jonnie, you're not in love with her, are you?'

'Don't be so damn silly!' The words came

107

out roughly and his tone frightened Beverly.

'Well, it may have seemed a silly question to you, but not to me. She must mean something to you for you to prefer her company to mine.'

'She's just a friend,' Jonnie lied quickly.

'Then you believe men and women can have platonic friendships?' Beverly asked pointedly.

'Why not? I suppose you and this Forbes fellow are friends? Just because you asked him back to tea, I don't imagine you've been falling into bed with him.'

'Jonnie!' Beverly's voice was shocked. 'That really is silly. I only met him this afternoon. As if I'd even consider Allan Forbes in that way.'

'Then why attribute ulterior motives to my friendship with Elinor Wilmot?'

'I suppose because I'm just jealous,' Beverly said miserably. 'But if your friendship with her is so innocent, why did you lie to me about being at the club?'

'Because I knew you'd make a scene if I told you I'd been with her,' Jonnie said. 'Now let's put an end to this, Beverly. I've told you I'll take you out tomorrow. Isn't that enough?'

'I don't know!' Beverly's voice was almost a whisper. 'I think I'd rather you said "I love *you* . . . that's why she doesn't mean anything to me." Oh, Jonnie, don't turn away like that. I don't mean to nag about this, but nothing will ever be right again between us until I'm sure. Are you going to see her again?'

'Are you going to see Allan Forbes again?'

'Yes, but I wouldn't if you asked me not to; if I thought you were really jealous.'

'Then I think you should grant me the same freedom. I may very well see Elinor again or I may not. But you've nothing to be afraid of. I've no intention of walking out on you and the children.'

This last remark, more than anything else Jonnie had said so far, shocked Beverly. For him to have said such a thing was in itself an indication of how far in his own mind he had been thinking about Elinor Wilmot. He had *felt it necessary to reassure his wife that he wasn't going to leave her* . . . as if it had ever entered her mind.

She was silenced at last. Slowly, thoughtfully, she got up from her chair and, without looking at Jonnie, went up to their room to tidy herself and try to remove the traces of tears. Annette was putting the children to bed and they called out to her, but for the moment she could not face them. Without any real consciousness of her actions, she once again took her pillow and night-things from the bed where she had replaced them that morning, and went with them into the spare room. She couldn't bear the thought of lying beside Jonnie while her mind was in this turmoil. She wanted to be alone to sort things out. Or at least, sort out the facts she knew. And even then, Beverly asked herself bitterly, did she know half the truth? Elinor

Wilmot! Elinor Wilmot! The very name rang like a warning bell in her ears.

CHAPTER SEVEN

'Elinor, I can't see you again. It's got to end now before something awful happens!'

Jonnie walked away from her where he could no longer feel the touch of her hands on his arm, nor look at that provocative mouth so close to his own.

'Something awful? What are you trying to say, honey?'

Even across the width of the room, he could still smell that heady perfume of hers. He felt desperate and utterly miserable. The day had been a terrible strain both on him and, as he rightly guessed, on Beverly. He had kept his promise to take them on a picnic, and the children had been wildly excited. Fortunately, their eager chatter had made it unnecessary for him and Beverly to talk to each other. Beverly was very quiet. There were great dark rings of violet beneath her eyes and he guessed that she, too, had had another sleepless night. If it hadn't been for the tension between them, the day would have been so perfect. The weather was warm, sunny and soft. The kids had been allowed to discard cardigans and run about with their faces upturned to the

110

sunshine or bent studiously over hot handfuls of wild flowers they had gathered. It could all have been so perfect if only he had not had Elinor crowding every thought; making him feel guilty and a cheat. How he hated himself! How right Beverly was to hate him!

When at last the day was over and they were home and the children tucked up in bed, Jonnie had known he could not go on like this any longer. He had to put an end to his association with Elinor, or else see his marriage break up. He couldn't go on deceiving Beverly, seeing her pale and miserable and suspicious, knowing something was horribly wrong. Sooner or later she would find out what it was, and then he knew he would have to face up to a decision; unless Beverly made it for him and asked for a divorce.

But he didn't want a divorce; he never had. He only wanted Elinor—sometimes. She'd never suggested marriage to him and he'd never contemplated it.

'Beverly knows I was with you yesterday. It can't go on, Elinor. I'm no good at this hole-in-the-corner kind of affair.'

Elinor looked at him sharply. She knew that she would have to play her cards carefully if she were not to lose him. And she had no intention of losing him yet awhile, anyway. Their affair had barely begun.

'That's only because it's the first time you've

been unfaithful,' she said calmly, matter-of-factly. 'It comes easier after you get used to the idea. Still, if you want it to be goodbye, I'm not going to try to prevent you. You're a man, not a boy, and you know what's best.'

Jonnie swung round, his face twisted. 'That's just it, Elinor. I don't know any more what is best. I know we are absolutely right for each other; that we must have been made for each other. You said so yesterday, remember. It's as perfect for you as for me, isn't it?'

Elinor smiled at him. 'Why, you don't have to ask me, honey. No man has ever made me as happy as you do. I guess there never will be anyone else quite the same.'

'No, but there probably will be someone else. That's the trouble, Elinor; you don't feel the same way about all this as I do. You aren't in love with me. You just want me.'

'Sure I want you. Is there anything wrong in that? Love—well, I thought you wouldn't want my love, Jonnie . . . that's why I never told you I loved you. I didn't want to make things more difficult for you. After all, you've been very fair with me. I've known all along you were married and that you didn't intend to leave your wife for me. It hardly seemed my place to ask you for love.'

Jonnie felt even more of a heel. He wasn't sure he had wanted love from Elinor, but pride demanded that he meant more to her than just a casual lover.

'Then you do care?' he persisted, taking her in his arms and looking deep into her strange, inscrutable eyes.

'Shall I show you how I care?'

'No, no!' Jonnie said quickly, drawing away again. 'You mustn't tempt me, Elinor. You've got to help me to be strong about this. I just can't go on being unfaithful to Beverly. Don't you think . . . Elinor, can't we just be friends?'

For a moment she began to laugh, but seeing the expression in his eyes, she quelled the laughter quickly and said:

'I guess not, Jonnie; not if we're going to be honest about all this. I think the link between us is too strong. But I'll try, darling. I'll try real hard rather than lose you altogether.'

Jonnie felt like a man reprieved from the gallows. He need not lose her completely, and at the same time he could still play fair with Beverly. If he were not actually unfaithful to his wife, he need have no conscience about her or the children.

'I don't know why you bother with me,' he said meekly. 'It can't be much fun for you, darling.'

'I'd go through a great deal just for an hour or two alone with you, Jonnie. That's how much you mean to me.'

'Oh, Elinor, darling!'

She was back in his arms now and he was kissing her mouth, trying to keep a brake on his emotions and on hers. He could quite understand that it would be more difficult for her. She had no reason to hold back, no one to whom she would be unfaithful when she gave herself to him. But he had to be strong for both of them, for Beverly's sake; or if not for her directly, for his marriage.

'Elinor, I'd better go home. We'll both be weak if I stay here now. Let me go, darling!'

She gave in easily, too clever to reproach him or to try to take a further trick. It sufficed for the time being that she had prevented him breaking with her completely. Jonnie was weak . . . he'd give way again soon enough. Meantime, his uncertainty gave an added piquancy to their relationship, at least as far as she was concerned. She was bored with the man who too easily and too readily became her slave. It was really the 'hunt' she enjoyed, and then the fruits of victory were all the sweeter for being delayed. She never gave Beverly a thought. If a woman couldn't keep her husband's affections, that was her folly, her misfortune. It had nothing to do with Elinor. If Beverly wanted to keep Jonnie, let her fight for him. But somehow Elinor didn't think she need worry much about her opponent.

Jonnie returned home feeling virtuous and for once able to look Beverly squarely in the eyes. But Beverly had gone to bed in the spare room, and he had no opportunity to talk to her. It was frustrating to say the least. Moodily, he went along to their bedroom and alone to bed.

*　　　*　　　*

By the Wednesday of half term, no further word had been spoken about the holiday except for Beverly's brief comment that she had decided against going alone. Jonnie announced that he might be late home from the office that night.

'I may be late home myself, anyway,' Beverly replied coolly. 'Allan Forbes rang up on Monday afternoon and he has asked Nick and me to tea.'

Jonnie felt a pang of annoyance. It was a bit much to swallow that Beverly should be able to go off and have tea-parties until all hours while he slaved away at his desk. And he really was working late on that Wednesday. He decided he did not like Allan Forbes. Nick had developed an annoying habit of mentioning him on every possible occasion, and he was sick of the man's name.

'Personally, I think Forbes had better pull up his socks a bit; you can tell him I said so,' he told Beverly at Wednesday morning breakfast. 'Nick's manners are getting worse and worse. He only just stops short of being rude to me every time I speak to him.'

Beverly raised her eyebrows. 'I don't see what that has to do with Allan Forbes. He's supposed to teach Nick lessons, not manners.

That's our job, Jonnie.'

Jonnie flushed and his lips tightened. 'Well, a little more discipline at school wouldn't be a bad thing,' he said, and left the room. Beverly had a way of turning a phrase so that it always seemed as if *he* were in the wrong. It was her job more than his to see to Nick's manners. He was not home enough to be able to control the boy properly. If Beverly didn't take care, he'd begin to think he was being a fool to deny himself the full pleasure of Elinor's company for her sake. If Beverly wanted him around more, then it was time she tried to make things a little more pleasant for him.

Beverly was preoccupied with similar thoughts as she and Nick walked across the fields in the direction of Allan's cottage. She hadn't seen him again since the Saturday, yet somehow she felt as if she were going to tea with an old friend. Maybe it was because Nick talked about him so much. It seemed that Nick must always have someone to fill his universe. Once it had been Jonnie with 'Daddy says . . . Daddy does . . .' until she nearly went crazy. Then it had been Paul Marshel until Allan deflated that bubble by showing Nick the older boy really wasn't so clever after all. Now it was Allan himself. 'Mr Forbes said I could read the best in the class . . . Mr Forbes said I might go up to Form II next term if I keep on working so hard. Mr Forbes said he'd show me a Bowline knot and a Surgeon's knot when we

116

go to tea on Wednesday . . . Mr Forbes has got an aviary full of budgerigars and he's got a pet one that talks . . .'

She'd learned a lot about Allan Forbes since their last meeting.

He came to meet them, walking across the fields towards them with long, easy strides. Beverly watched him approach with a sudden unaccountable shyness. Maybe it was because Jonnie had flung it in her face that this man was a possible 'boy-friend'—a hateful thing to have said.

'Hullo, Mrs Colt. Hullo, Nick!' He seemed quite at ease and he chatted quietly, as if aware of Beverly's shyness, and wanted to put her at ease as well.

'It's another beautiful day,' he commented as Nick swooped ahead of them to chase a large Brimstone butterfly. 'Nick seems to be full of his usual good spirits.'

'He's been so looking forward to today,' Beverly said. 'He has talked of little else. Moreover, he's been as good as gold since you spoke to him that afternoon. What did you say to bring about such a transformation?'

Allan smiled. 'I just told him mothers were there to be loved and taken care of. I don't think it ever occurs to young children that their parents need looking after, unless it is pointed out to them, either by word or example.'

Beverly understood what he meant. A boy

117

copied his father in such matters and Jonnie's abrupt, uncaring attitude to her had been Nick's yardstick for the last six months. She was not sure whether she resented Allan Forbes' implied criticism of her husband. It was too near the truth and he had no right to say it!

As if guessing her thoughts, Allan said quietly: 'I hope you don't think I'm criticizing Nick's home in any way, Mrs Colt. He's one of the lucky ones. So many of the lads I deal with come from broken homes, or their fathers drink, or the mothers just don't care. You'd be horrified if you knew how many such homes there are. I suppose it is the inevitable aftermath of war, but it seems as if people can't be satisfied any more with the simple things of life . . . the beautiful things. All they want are bigger cars, television sets, money to spend on this or that. Of course, there are many very good homes—far more than bad ones. But it always upsets me when I learn of another broken home. It so often means a broken child, too.'

'You are an idealist, Mr Forbes. I suppose I am, too. But life isn't kind to idealists. I think one needs to be a realist these days, and, you know, it isn't as easy as you suppose to be happy on twopence. I used to think my mother was being old-fashioned and narrow-minded when she warned me that love flies out when poverty flies in, but now I'm not so sure.'

'Of course, money makes things easier,' the man agreed. 'But it can't make two people happier if they can't get along with each other.'

Beverly felt her heart beating with a strange rapidity. This man was so wise, so sympathetic. Why not confide in him her fears for her own marriage? But Jonnie would hate to think she had discussed their marriage with an outsider. And he would feel Allan was an outsider. Strangely, she did not.

'You don't agree with me?' Allan prompted, watching the changing expressions on her mobile face.

'Yes, I think I do! But you can't always see all the facts from the outside. You condemn those parents who break up their homes—but do you really know what caused the break-up?'

'Whatever little thing caused the final break, it can only really be because two adults are unable to reach a compromise; that they have failed in their efforts to live together. Surely if they have children, they should realize that their own desires must come second to their children's need.'

They had reached Allan's cottage now and Nick had seen the aviary. He was staring into the wire cage, entranced.

'You can go inside if you want, Nick!' Allan said. 'Some of the birds are quite tame and if you keep very still, they'll come and perch on your arm or shoulder. Then you can look round the garden and see if you can find some groundsel for them.'

Nick nodded in delight and Allan indicated to Beverly the two deck-chairs placed on the flagstone terrace.

'I'll show you the cottage in a moment,' he said. 'Let's enjoy the sunshine here for a few moments. Tell me, Beverly, what is it that is troubling you? Perhaps I can help?'

His use of her Christian name seemed as natural as his incredible sensitivity to her thoughts and moods. She noticed both but neither seemed strange.

'I . . . I want to talk about myself, but somehow it seems disloyal, in a way. Allan . . .' She turned to him and looked directly into his eyes, her own bewildered and unhappy. 'Allan, although in one way it seems as if you and I have been friends for a lifetime, yet I know we are comparative strangers. Would it be right for me to discuss my marriage with you?'

Allan Forbes looked away. He had invited her confidence, had encouraged her to say what was on her mind. Yet could it be right for her to discuss her husband with him? He wanted so much to help her and to see her radiant and happy. How could he achieve this without knowing what was wrong? He'd thought so much about her since that first meeting.

I'm falling in love with her! he thought. She doesn't know it, but she senses it. I love her because she is like Louise. I feel the same desire to protect her, care for her, worship her. But such a love can only hurt her. She belongs to another man.

He stared down at his hands, clasped together loosely between his knees. Fulfilment obviously was not meant for him in this lifetime. The thought saddened him but could not make him bitter. This girl with her beauty and her sadness, her smile and her spirit was like a ghost from the past, evoking memories and stirring desires. As long as he remembered that his love was gone for ever, he could not harm her by giving her his devotion, his sympathy, his understanding.

'Whatever it is that is causing you so much worry will not go on, Beverly,' he said slowly. 'Nothing in life stands still, even when we would have it so. It will get better or worse.'

'But it's the not knowing!' Beverly cried out. 'I cannot live with this uncertainty. Allan, I think my husband is falling in love with someone else. I think he is finding me, the children, and his home, a burden and not a pleasure. I'm afraid. I feel I must have failed him in some way and that it's my fault.'

It was said. If disloyalty it was, it was too late now to withdraw the words. She wasn't even sorry. Allan would never betray her confidence. She knew that without any assurance from him.

'It won't help to apportion blame, Beverly,' he said gently. 'What matters is the future.

You love him very much?'

Beverly drew in her breath sharply. 'I don't even know that any more. I loved him more than anyone in the world when I married him. I didn't believe it was possible for two people to be so happy. But now I feel as if he is a stranger. I don't understand him any more. He isn't the same person, Allan. He lied to me— once that I know of, but how many times I don't know about? How can you love someone who lies to you?'

'You would go on loving Nick how ever many lies he told.'

'Nick? Yes, but he's just a child, Allan.'

'And Jonnie? Perhaps he, too, is a child. Most men are, you know. He may only have lied to spare you hurt. I can't believe he means to leave you and the children.'

'Maybe not that. But he must have been thinking about it. What ought I to do, Allan? Try to go away for a while? Try to get him to go, too? Pretend I don't know what's going on? Or fight for what is mine?'

'Do you know "what is going on"?'

Beverly grimaced. 'Well, no. But I'm pretty sure. What I'm not sure of is what I should do. Shall I force the issue? Yet in a way, I feel it is my fault. I desperately wanted Jonnie to marry me when he did. We were both terribly young. There'd never been anyone else in either of our lives. Maybe I should have waited, let Jonnie sow a few wild oats before he settled down.'

'I can't sit in judgment on him, Beverly. You wouldn't want me to, and, anyway, I don't know your husband. I'm not sure what advice I should give you, if any. But I don't think it would be right for you to do anything at all until you are sure this is more than a passing attraction. It is surprising how attractive the unobtainable can be—to a man, anyway.'

'The forbidden fruit?' Beverly's voice was half serious, half amused.

'Yes. Especially to the young. Your husband is young, Beverly. I suspect that marriage has matured you but not yet done the same for him. Give him a little time. He must be a fine character for you to love him, and sooner or later he will find out for himself the unhappiness he is causing you.'

'I think he knows already. I'm not very good at hiding my feelings. Nor is he. Allan, do you believe a man can be unfaithful to his wife and still go on loving her?'

'Depends on the man. Personally, I could not. Love and sex go together. But I know that isn't so of all others. If you want your marriage to work out, you must have it in your heart to forgive. Forgiveness and love go together.'

Beverly made no reply. Would she be able to forgive Jonnie if she knew for a fact that he'd been unfaithful? Was she capable of the high-mindedness, the depth of love of which Allan spoke? She knew what he said was right;

true love can forgive and go on forgiving. Did she really love Jonnie? Had she ever really loved him with her whole being? Somehow, she could not truthfully find it in her heart to tell herself their love was of this enduring quality. They had both been too young to know or to understand.

'I was so sure!' she said, more to herself than to the man beside her. 'So sure!'

'It is only as we grow up that we become "unsure",' Allan replied. 'The more we learn of life, the less well based do our early convictions seem. Now, if you were to ask Nick what he would most like to have if he could choose the one thing to make him completely happy, he would probably name some object— a football or a model yacht. Ask him again in twenty years' time and he would say, "Love". Life would have taught him a set of values, just as it teaches all of us.'

'Then you don't think the young can ever judge what is best for them?'

'Not really. Only by instinct.'

'Then when do you think we can know? How old must we be?'

'I doubt if we ever know completely. How could we? I think we must simply trust in God.'

'Then you believe in God? Really believe, I mean?'

'Yes. There has to be Someone or some Reason. Nothing in life makes sense if there is no God and no life hereafter. When Louise died, I knew that she couldn't just have gone for ever.'

'Tell me about her,' Beverly said gently.

'I'm not sure if I can. To me she was all I wanted in a woman. To look at—well, you are very like her. Perhaps that is why I wish so much to be able to help you.'

'You have helped me with Nick already. He admires you tremendously. I don't think he could have been more fortunate in his school-teacher!'

'Thank you!' Allan said, smiling. 'But it isn't entirely motiveless, you know. A happy child is a good worker.'

Beverly smiled back. 'Even if he were not in your class at school, I believe you would do as much for him.'

'But that, if it is true, might also have another motive. I might be anxious to please you so that you can recommend me at a later date for a headmastership. Now, let me show you the cottage. It's simple, but I think has a lot of charm.'

Bored now with the aviary, Nick came running up to them. Allan suggested a brief tour of the cottage and Beverly was enchanted with it. His innate good taste had chosen the right colours, materials, rugs. There were flowers arranged in a vase on the polished circular oak table. It was clear that here was a man who loved beautiful things and most of all the beauties of nature.

'You must be very happy living here,' she said as they went once more into the sunlit garden, each carrying a tray of tea things.

Allan did not reply. It was true he had found happiness here, of a kind. But it was of a lonely kind.

The same thought had struck Beverly and she wished her remark unsaid. Somehow she must contrive to see he was less lonely.

The rest of the afternoon gave no further opportunity for such talk, as Nick was with them, demanding his share of attention. Beverly sat quietly, listening to her small son and his companion who were obviously already such very good friends.

She had no wish to do so, but against her will she found herself comparing Allan again with Jonnie, and the comparison was always in Allan Forbes' favour. She liked his quiet, slow voice; the things he said; the sensitive hands as his fingers manipulated the intricate knots Nick wished to tie; the unconscious good manners towards both of his visitors; the gentle smile that occasionally flooded across his face. Everything about him was gentle, kind, and above all, peaceful. With this man she could relax completely and feel as if the outside world with its haste, its bustle, its worries and perplexities no longer mattered.

'You'll come again, won't you?' Allan asked her as he walked part of the way home with them. 'I have enjoyed our afternoon.'

'And so have I,' Beverly said truthfully. 'It has been a kind of escape from reality. I love your cottage.'

'It's there, whenever you feel the need to escape again,' Allan said with his friendly smile. But she knew that he did not mean the cottage only—he meant his friendship was waiting, too.

She felt a sudden premonition of danger.

'It's not always easy for me to find the time to get away from home,' she said in a sudden flurry of nervousness. 'But I will try.'

He did not press the invitation and they parted quietly, leaving Nick to do the talking as usual.

'I wish . . .' said Nick as they rounded a bend in the lane so losing sight of Allan's tall figure. 'I don't half wish *he* was my father. Don't you, Mum?'

Beverly looked at her small son in quick horror. How could he be so disloyal, so unkind to Jonnie. Sensing her disapproval, Nick said sullenly:

'Well, it's true. And, anyway, he's much nicer than Dad.'

'Nick!' Beverly pulled him up before he could say more. But even as she did so, she felt her heart hesitate. Wasn't Nick right after all? Allan was 'nicer' than Jonnie to Nick. And perhaps, given different circumstances, he would have been far 'nicer' to her, too.

Hurriedly, she took her small son home.

CHAPTER EIGHT

As they entered the house, Beverly felt strangely guilty. Jonnie had come home from the office early after all. She could hear him playing with the younger children in the sitting-room. The noise was uproarious and she knew, with the familiar sinking of her heart, that the children would be difficult to calm down and get to bed. All the same, she had been silently criticizing Jonnie in her mind for neglecting the children and here he was, home early, presumably in order to play with them.

The noise stopped abruptly as she opened the door. Jonnie looked up from the floor where he was lying and the smile died on his face.

'So you're back,' he said shortly, removing the twins' hands from his jacket and climbing to his feet. 'Do you realize it's after six?'

'Is it? I'd no idea it was so late,' Beverly said truthfully. 'I'm sorry, Jonnie. Have you been home long? Did Annette give you some tea?'

'Annette had quite enough to do giving the kids their tea!' Jonnie retorted, his face sullen and angry. He had known she and Nick would be out to tea with Forbes, but he'd forgotten it when he had decided on the spur of the moment to give the office a break for once and go home early. When he reached home he was furious with himself for forgetting and with Beverly for going.

Beverly felt resentment rising in her at his tone of voice.

'I suppose if you feel it is too much for Annette to give four children their tea, it wouldn't also occur to you that it might be too much for your wife to give five children breakfast, lunch and tea on Annette's day off? If so, I'm surprised it hasn't also occurred to you to stay home and help rather than play golf all afternoon with your American girlfriend!'

Jonnie's face flushed. 'If you're going to start that—'

Aware of the children's curious glances, Beverly broke in quickly, 'Let's finish this conversation after I've got the children to bed!'

'No, we'll finish it now,' Jonnie said, knowing Beverly was right not wishing to argue in front of the children, yet unable to curb his temper.

'I said later,' Beverly replied quietly, and, taking Philip's and Julia's hands, she led them quickly out of the room.

Her self-control fired Jonnie still further. For a moment, he considered going after her, having it out there and then. But on reflection, he decided not to. There was a better way to deal with Beverly; he'd not be here when she felt ready to talk.

He went to the bottom of the stairs and called up in a loud voice: 'I'm going out. I won't be back to supper.'

There was no reply, but Jonnie felt sure she must have heard. He waited a moment for her to call him back, but no sound came from the landing, and furiously he flung on his jacket and went out banging the front door behind him.

As he drove automatically towards the club-house, he fanned his irritation into a real grievance. It wasn't that Beverly had been out to tea. No, it was her attitude to him that made their life together impossible nowadays. She was always critical, coolly and maddeningly critical. It undermined a fellow's belief in himself to have a wife who continually criticized him. Nothing he did was right any more. And it was all the more unfair since he'd decided of his own free will to give up Elinor, or at least, give up any idea of taking what he wanted from her. Beverly's attitude was hardly helping the situation. She should have been grateful, understanding, admiring. Instead of which, she taunted him with Elinor's name!

Well, she could take the consequences. Other fellows had a bit of fun outside their homes and now he was beginning to understand why. They probably had wives who

130

went for them the way Beverly was always going for him. It was enough to push a chap into another woman's arms, especially if the other woman was like Elinor, sweet and thoughtful and knowing how to treat a man.

It was one thing to want to stay faithful to a wife you knew loved you. But it was becoming increasingly obvious that Beverly wasn't in love with him any more. It had begun the night she'd moved into the spare room and locked the door against him; that showed the way her mind was working.

Jonnie conveniently forgot the reason Beverly had moved into the spare room—a reason well founded, although she wasn't to know it. The why was not important. That she had done so was, for it helped him convince himself she didn't care. He didn't want her to care. Her love for him had kept him from having what he wanted.

If she goes on much longer, I shall tell Elinor I've changed my mind, Jonnie told himself as he drove into the car park.

He really meant to stay there an hour or two, have a couple of drinks with someone at the bar, have a meal and go home. That Elinor should be in the bar, alone, was an unlucky if not unlikely coincidence since she spent so much of her time at the club-house. He wasn't to know it had been deliberately planned by her. She'd rung his office, hoping to persuade him to drop in for a drink on the way home.

When Jonnie's typist had told her he'd already left, Elinor jumped to the conclusion he might be coming to see her. She'd waited at home for an hour, and then hopefully gone along to the club-house. She hadn't been there ten minutes when Jonnie arrived.

'Surprise—nice one!' she said as he seated himself on the bar stool beside her. 'I'll even buy you a drink, honey!'

'I could use one,' Jonnie said, warmed by her obvious pleasure in seeing him.

Elinor's thin-painted eyebrows were raised questioningly. His tone of voice indicated his frame of mind. Her eyes narrowed. 'Sound as if you'd had a bad day. Here, drink this!' She pushed a cocktail glass into his hand. 'It's one of Mike's special cocktails . . . my recipe,' she said, smiling as she watched him drink it and quickly ordering two more from the barman.

Within half an hour, Jonnie was feeling a little more than light-headed. He knew he shouldn't have drunk so many cocktails on an empty stomach, but in the mood he'd been in, he just hadn't cared. Now he wasn't in a mood any longer. He felt light-hearted as well as light-headed and everything Elinor was saying to him was making him laugh. He felt nothing but goodwill towards the world now, and towards Elinor in particular. Trust her to know when a fellow needed a drink. She understood men all right.

'You unner-sshand me,' he told her, leaning

his head close against hers. 'Beverly doesn't . . . always cross. T'shn't fair!'

'You've had enough, Jonnie,' Elinor said, her voice suddenly sharpening. She didn't want him too drunk.

'S'right! Had enough—enough of being boshed about. Do what I want now . . . I'll show her . . . I show you all!'

He swept out an arm and knocked over a glass and grinned sheepishly at Elinor.

'Come on, honey. We'll go home and have some coffee . . . and something to eat. You must be hungry!'

Jonnie acquiesced without argument. He didn't want the coffee but he could do with a meal.

Half an hour later, he began to sober up. A plate of cold chicken and two large cups of black coffee had done the trick. His head began to clear and he looked up from the deep sofa in which he was lying and caught sight of the clock on Elinor's mantelpiece. It was eight o'clock.

'Gosh, I'd better be off!' he said. But Elinor's arms were round his neck and he was suddenly aware of her soft slim body lying against his own.

'Not yet, Jonnie . . . not yet!' she whispered, her voice husky in his ear. 'There's no hurry! Your wife won't care if you're late. After all, she was late home from her assignation.'

Jonnie had been talking as well as drinking.

He began to remember what had brought him here, back with Elinor again. She was right, of course. Why should he hurry? Beverly had stayed as long as she wanted with Forbes! But it wasn't true she wouldn't care if he stayed on here with Elinor. He knew it, even if Elinor didn't. Beverly would be jealous all right. Would she be hurt? Could you be hurt if you weren't in love?

'Jonnie darling, you need me. I only want to make you happy. It can't hurt anyone—you know that. Kiss me . . . please, Jonnie.'

One kiss, Jonnie thought, then I will go, before it's too late. But Elinor wasn't content with one kiss, nor with several. Her body was alight and his caught fire from hers. He knew it was wrong; knew it was weakness, madness, but he couldn't stop himself. Her perfume was all about him, weakening his senses as the drink had done earlier, and there was no cooling the ardour that was in this vital woman who lay in his arms.

'Jonnie, I want you. Take me, darling!'

'I love you!' he cried, as he crushed her closer and closer against him. He didn't stop to wonder if it were true. Beverly didn't care—it didn't matter. Nothing mattered any more but the complete surrender to their desire.

*   *   *

It was nearly midnight when Jonnie drove

himself slowly home. He was sober enough now. Although he felt physically completely inert, his mind seemed charged with electricity as one thought after another chased round his head.

It was wrong. He'd known all along it was madness to give way to Elinor and to his own desires. It wasn't all Elinor's fault. He'd wanted her as much as she had wanted him; and in a strange way, their union had been perfect. No—not perfect, there was a savagery in Elinor's caresses that were frightening even while they stimulated him. He'd felt almost as he might have felt in the presence of black magic. There was a primitiveness in Elinor that spoke of the jungle, of times before man and woman became civilized. Was sex meant to be like this? Exciting, yes! But lacking in gentleness, in tenderness, in love?

Did Beverly still love him? The thought of her made him despise himself for what had just happened. She must never know. She couldn't possibly understand. She was so different from Elinor. He disliked himself for making comparisons and yet he could not stop his thoughts. Beverly was nicer than Elinor. Deep down he did not really *like* the American and yet she had this strange hold on him. He knew he'd want her again, yet it couldn't go on, how could it? Beverly would be sure to find out and then—well, did he want to be divorced? Did he want to lose his home, his wife, his children? Did he really want to spend his life with Elinor?

He knew he did not. This was playing with fire and he had to put a stop to it.

Uncontrollably, his thoughts went back to the woman he had just left. He saw her naked, milk-white body stretched out among the cushions on that large sofa, saw the soft arms held out to him and the wild, strange expression of her eyes. What a woman! And it seemed she found him as satisfying as he had found her. She made him feel special, important, all man. Beverly lately made him feel like a silly schoolboy. Well, it was a pity she couldn't learn a few lessons from Elinor. Then he might not have been unfaithful to her.

Blaming Beverly helped him to stifle his conscience—but not for long. When he reached home, he found himself tiptoeing up the stairs, his heart in his mouth as if he were an escaped criminal. He felt unclean and it was not until he had locked himself into the privacy of the room he had once shared with Beverly that he felt he could breathe normally again. But he could not sleep. Dawn came before he dozed off and then the twins woke and he heard Beverly go along the passage to their room and try to quieten them before they woke the entire household. For a moment, he felt a desperate urge to get up and go to her; to tell her what had happened and beg her to forgive him, to give him a chance to start again. But even as the feeling swept over him, it passed away. He couldn't tell her . . . couldn't face up to the look in her eyes. And what good could it do? It wouldn't make her more loving—he could hardly expect that. It couldn't stop him wanting Elinor, damn her!

Jonnie buried his face in his pillow and fell into a deep sleep.

*   *   *

By the time he had washed and shaved next day, Jonnie had thought out his explanation of his late arrival home. When Beverly looked over the coffee-pot at breakfast and asked him coolly:

'What time did you come home? I didn't hear you!' he had his answer ready.

'I was pretty late. I had a few too many drinks at the club and slept it off in the car before driving home.'

His voice, despite his efforts, sounded sheepish and he was unable to meet her direct gaze. She knew he was lying and he guessed she knew. But she didn't question him. She said:

'You'd better hurry or you'll miss your train!'

After he had left the house, Beverly went up to her room—the spare room—and sat down on her bed. She knew that last night had

137

brought things to a head. Something would have to happen now. They couldn't go on like this, living as two strangers.

She was quite sure Jonnie had not been telling the truth, and she knew she could find out. She had only to phone the club and find out when he had left. If, as he said, he'd got slightly drunk and had decided to sleep it off in the car before driving home, his car would have remained in the car park and someone must have seen him. The club-house was shut up at 11 p.m. and the steward would have gone through the car park on his way home. He would certainly have noticed Jonnie asleep in his car!

But did she want to know? If he hadn't been there, it meant he had been somewhere else and somewhere he should not have been since he felt it worth lying. Elinor! Suppose he had been at Elinor's cottage. What had he been doing till midnight? Talking? Or making love?

Beverly felt sick with her own thoughts. Jonnie, her husband, and another woman. If it were true, she didn't want to know. She couldn't bear to live with it! Yet how could she go on with these horrible suspicions unanswered and poisoning her whole life with Jonnie?

I wish Mother was here! she thought. Yet she knew even if Mrs Bampton were in the room now, she couldn't bring herself to admit she thought her husband was being unfaithful.

It was too humiliating. This was something she must fight alone.

'But I can't! I don't know what to do!' Beverly whispered aloud. This was something that happened in books, not to her and Jonnie. What would she do if it were true? Divorce him? Did she want to spend the rest of her life alone with five children? Did she really want Jonnie out of her life?

Beverly stood up suddenly, her face white and determined. It was far worse to imagine these things than to know. She would telephone the club.

Before she could change her mind, she went quickly into Jonnie's and her bedroom where there was a telephone extension. Trying not to see the large double bed where she had spent so many nights in Jonnie's arms, she put a call through to the club-house.

'This is Mrs Colt,' she said when the steward answered. 'My husband thinks he might have left his clubs in the bar last night and asked me to ring you and see if you have found them.'

'His clubs, Madam? I don't think he had them with him when he came in. Let me see . . . no I remember now, he came straight to the bar when he came in and—yes, that's right— he joined Mrs Wilmot. I was serving them one of Madam's special cocktails. I'm sure he hadn't his clubs with him.'

'He might have put them on the floor!'

Beverly said, her voice carefully controlled and casual. 'Did you notice when he left?'

'I'm afraid I didn't actually see him go. I was cutting sandwiches for a foursome who couldn't wait for dinner to be served. When I came back to the bar, Mr Colt and Mrs Wilmot had both gone.'

'That's right; they came back here to a dinner. Well, if you find them, perhaps you would give my husband a ring!'

Beverly put down the phone and sat down on the bed. It was easy, so easy to find out the truth. Surely Jonnie must have known she would find out. Perhaps he didn't care. Perhaps he wanted her to know. Perhaps he wanted a divorce, so he could marry Elinor.

'I hate her . . . I hate her!' Beverly thought, tears trembling on her cheeks. 'She can have him. I never want to see him again!'

There was a knock on the door and Annette came in. She looked at Beverly curiously.

'The children are gone away to school, Madame, and I have washed the breakfast things. What should I do now?'

Beverly tried to give her mind to the domestic routine. That had to go on even if her whole life was being broken into little pieces. There was still the washing, the cooking, the ironing, the shopping.

'The shopping, I think, Annette!' she said as calmly as she could. 'Take the twins in the pram with you. I'll get on with the washing

140

while you are out. You'll find the list on the kitchen table, and some money.'

With Annette out of the way, she could at least have time to think.

As the morning wore on, Beverly tried to make herself believe that she was jumping to the wrong conclusions. Just because Jonnie had spent an hour or two with Elinor there was no reason to condemn him completely. He'd been annoyed and he might just have wanted to teach her a lesson and make her jealous! Jonnie wouldn't be unfaithful to her. He couldn't want to break up their home and leave her and the children.

'I don't care for myself!' she told herself. 'It's the children I mind about. Why should they have their home broken! I won't let Jonnie do it for any American female.'

It was all Elinor's fault. Ever since Jonnie had met her, their life had begun to go wrong. They'd been quite happy until then.

Impulsively, Beverly flung down the bundle of washing she had been about to put into the machine, and went to the hall telephone. She was annoyed to find her hands trembling violently as she leafed through the pages of the local directory for Elinor's number. But eventually she found it and dialled it.

'20315, Mrs Elinor Wilmot speaking.'

'This is Beverly Colt. If it's convenient, I'd like to come round and see you!' Beverly was proud of her cool tone. Her heart might be thumping nervously but at least her voice did not betray her.

There was a moment's pause, and then Elinor's light nasal laugh. 'Sure, honey. Come right over! I'm not up yet but I'll pull myself out of bed and make some coffee.'

'Don't trouble, please!' Beverly said with icy politeness. 'It doesn't matter to me what you look like and I don't want coffee, thank you!' Not quite so polite but Elinor might as well know this was not a social call.

'I'll be seeing you!' was the amused rejoinder and the line went dead.

It took Beverly ten minutes to walk to the station and pick up the car Jonnie left in the yard. Twenty minutes later, she pulled up outside Elinor's cottage and by now was regretting the impulse that had brought her here. Suppose she was wrong? Suppose Elinor wasn't interested in Jonnie! How gauche and stupid she would think her coming here like this! But better Elinor's poor opinion than to go on in uncertainty.

In the half hour since Beverly had phoned, Elinor must have bathed and dressed. She was carefully and skilfully made up. The face she presented to the younger woman was sophisticated and had the same amused look that must have been there when Beverly phoned.

'Come right in and make yourself at home! I've made coffee good and strong and black

. . . I need it. Sure you wouldn't like some?'

'*I* haven't a hangover!' Beverly said childishly and sat down awkwardly in the arm-chair, putting herself at a physical disadvantage for Elinor now stood poised gracefully by the table, looking down at her.

'Well, what did you want to talk to me about, Mrs Colt?'

'About my husband!' Beverly said on an indrawn breath.

'Does Jonnie know you're here?'

Beverly shook her head.

'Of course not, Mrs Wilmot.' She stopped short to look up at Elinor's face, her own suddenly appealing as she met those cool grey eyes. 'Mrs Wilmot, was Jonnie here with you last night?'

'Not if Jonnie says he wasn't!'

'Then you mean he was?' As Elinor did not reply, Beverly went on haltingly: 'You see, I have to know the truth. If you are having an affair with Jonnie, I'd rather know!'

'And if I'm prepared to say we are, what then?'

Elinor lit a cigarette which she put in a long amber holder and studied Beverly's white face through the smoke. She felt no pity for the girl—only a mild contempt. She must know this wasn't the way to get Jonnie back. He'd be furious when he knew his wife had been prying into his private affairs. If the girl didn't want to lose him altogether, she'd better change her

143

tactics. It didn't occur to Elinor, who was always working out some preconceived plan, that Beverly was acting on impulse, from the heart and without reason.

'I . . . I don't know!'

'You want a divorce?'

Beverly was stung into feeling. How dare this woman question her about a divorce!

'Perhaps you aren't aware of the fact that Jonnie and I have five children!' she flung at her companion.

'Poor Jonnie! No wonder he feels the need for a change.'

Beverly flushed. 'I'm not going to stay here to be insulted by you,' she said violently. 'I just wanted to know—'

'If Jonnie and I had been having an affair. Well, I'll tell you, just to satisfy your wifely curiosity. We've started an affair and if I have my way, it will continue. Now you know.'

Beverly was once more shocked into anger. 'Don't you care about anything but your own horrible feelings?' she cried. 'Doesn't it matter at all that you are breaking up my home and my marriage?'

'Care? Why should I care? You don't mean a thing to me. It's up to Jonnie, honey! If he wants me, I'm here. You can tell him I said so. It isn't my fault if he's bored with you!'

Beverly stood up and with a last horrified look at the woman Jonnie presumably loved, she turned and ran out of the room. Behind her, she heard Elinor laugh and one half of her mind was capable of sheer amazement at this woman's callousness. It didn't seem possible that any real person *could* speak as Elinor had done. She hadn't an atom of shame, embarrassment, feeling for anyone—unless it were herself and Jonnie.

Jonnie! Beverly felt sick with shame and humiliation. How could he? How could any man enjoy this woman's company?

Again, one half of her mind remained aloof from her heart, coolly accepting that Elinor was attractive, that there was something feline and powerful about her that made her a dangerous rival; she was ruthless, too. She would break up a home and a marriage as easily as she would crush a fly if it suited her.

She shan't have him! Beverly thought furiously. Not if I can stop it! He can't marry her unless I divorce him and I won't, I won't! Why should I make it easy for them? I won't ever divorce him.

She had a sudden appalling vision of her future, married for the rest of her life to a man who loved someone else. She felt cheapened, revolted and desperately afraid. It was too late now to wish she'd never come, never found out the truth. At least while she was ignorant, she had some hope her suspicions were unfounded. Now there was none. Tonight, Jonnie would come home and they'd have to have it out. Elinor would surely tell him of her visit even if she did not do so herself. What would they say to each other? What was there to say? Jonnie would ask for his freedom and she would refuse him. Or maybe he would be penitent, sorry, ask for her forgiveness. As if she ever could forgive him or ever be a real wife to him again after this!

The day wore on interminably, Beverly alternately longing for the sound of Jonnie's return and then dreading it. Nick and Philip returned from school and momentarily at least she was too occupied with them to think of much else. But even as she played with them, her mind kept thinking, weighing up, trying to consider what she should do with her life and say to her husband. Perhaps he wouldn't come back! Perhaps he'd go straight to that horrible woman and only come back in the early hours of the morning.

If he does, he won't find me here! Beverly thought violently. Yet immediately followed the question, where could she go? How could she walk out and leave Annette with the responsibility of the five children. What would they think? It wasn't so easy to end a marriage. A mother couldn't just walk out.

I can lock the door against him so he can't come back! Beverly thought. He's forfeited any right to his home and his children.

Yet she had only Elinor's word for it. It wasn't inconceivable that Elinor had lied about last night. She couldn't be sure until

Jonnie admitted it.

*   *   *

Shall I tell her? Jonnie was thinking as his train neared home. Wouldn't it be better to tell her? Then I can't be tempted to see Elinor again. Once Beverly knows, she'll make it a condition I never see Elinor again. I'd have to give my word, and then it would all be over.

But did he want it to be over? Wasn't it better to leave things as they were until he was sure what he wanted? He could go and see Elinor and talk it over with her. But that was just an excuse. He knew what would happen when he got inside her house. They couldn't be alone together without passion flaring up between them.

In a few minutes, he'd have to face Beverly. What could he talk about? What lies would he be forced to tell if she questioned him again about last night? He felt mean and utterly miserable. It would have to end. He couldn't go on like this. It had been a rotten day at the office. Everything had gone wrong and he knew he hadn't been concentrating and that most of the mistakes had been of his own making. He was tired and ashamed and appalled by the burning need to see Elinor again soon. At least he might have hoped for some respite after last night.

Jonnie was first surprised and then furious

147

when he found the car had gone from the station. It meant he'd have to walk home. Twice before it had happened when Beverly had needed the car urgently and it was understood between them that she would only take the car without telling him when something unexpected cropped up. What could have happened today?

Jonnie stood stock-still in the station yard as a sudden thought struck him. Had Beverly found out the truth and left him? Had she wanted the car to take herself and the children away to her mother's perhaps?

He was frightened and because he was frightened, he was angry when he reached home and saw the car in the garage. He flung open the front door and shouted for Beverly.

'Why wasn't the car at the station?'

Beverly came to the kitchen door and surveyed Jonnie's flushed face with a curious calm. His anger steadied her.

'Because I needed it!' she said coolly.

'So I have to walk home!' Jonnie said furiously. 'If this is your way of teaching me a lesson, I can tell you I shan't put up with it.'

'Won't you, Jonnie? Maybe you won't have to much longer!'

'And what's that supposed to mean?' Jonnie asked, following his wife's retreating figure into the kitchen.

'Simply what it suggests; that you may not have to put up with me any longer.'

'And why, if I may ask, this hysterical outburst?'

Beverly hesitated. It had come, the moment when she must tell him and he must answer. Perhaps he'd try to lie. But she'd know.

'Jonnie, I took the car today to go and see Elinor Wilmot. She admitted you were having an affair with her. She took care to point out that it had only just begun. Well, I think you should know without me telling you that I'm not going to be the kind of wife who sits quietly in the background and turns a blind eye. Those are the women who want to keep their husbands at any price. I don't want you at any price, Jonnie. That's what I'm telling you.'

Jonnie was astounded. He'd never once thought Beverly might go to Elinor. And how could Elinor have been so crazy as to admit the truth?

'Don't try to think up a lie, Jonnie. It's a waste of time. I know what time you went to her house last night and I know what time you left. I'm not so naive I think you sat and played rummy all that time!'

She held her breath, waiting for Jonnie's indignant denial, but it didn't come. Her heart sank. She could not meet his eyes.

'I'm sorry, Beverly. I never meant it to happen. I got a bit tight and—'

'Oh, shut up!' Beverly cried, her nerves at breaking point. 'I don't want to hear your apologies or your excuses. I think you're disgusting and contemptible. I hate you! Hate you!'

She pushed past him, and ran out of the room.

'Hell!' Jonnie walked over to the window and stood looking out unseeingly at the garden.

He felt ashamed and unnerved. He knew Beverly would be on her bed crying; he knew that he really ought to pull himself together and try to patch things up. Yet he dreaded the thought of her accusing eyes, her justifiable complaints. He hadn't been such a bad husband, except for this one lapse. Beverly could at least show a little tolerance and understanding. If she tried to help him now, maybe he could get over Elinor! If she'd flung her arms round him, begged him not to do it again, told him she loved him, he would have *wanted* to please her.

What did she mean to do now? Would she ask for a divorce? He was suddenly afraid again. Better go up and see what she intended to do.

He knocked on her door twice before she answered in a muffled voice, 'What do you want?'

'Let me in, Beverly. I can't talk out here on the landing.'

Beverly unlocked the door and Jonnie went in. They faced one another in an embarrassed silence.

150

'What do you want?' Beverly said again. Her face was streaked with tears and she knew she looked far from attractive. But she didn't care . . . she wasn't going to care.

'That's what I was going to ask you. What you want to do, Beverly. Do you want a divorce?'

'Do you?'

'No! Apart from us there are the children. I've said I'm sorry, Beverly.'

'Go on, say it won't ever happen again. I wouldn't believe you. I'll never believe anything you say again, Jonnie. I just don't understand you any more. *How could you?* Are you in love with her? Do you want to marry her?'

'Good God, no!' That at least he was sure of. 'It's so difficult to explain, Beverly. I don't expect you to understand. It's just that there's something between Elinor and me that we can't deny. We've fought against it and I swear that's true. I never meant it to happen.'

'But you wanted it to happen!' Beverly said. 'Deep inside you wanted her, Jonnie, the way you once wanted me.'

'No, it wasn't the same!' Jonnie said with conviction. 'There is no love, Beverly. Try to understand.'

Beverly drew in her breath sharply. 'I don't think I want to understand. I find it all quite revolting. I suppose it's all sex if it isn't love. That makes it more disgusting in a way. You've betrayed me and the children for something completely worthless.'

'I . . . I suppose you're right. It won't happen again.'

'Won't it? How do I know? How do *you* know, Jonnie? You said you fought against it. Yet you weakened in the end. It could happen again, and again, and again. I'm not sharing you, Jonnie, understand that. You've got to choose between your American mistress and your wife. She might be willing to share, but I'm not. Either we move house or she does. If the attraction between you two is so devastating, then the greater the distance between you the better.'

Jonnie shrugged his shoulders. 'I don't see how it can be done. We can't afford to move house and Elinor certainly won't go just because you or I ask her to. You'll just have to trust me, Beverly.'

'Trust you?' Beverly cried. 'How can I? You've lied and cheated, Jonnie. It'll be a long time before I trust you again.'

'I see! It's pretty obvious the pleasant choice I'm faced with; to continue this wretched kind of existence with a wife who's always suspicious of every moment I'm not with her, who admits she no longer cares about me; or to lose my home and children if I want to be with the woman who does love and appreciate me.'

'Appreciate you? In bed, I suppose you

mean. I agree you make a very good lover, Jonnie, and no doubt you excel yourself with your precious Elinor. But love? I doubt if you or she know the meaning of the word. I don't see how you can expect me to love you again. Not a very happy prospect for me, either. But it's a decision of your own making. I hope you're very very happy about it.'

Jonnie hesitated. In a way it was such a tremendous relief not having to lie any more, that he couldn't feel as appalled as he knew he should have done. Now at least he could look his wife in the face.

'Look, Beverly, I *know* I've behaved rottenly. I know how terrible it must seem to you. I understand how you must hate me. Try to believe me when I tell you that I hate myself probably much more than you do. I've betrayed everything we both valued and I know it. But can't you *try* to understand? I don't love her; I don't want to break up our home and leave you and the kids. It's just that . . . well, I couldn't promise never to see her again. I don't know if I could keep that promise. I've been trying for weeks to fight against this need for her. Give me a little time; let me fight it my way.'

Beverly clenched her hands against her sides, her mind in a turmoil of doubt and indecision. The more mature side of her nature spoke a warning: You don't want to lose him. Do as he asks and don't force the issue.

He says he doesn't really want her, but the passionate, impulsive, loving side cried out in bitterness. Why should he get away with this? What right had he to hurt her, humiliate her? What kind of a woman could this be to try to take a man deliberately from his wife, his children; smash up a home as if it meant no more than a pack of cards? And for this female, Jonnie was asking her to sit back and take second place.

'There isn't going to be a fight, Jonnie. I'm not going to wrangle with any woman for my husband. It's really quite simple. Give her up and we'll try to make a new life out of the ruins. Go on seeing her, making love to her, and I'll divorce you. I won't *share* you, Jonnie.'

Her voice was vibrant with feeling, her cheeks flushed a bright red, her eyes flashing with the outraged feeling that hurt pride had brought to the fore. Inopportunely, Jonnie thought suddenly: How pretty she is! Then the meaning of her words sank into his consciousness and he knew that she was giving him an ultimatum.

'But I don't like ultimatums!' He spoke his thoughts aloud, his voice strangely quiet, cool.

'Oh, no!' Beverly cried scathingly. 'You want your cake and you want to eat it as well!' Jonnie remembered Elinor's use of the same quotation. 'Well, you're my husband, Jonnie, and if you want another woman in your life, then you can pay the price. I'll divorce you all right. And I'll get the children. You aren't fit to be their father. No wonder Nick's growing up the way he is. A fine example you turned out to be . . .' Suddenly her voice broke and, without warning, the tears coursed down her cheeks. Angrily, she brushed them away, and, pushing past Jonnie, she left the room.

'Hell!' Jonnie said aloud to the empty room. 'Damn, blast and *hell*!' and hurried downstairs to the dining-room.

He walked across to the sideboard and poured himself a stiff drink. It steadied him and stilled the desire to run after Beverly. Let her go! Let her think for a moment what divorce would mean. Once she realized its implications, she wouldn't think it such a fine thing. Where would his income go with two homes to run? It was all very well for Elinor to say *she* had money. As if Beverly would ever touch a penny of her money. Or would she? Maybe she would get every penny she could from Elinor. Enticement, wasn't it? But he'd hate to think of Elinor's money helping to raise his children.

The kids . . . always the kids. Divorce might be easy enough when there were no children. But they had *five* and he loved them. Whatever Beverly said about him being a bad father, he'd always loved them.

White-faced, Jonnie paced the room. His anger turned against Elinor. This was all her fault. Until she'd put in an appearance, his life had been pretty trouble free. Oh, it had been difficult at times and dull, maybe, and devoid of that heady excitement. But at least it had been a calm, ordered life without these ghastly rows and scenes. They couldn't go on. In a way Beverly was right. There wasn't a compromise. Either he must give up Elinor or give up his home.

'I'll give her up!' Jonnie thought, suddenly calm. 'I'll go now and tell her it's all over. *She* won't make a scene. I'll do it now, this minute, before I grow weak again.'

He went to the kitchen door and as calmly as he could, told Annette he was going out for an hour.

He drove to Elinor's cottage in five minutes flat. This time he felt no anxiety as to whether the car would be seen, recognized. He slammed the car door and without knocking or ringing, strode into the living-room.

Elinor was stretched out on the hearthrug like a large Persian cat. Her hair, which she was drying before an electric fire, was spread all around her bare shoulders. A loose towelling bath-robe had slipped down so that it only half covered her beautiful up-turned breasts. She didn't move her body, only turning her head to smile at him lazily and say in that deep-throated voice of hers:

'Jonnie, *darling*! What a lovely surprise.'

'God, you're beautiful!' he said, standing there, staring at her, knowing that he must

156

never hold that body in his arms again, never possess her again, never be possessed. The mere thought only increased her desirability. Had she been forewarned of Jonnie's arrival, she could not have put herself in a more favourable light. The glow of the electric fire flickered on her shoulders, was softening to the lines about her mouth and eyes. The gentle flow of hair was somehow young, innocent looking. Never had she looked less evil.

And I had been telling myself she was bad, bad! Jonnie thought.

'Well, come and sit down, my sweet!' Elinor said, holding out her arms invitingly. 'Why, Jonnie, what's the matter? Aren't you well?'

'It's Beverly!' Jonnie said flatly, dramatically. 'She knows everything, Elinor. I've come to say goodbye!'

Elinor picked up her hairbrush and slowly began to brush her hair in steady, smooth strokes. Her face was turned away from him now, in profile. He believed she was suffering from shock and trying to control her unhappiness. In actual fact, her mind was teeming with conflicting thoughts.

What a bore this is! Why can't he forget about that stupid girl he married? He's so young—so immature! But that's what I like about him too. He doesn't know all the answers; he's gentle and kind and romantic. It's such a lovely change after . . . But this is too tiresome, this hopping about between us. Is he worth fighting for any more? We have fun . . . there's no one else and he's young and sweet.

'Elinor, for pity's sake say something. Say you understand.'

He wanted her to reject him and to make going easier for him. She knew it but her ears were deliberately deaf to the appeal in his voice. She said softly:

'You've always been straight with me, Jonnie. You never pretended you loved me. I can't blame you. I don't want to. I just want to go on loving you, Jonnie. Oh, life is so unfair!'

He saw her suddenly quite differently. This was no longer the sophisticated, self-assured young widow. This was a lonely, unwanted woman rich in everything but love. He knew he was hurting her, and hated himself for it just as he had hated himself for hurting Beverly. What a mess he'd made of it all!

'Elinor, you've got to understand. Beverly's given me an ultimatum. If I go on seeing you, she'll divorce me. I'll lose my children.'

He went across the room and, kneeling beside her, took her two hands in his own. Her hair was falling across her face and he could not see if she was crying though he felt her body shaking.

'Elinor, you'll find someone else, you're so lovely. If you knew how lovely, how utterly desirable you are . . .'

She lifted her face then, and a moment later she was lying against him, her arms holding him tightly, her body pressed against his own.

'I don't expect your love, Jonnie. I've always known I had no right to that. I don't ask you to divorce her. I only want to be able to see you sometimes, be with you, be close to you. Surely she can't deny me this small part of you? She can't be so selfish that she wants to deny you everything. She doesn't need you the way I do.'

Jonnie struggled against his own desperate weakness.

'Don't you see, it isn't like that, Elinor? She has been brought up differently. She could never accept the kind of terms you are willing to accept. She's my wife and she has a right to expect me to—to be faithful.'

'Has she, Jonnie? Does a piece of paper and a ring give her the right to own you, body and soul? Isn't it really only love that gives a person that right over another human being? Does she love you? Can she love you the way I do?'

'No, no, it's not your way.' The words broke from him. 'It's different, Elinor, but it means as much to her.'

'I wonder if it does,' Elinor said softly. 'Real love means giving, doesn't it, Jonnie? If she really loved you the way you seem to think she does, she'd want you to be happy. Even if it meant she had to give up one of her ideals. I'd give you up, Jonnie. I won't try to keep you, not if that's the way I *know* you want it. You've got to convince me that you don't want me or need me any more. Don't you, Jonnie? Look at me, darling. Say you don't care.'

'I can't, I can't!' The man all but groaned the words. 'When I'm with you, only this seems right. Everything else pales into insignificance beside my need for you. I don't know if it's love—I don't know what love is any more. But when we're not together I know this is wrong.'

'How can it be wrong?' Elinor said softly, one hand gently stroking his hair from his forehead, the other warm and soft against the back of his neck. 'We're meant for each other, we were made for each other. You know that and I know it. We can't be apart, Jonnie.'

Suddenly, abruptly, he stood up, pulling her hands roughly away from him. His face was chalk-white; his whole body trembled as he said: 'I've got to try to live without you. I've got to. Maybe I won't succeed. Maybe I'll be back, if you still want me. But I must try . . . I must.'

He'd given her the one loop-hole she needed, the one card left to play.

Slowly, gracefully, like a cat, she rose to her feet. Gently, she bent forward and kissed him, the mere touch of a kiss against his lips. 'All right,' she whispered. 'I know in my heart you'll come back, and I'll be waiting, Jonnie. I'll be waiting all the time.'

With one last tortured look at her, Jonnie fled from the room.

Smiling, Elinor heard the door bang, then the car door, and finally the sound of the car engine disappearing into the distance. All men were weak, Jonnie more than most. 'Maybe I'll be back . . .' he had said, even at the moment of going. Yes, he'd be back, and next time he returned, it would be for keeps.

She curled herself once more in front of the fire and slowly began again to brush her hair.

*   *   *

Beverly heard the front door close behind Jonnie and a sudden icy chill settled over her heart. What had she done? What had she done? He'd asked for her help, her understanding, and she'd given him neither. Now he'd gone. Perhaps for always. Perhaps this was the end—the end of love, of marriage.

'Did . . . did Mr Colt say where he was going?' she asked the startled Annette.

'He just said that he was going out for one hour,' Annette said in her halting English. 'At least, I think he said for one hour. Is something wrong, Madame?'

Beverly did not answer. What could she answer? Jonnie had gone. He could only have gone to Elinor. She had sent him there. She had no one but herself to blame.

What can I do, what can I *do*? she thought frantically. To whom to turn for help, for advice? Her very nature demanded action—

any action. It would be a physical impossibility to sit here in this house, waiting to see if Jonnie was coming back.

She could phone her mother. But she knew what her mother would say. She'd say that Beverly must wait, and when Jonnie came in, behave as if nothing had happened; wait for him to show his hand. He'd said he didn't want a divorce. He couldn't get free unless she chose to divorce him and she wouldn't—not ever. Elinor should never have him.

But it wasn't true that he couldn't go. He'd gone. Maybe he didn't care about a divorce. Maybe Elinor didn't even want to marry him. She had cast some spell over him so that he'd lost all decency, all knowledge of what was right and wrong. He might be with her now, holding her in his arms . . .

'Annette, I have to go out for a little while. There is nothing to worry about. It's . . . it's Mrs Adams,' she lied swiftly, easily. 'She isn't very well and we are all rather concerned.'

'But of course I manage,' Annette said imperturbably. 'Please not to worry, Madame. All will come well to the end.'

Slipping a coat over her shoulders, Beverly ran out of the house. In the cool darkness, she paused, uncertainly. She'd meant to go to Sue, but now that her first steps were turned towards Sue's house, she knew she couldn't go. Pride forbade it. Sue would feel so sorry for her and she couldn't bear anyone's pity.

Then where else? She had so few really close friends. Allan? Allan Forbes? He would understand, guard her secret. He would tell her what to do.

She began to run, increasing her pace as a kind of hysterical panic took control of her. Now the night had suddenly become an enemy. The half-light seemed full of shadows, the branches of the trees long, ghostly arms that were reaching for her, to clutch at her and prevent her escape.

Blindly, she ran on until the narrowness of the lane that led to Allan's cottage forced her to slow her pace. Her heart still raced and her thoughts were still incoherent but somehow she managed to stumble forward, tearing her stockings on hedgerow brambles, uncaring, unseeing.

When at last she saw the orange square of light shining from the window of Allan's cottage, she gave a gasp of relief. He was there; it was all that mattered. Allan was there and soon she would be safe.

When he opened the front door to her feverish knocking, the man stared aghast at the dishevelled figure who fell forward into his arms.

'Beverly!' he said in a shocked voice. 'My dear, whatever has happened?'

He drew her quickly inside the room and closed the door against the darkness. Then he led her towards his own easy-chair and gently pushed her into it, smoothing the tangle of her hair back from her forehead and then turning away from her to switch on the electric fire.

Beverly watched him with a rapt concentration, unaware of the tears running down her cheeks. She knew she was shivering and she was so glad of the fire. It was all she could think about, she felt so cold.

'I'm going to make a cup of tea and lace it with brandy,' Allan said with a calmness he was far from feeling. 'I won't be long. Wait here.'

'No, no, don't go, don't leave me alone!'

Her voice arrested him half-way to the door. More quietly, she added:

'I don't want anything, really, Allan. I'm so sorry. I shouldn't have come . . .'

Despite her protest, he went to the corner cupboard and poured her a glass of brandy. Then he stood by her until she had had at least three mouthfuls. Slowly, the colour began to return to her cheeks, burning more brightly until they were a feverish red. His anxiety for her mounted. What could have happened?

'Feeling any better?' he asked, his voice so full of his concern for her that suddenly Beverly felt she could not bear it. Kindness now was too much. This time she cried openly, noisily, like a child.

His face twisting with the sudden rush of emotions that had overcome him, Allan leant forward and took her in his arms.

'Don't, don't!' he whispered. 'I can't bear to see you like this. Beverly, *darling*. Don't cry. Whatever it is will be all right, I promise it will. I'll make it all right.'

In the midst of her own hysteria, she heard his voice, his words, and knew suddenly that this man loved her. It surprised yet somehow did not shock her. Deep inside, she felt she must always have known how he felt.

That's why I came to him, she thought, her mind suddenly cool and clear. I knew deep down inside that I could trust him, that he'd help me.

'Oh, Allan!' she whispered. 'I know I shouldn't have come. I'm so sorry, but I . . . I needed you so.'

'I'm glad you came.' She heard his voice, filled with tenderness, against her hair.

Gently, he released her and, walking away from her, sat down on the other side of the fireplace, looking down at his hands for a moment. Then, with studied calm, he began to fill his pipe. By the time he had it lit, both were once more in control of themselves.

'Want to talk about it?' he asked as casually as he could. 'Maybe I can help?'

Beverly pushed the hair away from her eyes and drew a deep, trembling breath.

'I do want . . . I came . . . it's . . .' She saw his eyes crinkle at the corners in that sudden sweet smile, and then she too was smiling. 'I'll try again. Allan, I came because I couldn't think who else to turn to. I just rushed out of the house in a kind of blind, crazy panic. I didn't know what to do, you see, and I could only think of you. You've been so kind . . .'

Her voice trailed away uncertainly.

'Beverly, I'm *glad* you came. Let us be completely honest with each other and trust one another. I think you came because you knew how I felt about you. I've tried not to admit it even to myself, but when I saw you in the doorway just now, I couldn't deny the truth. I love you. I think I loved you the very first time I saw you. I know you don't feel this way about me and that's a good thing, for we have no right to love one another. You're someone else's wife and I've never forgotten that. I want only that you should know of my feelings so that you will understand that you can ask me anything, tell me anything, trust me. There isn't anything in the world I wouldn't do for you.'

'Oh, Allan,' Beverly whispered. 'I know I ought not to be glad, but I am, I am. I can't be a very nice person, can I? To be pleased about something like this? I suppose it's vanity. But if you knew what had just happened to me, maybe you'd understand.'

Allan drew deeply on his pipe and looked across at her.

'Then tell me. Clearly you'd had a shock, a bad one. You are not the kind of woman to rush out of your house at this time of night

166

without cause. Beverly, your husband hasn't *hit* you? If he did, I'll—'

'No, no, no!' Beverly broke in. 'Jonnie hasn't touched me. It's just that . . . Allan, I think he's gone to Elinor for good. He's been having an affair with her for some time. I guessed it but I wasn't sure. Today I went to see her. It was a stupid thing to do. She admitted everything. This evening, Jonnie and I had it out. He told me she had some kind of hold over him, that he couldn't promise to give her up. He said he didn't want a divorce, but still he wouldn't promise not to go on seeing her. Allan, how can a man expect his wife to *share* him with another woman? I couldn't. I know in books and magazines and things, they say the wife who wants to keep her husband should turn a blind eye, be that much nicer, even more understanding, make herself more attractive. But it isn't like that in real life . . . it isn't!'

Appalled, Allan listened to the rush of words, hearing them and believing them, yet still not understanding how any man could behave towards his wife in such a way and to Beverly of all people, who was so unsophisticated, so unworldly wise. What kind of a man must he be to ask his wife to *share* him with his mistress. No wonder she was so shocked, so hurt.

'And when you told him he had to choose, he chose *her*?' he asked quietly.

Beverly shook her head.

'No! He said he didn't want a divorce or to leave me and the children. He even said he didn't love her. He wanted time to fight against his own weakness for her, I suppose. But I had to know one way or another. I couldn't have gone on living in the same house, never knowing if he was going to give her up or leave me. I told him he must choose or I'd divorce him. Then he left the house and I know he went straight to her. I made him, Allan, that's the awful thing. Perhaps if I had given him time, he'd have stayed.'

'Then you do still love him?'

'I hate him!' Beverly cried violently; then, more calmly, she said: 'I don't know. I suppose I must still care to mind so desperately and to be so hurt. How could he, Allan? After all this time? I know I'm far from perfect; there's lots of ways I must have irritated him and failed him. But I've never looked at anyone else, and never once in my life considered anything or anyone but Jonnie and the children. They've *been* my life. I knew something was wrong between us a long time ago and that we'd grown apart some way. I just didn't know what was causing it. I thought if we could get away together alone for a bit, without the children, it would all come right. I never once imagined it was anything serious. Jonnie promised he'd come. I'd made all the arrangements, and then at the last moment he called off. Because of *her.* I see now, but I couldn't see it then. Allan, what am I to do? Should I let him go? Should I give him his divorce? What about the children?'

Allan Forbes remained silent. As she was speaking, the wild thought rushed through his mind. If she divorced her husband, she would be free to marry me. I'd make her happy and be a good father to those children. I could love them, too, since they are part of her. I'd never be lonely again. My life would have meaning and purpose . . .

But he couldn't say these things to her. He had no right to influence her to such a decision. He was sufficiently modern in his outlook to know that divorce was sometimes necessary, but when there were children it must always be the very last resort. Besides, he was far from certain that Beverly was out of love with her husband. Disillusioned she might be and deeply hurt, but that need not necessarily destroy love; not a real, deep-rooted love between a man and a woman.

'I think you should do nothing at all, at the moment,' he said at last. 'I realize that isn't easy. But from all you've said, my dear, it doesn't sound as if Jonnie really wants to bust up his home. I think if you can find some way to give him a little time, he'll give her up. There's no need to *share.* Just stay quietly for a week or two somewhere in the background.'

'But I don't know if I *want* to be there!'

Beverly cried passionately. 'Why should I sit back and wait for Jonnie to come home? I don't know if I *want* him back.'

'That's something else you have to think about, carefully,' Allan said with deep sincerity. 'You speak now from hurt pride. Do you really want to lose him? He's the father of your children. Have you a right to take them away from him?'

'He's forfeited all right to them,' Beverly cried.

'Yes, but *they've* done nothing to deserve the loss of their father,' Allan said with a calm he was far from feeling. 'You have to decide for all of them as well as for yourself.'

'I thought *you* might understand,' Beverly said bitterly. 'Apparently you think a man has a right to do this to a woman and get away with it. Suppose I had been unfaithful to Jonnie? Everyone would condemn me because I am a woman. It's different for a man. But why?'

'I think it's just that men and women are different and that probably most women are stronger than men and that they love more deeply. It makes it easier for them to be faithful.'

'I think it's horrible!' Beverly burst out. 'I couldn't ever trust him or respect him again. Yet I don't want my home broken up. I don't think I could bring up five children alone. I'm not strong enough. I know boys need a father—not that Jonnie's been much of a father lately. And there's the money side of it, too. We're not well off. If I divorced Jonnie, I suppose all that would be worse still.'

'You might marry again,' Allan said hesitantly. 'You're young and very attractive.'

Beverly gave a sardonic laugh. 'Jonnie doesn't seem to have found me so. And, besides, who'd take on five children? No, Jonnie has it all his way. He must have known all along how dependent I am on him. It isn't fair, Allan. Even if I wanted to divorce him, you've shown me I couldn't afford it.'

Allan looked at the flushed face before him, the hurt, bewildered, unhappy face of a little girl. She looked so incredibly young with her nose shining and the tears still wet on her cheeks. Inconsequently, he said:

'Most women look awful when they cry. You look about six years old, and very sweet!'

Suddenly she was crying again, this time in his arms.

'It isn't fair,' she sobbed. 'Life isn't fair.'

With great tenderness, he turned her face upwards and touched her lips with his own.

'I used to say that,' he said softly. 'After Louise and my boy died. But life has its compensations. You and I at least have known love, even if we both have lost it. Do you know that poem, Beverly, called "The Penalty of Love"?'

'No, say it to me.' She chocked against another sob.

171

'All right. It goes like this:

"If love should count you worthy, and
    should deign
One day to seek your door and be your
    guest,
Pause! ere you draw the bolt and bid him
    rest,
If in your old content you would remain,
For not alone he enters; in his train
Are angels of the mist, the lonely quest,
Dreams of the unfulfilled and unpossessed,
And sorrow, and Life's immemorial pain.

He wakes desires you never may forget,
He shows you stars you never saw before,
He makes you share with him, for evermore,
The burden of the world's divine regret.
How wise you were to open not! and yet,
How poor if you should turn him from the
    door!" '

Neither spoke for a moment as Allan's voice
ceased. Then Beverly looked up, smiling
through her tears, and said:
   'It's said, and yet it's true, too. I wish I'd met
you before—years ago. I feel somehow as if we
have understood each other . . . been very
close to each other. You said just now you
loved me, yet we are strangers in fact. But I
can understand, because somewhere inside
me, I, too, have a strange feeling of belonging.

Allan, would we have been happy? Would *you* have grown tired of me. Bored with me? Found someone else?'

'I can't answer that,' Allan said with a smile. 'I believed there was only one love for each person in this strange world of ours. When I met and married Louise, I knew I had found my love; that I could never want anyone else ever; that I could never love anyone else. Yet here I am, as much in love with you, my dear, as I ever was with her. Don't you remember the old song, "It's when you think you're past love, then you meet your last love, and you love her as you never loved before".'

'Oh, Allan,' Beverly said. 'I know I ought not to be glad—in a way it only complicates everything still more . . . but I am glad you love me. I can't help it. It isn't just because . . . well, because it's flattering to my vanity after the kind of knock mine has had. It's more than that. I like you so much. When I'm with you, everything seems so right, so much what it should be. Does that sound crazy? It's a kind of peace you bring me. When I'm not with you, I feel like a bit of elastic stretched to breaking point. Now, like this, it's as if I have been released.'

She lifted her head and looked into his face with sudden curiosity.

'This seems so strange, so unbelievable!' she said softly. 'I don't understand anything any

173

more. I don't know what made me come to you; I'd no real plan in mind. I had no idea when I rushed out of the house that you loved me.'

Allan gave a half-smile. 'Would it have made any difference if you had known? I hope not! I hope you'll always turn to me when you're in trouble.'

'It seems so selfish to say "of course, I will!" Allan, what is going to happen? It's all such a mess. You say I should go back and wait for Jonnie to come to his senses. But I don't want to do that. I'm not even sure I *care* whether Jonnie comes back at all.'

He looked into the green uncertain depths of her eyes. He could see the pain, the bewilderment as clearly as he could read their beauty and innocence. What was this husband of hers *really* like? Would he be right to send her back to more humiliation? Or could he tell her to stay here, with him, to be looked after, protected, warmed back to life again.

'You must go back!' he said, his voice suddenly harsh. 'You have to think of your children first, Beverly. Besides, the vows we make on our wedding day are for better *or for worse*. For worse, too, my dear. You must try to forgive, to start again. I'm sure it will come right and that you will find your love for your husband again.'

'Will I?' Beverly asked doubtfully, her voice so like that of a small, frightened child, that for a moment Allan was desperately tempted to hold her to him in a passion of protective love. But he mustn't. Neither must he allow his own feelings for her to influence her against her duty. Perhaps already, by speaking of his love for her, he had done her marriage harm.

Abruptly, he walked away from her and stood with his back towards her, staring out of the uncurtained window into the darkness.

'I'm going to take you home,' he said quietly. 'You can't stay here, Beverly. I'm the respected local schoolmaster. I'd get the sack for harbouring a beautiful married woman in my house at this time of night.'

His voice was casual, almost bantering, and Beverly looked at the strong, squared shoulders uncertainly.

Of course she could not stay here. She should not really have come at all. Poor Allan—inflicted with an hysterical woman at this time of night. She glanced at the clock over the mantelpiece. Ten fifteen. Annette would be wondering where she was. And for the first time in her life, she hadn't kissed the children good night.

'Yes, I'll go back now,' she said. 'I can go by myself, Allan. There's no need for you to come.'

He turned towards her again, his face strangely twisted. 'You don't think I'd let you go alone? Here's your coat. Would you like to tidy up a little first?'

Obediently, Beverly went to the bathroom and tidied her hair, washed her face. She felt calmer, certain at least that whatever tomorrow might hold for her, she *would go* back now, tonight. Maybe Jonnie had come home. And if he had? Her thoughts ended there. She did not want to think about Jonnie.

'Coming?' Allan's voice, quiet and matter of fact, steadied her. Together they went out of the house into the darkness. At once, she felt Allan's hand reach for her own and hold it tight. As her eyes became accustomed to the dark, she could see the firm, true lines of his profile. Quite suddenly, she felt a new rush of emotion assail her—a kind of electric current passing through their joined hands from one to the other.

What is happening to me? she thought. This is the first time in my life I've felt this way towards any man but Jonnie. What does Allan really mean to me? He has said he loves me. How can he know? We've only seen each other twice before this. Is my whole world going completely mad?

Of course, Allan must be terribly lonely. He'd lost the wife and child he loved and she reminded him of Louise. Was this bad for him? Was she inadvertently going to bring him a new loneliness, a fresh pain, just when he had learned to accept life as it was?

'Allan, are you happy?' she asked suddenly, breaking the silence between them.

She felt the pressure of his hand on hers and heard the quick intake of his breath.

'Like this, walking in the dark with you, yes! But I could not be completely happy unless I thought you were happy, too. It's all I want, my dear, your happiness. Do you believe that?'

'Yes, yes I do!' Beverly said. 'But you mustn't be too unselfish, Allan. If we . . . if we're going to be friends, you must let me do some of the giving, too. I should be miserable if I thought that in any way you were unhappy because of me.'

'I know. You don't have to say these things. I understand. And, Beverly, it isn't "*if*" we are going to be friends. We are—we were right from the start. That is true, isn't it?'

'Yes!'

They walked on, not hurrying their steps. To the girl, it was now as if she were in some kind of prolonged dream. It had begun as a nightmare—truly that wild rush along this same path had been a nightmare—but now all fear had gone and there was only peace. Nothing had been solved, yet her mind and heart were calmed and even happy. She knew this was because of Allan. Further, she would not question.

As they came to the end of the footpath where it joined the road, they both stopped as if by mutual consent. They turned towards one another and once more, as if in a dream, Beverly lifted her arms round Allan's neck and

177

a moment later his lips were warm and hard against her own.

It had been a long time since any man had kissed her with love. Warm-hearted and passionate by nature, Beverly felt her whole body respond to this man with desperate need.

Why not? she thought wildly. Jonnie doesn't want me. He's found someone else. Allan needs me. We've both been alone.

For Allan, it was a brief moment of weakness, too. He'd never meant to kiss her. Beverly was another man's wife and could never belong to *him*. Perhaps it was this very knowledge that made him weak. As their steps had slowed at the end of the footpath, he'd known that he must soon lose her; that they might never be so close together again. When her arms went round him, he felt such a wild rush of longing for her, that his resistance was no more than momentary. But even as he felt her response, the demand of her mouth on his, her body soft and willing against his own, his conscience still told him that this was wrong. However right it might seem at this moment, he *knew* it was wrong.

'Beverly! Darling!' He drew away from her, trembling and deeply moved. 'Not this way, my very dear, my darling. I love you too much. It could only be right if we were free.'

The words hung between them, cold and factual. Slowly, Beverly's heart ceased its wild beating and she knew that Allan was right. She

178

wasn't free. She had no more right to kiss Allan, be kissed by him, than Jonnie had to kiss Elinor. She had despised him for the same weakness and his wrong could not make the principle any different for her and Allan.

'Beverly?' She knew without words that he was asking for her understanding. He wasn't withdrawing his love for her, his need for her.

'It's all right, I know!' she whispered. 'Dear Allan, I'm sorry.'

She could just discern the half-smile on his face. His voice was like that of a naughty schoolboy as he said:

'I'm not—not really. I wanted it so much. But now you *must* go home, Beverly. Next time, I might not have the strength to leave you.'

Reaching up, Beverly touched his lips very lightly with her own and then, before he had realized her intention, had run away from him into the darkness. He was about to follow her, afraid for her alone in the night at this late hour, but then remembered her house was only a few minutes' walk away. No harm would come to her and it was better this way. If he'd run into that husband of hers, he'd have surely done something wild and crazy.

Walking home, Allan tried to steady his thoughts. This whole evening had been so utterly unexpected. Had he been prepared, he could, perhaps, have controlled his emotions better. But with Beverly arriving as she had, shocked, hurt, unhappy and so much in need of him, how could he have denied his love for her?

And I do love her! he thought, without surprise, for now love had come to him a second time, it was almost as if he had never been without this deepest of all emotions. He tried to think of Louise but it was always Beverly's face that came into his mind. They were so alike. It had some strange effect on his mind and heart, as if the two were one. And because Louise was his—his love and his wife—it seemed as if Beverly must be, too, although he *knew* it was not so.

As he returned once more to his own sitting room; aware now of its emptiness, its quiet, yet filled with the memory of the girl who had been there, Allan fought with his heart. He knew he was hoping desperately that Beverly's marriage might crack completely. That was the only way he could have her. Yet he despised himself for the hope, the wish. He was as weak as that husband of hers. It was one thing to be strong and righteous when temptation wasn't there; another to be strong when one's whole mind, heart, body and soul, longed so deeply for what must not be.

It's madness to think this way! he told himself with an effort. She doesn't love me. She was just finding in my love a shadow of what she believed she had lost in Jonnie.

Despite her denials, she must still love her

180

husband. Otherwise she would have been indifferent to his unfaithfulness. You can only be hurt by another human being, deeply hurt, when you care for them. Your pride can be hurt, but not you, not deep down.

Suddenly terribly alone and unhappy, he leant his arms on the mantelshelf and bowed his head.

'Oh, Louise!' he whispered the words aloud. 'If you are somewhere now with God, pray for me, help me. Don't let me hope for what can never be mine.'

But it was Beverly's faint, elusive presence that filled the cottage and seemed to follow him to his own room, her face which haunted the shadows round his bed and finally his dreams.

CHAPTER NINE

Beverly opened the back door of her house and feeling her way across the kitchen switched on the light. The room was neat, tidy and warm from the boiler which Annette must have made up before going to bed. On the table top was a note.

Madame,
I have retired to bed. The tea-tray for the morning is on the dresser ready for

181

you. The children are asleep and all is well.

Annette

All is well! Beverly sighed and went across to the electric kettle and filled it to make a cup of tea. Presently, she would put it on a second time for her hot-water bottle.

As she held the kettle under the tap, she heard the kitchen door open. Swinging round, she saw Jonnie standing in the doorway. His face looked twisted and—she sought for the right word and found it—crumpled. In his hand was a half-empty glass. She knew then why he looked so different. He was tight—or drunk.

'So you've decided to come home?' His voice was slurred and he shifted uneasily on his feet.

Beverly bit her lip and forced herself to continue with her job of making tea. 'So have you, Jonnie. Now we're all here.'

'Where've you been?'

'Out!' Beverly said crisply. 'What about you?'

Her tone of voice checked him. She was different. This wasn't the tearful, strained Beverly he had left behind. This was a cool, collected young woman—someone strange. He wished he hadn't had so many whiskies and that he could think more clearly.

'Don't bother to answer that!' Beverly said

quickly. 'Obviously you've been with *her*. I hope you had a pleasant evening? I imagine she gave you a good dinner?'

Jonnie stared at her and shook his head. 'No dinner!' he mumbled. 'Thatsh the trouble.'

'Oh, I see! Too much champagne on an empty stomach. You're drunk, Jonnie.' As he came towards her, she backed away from him, some of her coolness and calm deserting her. 'Don't come near me! Don't touch me!'

He gave her a stupid smile. 'Thatsh no way to treat your husband. 'Sno way to keep him anyway. Your fault if I've drunk too much. Should have been home.'

Beverly's face whitened. 'Why? Sit back and wait for you to come back from *her*? No, thank you, Jonnie. I've better things to do.'

'Where've you been?' Jonnie asked again, slumping into a kitchen chair and leaning over the table.

'It's no concern of yours, Jonnie.'

'Afraid to tell me. With Forbes, I sh'pose. Not with Sue, anyway. Must have been lying. No need to lie if it was above board.' He was almost talking to himself, but suddenly he looked up and said sharply, 'Were you with Forbes?'

Beverly poured the now boiling water into the pot and spilled a little on the table as her hand shook.

'Yes, I was. He's one of the few friends I have. I needed a friend. You see, I didn't know

183

what to do, Jonnie. I thought my life was finished. I was all in pieces and I thought Allan could help me. He did.'

'Did he? Perhaps he can do the same for me.'

Beverly poured out two cups of tea and pushed one across the table at Jonnie. She might be behaving strangely towards him, but his behaviour, his words, were just as strange-sounding to her.

'Surely *you* don't need help?' she said, unable to prevent the sarcasm from sharpening her voice. 'It's really quite a simple decision for you, Jonnie. All you've got to do is make up your mind which of us you want: Elinor or me.'

'Made up my mind. S'all over!' Jonnie said sadly. 'Thas why I went to see her. To tell her s'all over.'

Beverly sat down suddenly and stared at Jonnie aghast. 'You mean you've finished with her? For always?'

'S'right!' He smiled again, stupidly.

Beverly stood up again, her mind whirling. It had happened. What she had wanted so much had happened. Jonnie had come back and it was all over. Now everything could be as it was before. *But could it?* Could it be the same? Did she still love him? Relief that now there was no longer any problem was there, uppermost in her mind. But what about her heart? Why couldn't she fling herself into

184

Jonnie's arms and tell him how happy she was; how wonderful it was of him to come back!

'Is Elinor going away?' she asked.

Jonnie looked surprised. 'Don't think so. Don't know. We didn't discush that.'

'Jonnie, drink that tea, please. Perhaps it will sober you up. I want to get this straight. You say it's all over. Is it? Have you stopped wanting her or have you just done this because I asked you?'

'Don't want to bust up the home. Got to think of the kids!' Jonnie said. Suddenly he laughed. 'My God, five of them, too. However did we have so many? Must have been mad.'

'Jonnie!' Her voice pulled him up and he stopped laughing.

'Whatsa matter?'

'Please drink that tea!'

He did so, shook his head as if trying to clear it and then said suddenly: 'Don't you want me back, Bev? What's happened? Don't you love me any more?'

Beverly felt a sudden desperate desire to cry. But she would not. This time she would not do so.

'I don't know, Jonnie,' she said honestly. 'I don't know. I want it all to be as if this hadn't ever happened. It all seems like some terrible dream from which I can't wake up. But I don't see how it can ever be the same as it was. Please don't think I'm not grateful that you want to keep the home together. I'm glad you

185

feel it's worth it. But love . . . you don't love me, Jonnie, do you? It's her you want.'

'I didn't want to—to want her. She's got something. I just can't explain it, Bev. You wouldn't understand. I don't think I'm in love with her, it's just that, when I'm with her, I don't seem to be able to help myself. I know you're worth ten of her. She isn't half as nice a person as you. I know that, but all the same, I don't seem to be able to leave her alone.'

Beverly listened white-faced. 'I suppose you're talking about sex, Jonnie. Maybe it's different for men; perhaps they *can* make love to women they don't even like. It's different for women—at least for me it's different. I'd have to be deeply fond of and respect any man who wanted to love me that way.'

'I said you couldn't understand!' Jonnie said helplessly.

'But what will happen?' Beverly asked. 'If she doesn't go away, you'll meet her again and it'll all start up again. How can I trust you, Jonnie, when you don't even trust yourself?'

'I don't know!' Jonnie said, his voice suddenly sober and reasonable. 'I don't suppose I've any right to ask you to have me back. You're fine, Beverly, and good and decent and strong. I'm not. I'm weak. But I mean to try.'

Beverly looked into Jonnie's face, trying to feel love for him, pity for him, *something*. But she seemed to be unable to rouse any emotion in herself.

'I don't understand!' she said, more to herself than to him. 'We don't seem the same people any more. I'm not strong, Jonnie. I found that out tonight. I don't know how to help you . . . help our marriage.'

'Can't we pretend this hasn't happened? Maybe in time we will forget. If you like, Bev, we'll take that holiday?'

'No!' The cry was wrung from her. How could she bear a holiday like that now? It was to have been a second honeymoon. What kind of time would they have, Jonnie wishing all the time she were Elinor, and Beverly knowing it?

'Can't I do anything to put things right?'

'Oh, Jonnie!' Beverly cried, suddenly weakened despite herself. He sounded so like Nick or Philip or Julia—'I've said I'm sorry, now can I have a sweet?'—it was the same tone of voice, the same childish reasoning. One could forgive the children because they were children. But Jonnie was a man; a husband, a father. Hadn't he really grown up at all? Must she spend the rest of her life looking after another child? She wanted to be looked after by him, to be able to lean on him, trust in him, above all respect him.

'It's all right!' she said with difficulty. 'Don't let's talk about it any more. We'll do as you say, Jonnie; pretend it never happened.'

Jonnie nodded his head. 'You're a good sport, Bev. Always thought so. Coming to

187

bed?'

Oh no! Beverly cried in her heart. Not that! That's no way to do things, Jonnie.

Aloud she said: 'Not just yet. I want to lay the breakfast things. Annette forgot. I'll be up presently.'

After he had gone, she sat down again at the table, unbearably tired and feeling once again as if she were made of elastic, stretched to breaking point. She knew that Jonnie's way was wrong. How could he expect her to make love when he had been so recently in another woman's arms? Maybe he hoped to use her body to still his own need for Elinor? No, she couldn't, couldn't! Yet if she denied him this part of her married life, how could she expect him to remain faithful?

And Allan? she told herself cruelly. What about those moments in Allan's arms? His kisses? How much are they affecting your emotions. If you'd never gone to Allan tonight, might you not be in Jonnie's arms now?

No, no! It wasn't so. Her need for Allan now was merely a desire for the same peace, the same relaxing of tension, the same ability to be utterly dependent. Allan had nothing to do with this. It would be better not to see Allan again for a while; not until her relationship with Jonnie was on a firmer footing. Because that was what she must do— rebuild their marriage. She must learn to trust him again, to love him again, to *want* him again as her lover.

Jonnie is lying up there, waiting for me, she thought. I ought to go to him, let him feel my love for him, let him see how much more I need him than Elinor ever can do. He's given her up; he deserves something in return. He needs me to help him be strong against her.

But I can't, I can't! she tortured herself. I don't want him to touch me. I couldn't in any way respond.

It'll be your fault if he goes back to her, she told herself. If you want to keep your marriage intact, you've *got* to mean to him what she means. Go up. Go to him. Show him you care.

Slowly, she picked up the tea-tray and with trembling hands carried it up to their room.

*   *   *

'Bev? Wake up, darling. Here's a cup of tea!'

Slowly, she opened her eyes and became conscious of Jonnie's voice.

'Cup of tea, my sweet. You were dead to the world so I made it. God, I've got a hang-over. Think I'll cut the office and stay home.'

Slowly, Beverly drank the tea, as she did so memories of last night flooded over her, bringing a hot blush to her cheeks. She could not look at Jonnie. Last night had been a wild, savage, unbelievable hour, at the end of which she had fallen swiftly and suddenly into a deep, almost drugged sleep. There had been no

189

tenderness, no love, no gentleness, completely different from any other time they had been together. It had seemed impossible to her that under such circumstances, she could have responded to Jonnie's demands of her. Yet, in the end, she had been as wild and uncontrolled and savage as he, deriving the same purely physical enjoyment and satisfaction.

Only now, her cheeks flushed, her head and eyes averted from Jonnie, did she wonder: Was that how it was with Elinor? Was that what he wants from me? It isn't love. I felt no love . . .

'Think I'll take a couple of alka-seltzers!' Jonnie was saying brightly. 'Shall I run you a bath, darling?'

His voice was affectionate, possessive, friendly. He was behaving as if there were nothing in the world that was wrong except his hang-over. Maybe that's how he felt. Maybe he believed that last night had put everything right. Was that really all Jonnie needed from her? Nothing of her heart? Only her body?

As if in direct reply to her thoughts, Jonnie suddenly leant forward and kissed her lightly on one bare shoulder.

'You look so tempting, lying there naked, only half awake. I've a good mind to get back into bed!'

'Jonnie!'

'Yes, darling?'

She couldn't after all talk to him and explain how she felt. He was so bright, so cheerful, so

190

obviously content. How could she take that happiness from him by saying, 'We can't build a marriage on this!'

'I would like that bath!' she substituted quickly.

She locked the bathroom door as soon as she was in it, locked it against Jonnie, hoping he would not realize the reason for it. In the past he would sometimes come and sit on the edge of the bath, smoking a cigarette and talking to her. It had seemed perfectly natural. But now she did not want him to see her nakedness.

What's the matter with me? she asked herself desperately. I ought to be so happy. I've got my husband back. That's what I wanted. He's given her up. Last night proved to him I can be what she is! But I can't—not really. *That* isn't what I wanted. But what right have I to everything? I married him. That's what Allan told me; for better or for worse. This must be enough. It always used to be. Jonnie hasn't changed and I mustn't. But I have, I have! I feel as if I've grown twenty years since this time yesterday.

Somehow, the day wore on. After lunch, Annette took the twins for a walk with Julia. Philip and Nick were at school. Mercifully, none of the children seemed in the least aware of the upset between their parents yesterday. They took Jonnie's unexpected day at home with unconcern and since he was obviously in a very happy frame of mind, they were delighted to have him there. It was as if Jonnie were trying to make amends to them, too. Anything they asked, he did. At four o'clock, Nick and Philip returned. Nick handed Beverly a letter. She knew at once it was from Allan and was glad that at that moment, Jonnie was in the garden with Julia. Nick ran out to join them and she was able to take Allan's letter to the privacy of her bedroom to read.

My dear,
I have found it hard to concentrate on twice two this morning. Every time I look at young Nick's face across the room, I've thought of you and wondered if you are all right. The trouble with twice two is that it can so easily make five in the moonlight. Not that there was a moon last night, but I think you know what I mean.
I meant everything I said to you, but I want you to know and believe that in your case twice two was making five. You were upset and shocked and alone and your reactions were perfectly normal for someone in your state. I was there and offered comfort and you took it. It meant no more than that. I'm afraid, you see, that you might just possibly begin to think it did mean more.
I think your husband loves you,

Beverly. Perhaps each of us loves in a different way according to our capabilities and our natures. A man can be unfaithful to his wife and still love her and need her. I hope very much you will both be able to find happiness again. I have great faith in you and I think you can be strong enough for both if you so choose.

If things go wrong, don't forget that you have one true friend who would do anything in the world to help you.

As always,
Allan

'Oh, Allan!' Beverly whispered to the empty room. 'How well you seem to know me! I had wondered about myself last night. It would be so very easy to fall in love with you. But you are right, of course. There can never be a love between us and it's best not to think about it even as a possibility. I'll concentrate on Jonnie, on his need for me, his love for me.'

Love! There again Allan was right. Each individual is capable of only so much loving. In his way, Jonnie *must* still care a lot or he would have left her for Elinor, of whom he'd said all along that her hold over him was purely physical; that he didn't love her.

She folded the letter and put it away in her writing case. Later, when she had read it again, she would burn it. Meanwhile, she must answer it, reassure Allan.

Dear Allan, she wrote, underlining the dear:

Thank you for your letter. It came at a moment when I was confused and you have helped, as usual, to straighten me out. I will never forget your kindness to me yesterday, nor will I forget that you helped me to grow up a little.

I suppose we must lose many of our ideals in life and that in doing so, we do grow up. I think I can face the future calmly. As you say, I believe Jonnie does love me in his way and he has given her up. Now it's up to me to build things up again.

I'm very happy to have your friendship. I hope you will feel we can meet and talk sometimes, as friends. Thank you again, dear Allan.

from
Beverly

Reading it through, it seemed somehow inadequate. It was complicated by his love for her. Knowing that he cared made it so hard to write without showing the depth of *her* affection for him. It wouldn't help either of them if she did so. Maybe it would be better not to meet again, for a long time. She didn't want to make things too hard for him. Yet he lived such a lonely life, and sometimes just to be together for a short while, with Nick, maybe . . .

I mustn't lean on him! Beverly thought as she hurriedly sealed the letter and stamped it. It would be wrong to become too dependent on their friendship, their understanding; to count too much on the strange bond between them.

The thought of his loneliness, the emptiness of his life, became suddenly unbearable to her. Impulsively, she leaned out of the window and called Nick in.

'Darling, I was going to post this, but if you like, you can run over to Mr Forbes with it. Maybe he'd like you to stay to tea. You can, if he asks you. Do you want to go?'

'Yes, I'll go, Mum. I say, Mum, he hasn't written about anything *bad* I've done at school, has he?'

'No!' Beverly smiled and ruffled Nick's hair. 'He said last time I spoke to him that you were being very good. Run along then, darling. Be back by bedtime.'

She felt happier when he had gone. Slowly, she walked downstairs and out into the garden. Philip and Julia were helping Jonnie build a vast bonfire. Not far away someone was mowing their lawn and the rhythmic sound drifted across the hedge. There was a sweet smell of honeysuckle from the plant which had spread itself through the clump of hazel trees. It was a beautiful afternoon, yet sad.

This day—this moment, is how I feel inside me, Beverly thought as she walked towards them. Before long, summer would be gone she told herself, the smoke from the bonfire reminding her of November.

Jonnie's mind must have been running on similar lines.

'We must have some really good fireworks this year,' he said as she came up to them. 'Let's make a party of it, Bev. We'll ask Sue and Pete and anyone else we can think of. I'll get some decent rockets in town and we'll give the kids a real bang-up show.'

He looked suddenly very young, very happy, very enthusiastic. There was no trace in his face of last night's drinking. It was almost as if all the lines of worry and tiredness had been wiped from him in one clean sweep. He looked young, clean, strong.

'Of course I'm still in love with him,' Beverly told herself quickly. 'It's just that it is a different kind of love now.'

Quickly, she stooped and gathering a handful of hedge cuttings threw them on to the pile. The leaves curled in the heat, twisted, crackled and burst in to flame.

CHAPTER TEN

A month later, Jonnie was clearing up in the office, hoping to catch the early train home, when one of the typists came in.

'There's a lady to see you, Mr Colt,' she said. 'I told her you were just leaving, but she said she had to see you urgently.'

'A lady?' Jonnie looked at the girl in annoyance. 'Didn't you ask her name?'

'Yes, I did, sir, but she said just to tell you she was there.'

Elinor! He knew it must be Elinor. There wasn't anyone else it could be. And the wretched girl had said he was still there. He didn't want to see her. She ought not to have come. Everything was all right at home and he couldn't risk another bust-up. Not even he could expect Beverly to forgive him a second time. He'd behaved pretty rottenly and he was damn sorry about it all. He'd just about convinced himself now that he didn't even *care* about losing Elinor. After all, it turned out so differently with Beverly; seemed she could attract him that same way, when she chose. *That*, he had convinced himself, was all that had been wrong with his marriage; all that had led him into Elinor's arms. They'd let that side of their life become humdrum and dull. Well, it was different now and he wanted to keep it that way.

'Can't you say I've gone?' he asked the girl desperately.

'You mustn't teach your staff to tell lies!'

Jonnie and the typist both flushed scarlet as Elinor walked into the room smiling. The girl ran out of the room making her escape, but Jonnie remained rooted to the floor.

Elinor gave a deep, throaty laugh. 'You look so *guilty*, darling,' she said easily, sitting down on the edge of his desk and toying with a paper knife. 'Tell me, why don't you want to see me?'

He could smell her perfume now, heady and strong. It made him think of—but he wasn't going to think about her that way.

'You know why I don't want to see you,' he said harshly. 'It's all over, Elinor. You must have known I meant it.'

Elinor nodded.

'But of course! All the same, I don't see why you have to avoid me as if I was the plague. You haven't been up to the club. I suppose in order not to see me. And now this. It's really rather *unkind* of you, darling.'

'Elinor, please!'

She looked very smart. She was wearing a tight-fitting skirt that clung to her slim hips, over it a loose jacket that seemed in some odd way to accentuate her femininity although it hid the lines of waist and breast. On her dark head was a tiny fluffy white hat, piquante, coquettish, somehow French and naughty.

'You're not *afraid* of me, are you?' she asked, looking up at him from between long, blackened lashes.

'Damn it, you know I am!' Jonnie burst out. 'It isn't playing fair, Elinor.'

'Oh, I see. Not cricket and all that, what!' Her American drawl had become a parody of Oxford English. 'But since when has love become a sport? I thought even you English agreed that all was fair in love and war.'

'I'm not afraid. It's just that I've got to go home. It can't do any good, coming here, Elinor. It's all over.'

'Well, I wasn't suggesting anything else, honey. I was passing by and I thought if I dropped in, you might stand me a drink for old time's sake, or something?'

'A drink?' Jonnie said stupidly. 'You want me to take you out for a drink?'

'Why not? Six o'clock and opening time. Surely you can spare me ten minutes, Jonnie?'

He felt stupid. He'd been fighting against her trying to re-open their affair and, all the time, she'd only wanted a drink.

Suddenly he laughed. 'It's really rather funny. Okay, we'll have a drink. Then I must get back. We've people coming to dinner tonight and I promised I wouldn't be late.'

'Poor old Jonny-boy; tied to the apron strings again. Well, we can always drink to your funeral, I suppose.'

'It isn't like that. They're my friends as well

199

as Beverly's. I asked them, as a matter of fact.'

Again Elinor laughed, her deep long laugh that seemed to come from somewhere right within her.

'You are touchy, darling. What's the matter with you? Surely your wife can't object to you having a drink with an ex-girlfriend. After all, I am an ex, aren't I? It's not as if she need be jealous any longer.'

Jonnie was reassured. Clearly Elinor did not intend to reopen their affair.

'I could do with that drink myself,' he said, reaching for his hat and brief-case. Elinor slipped gracefully off the edge of the desk and put her arm through Jonnie's. He could feel the warmth of her bare flesh between glove and cuff through the sleeve of his own jacket. His arm muscle jumped and pretending to need his arm for that purpose, he carefully and clumsily locked his office door.

Elinor preceded him downstairs, the eyes of both typists staring after them.

'Coo!' said the girl who had announced Elinor. 'What a stunner!'

'I think she looks like a cat or something!' the other girl said. 'I bet she purrs and scratches!'

'Go on! I think she's ever so smart. Wonder who she is?'

'*He* didn't want to see *her*, anyway,' said her companion. 'I would, if I were a man.'

'Well, he's married, so shut up!' was the

reply. 'Come on, or we'll miss the bus.'

At that moment, the telephone rang. 'Oh, bother it!' said the younger girl, but she picked up the receiver all the same. 'Who? Oh, Mrs Colt, I'm ever so sorry, he's just left. Is it important?'

'No, it doesn't matter, thank you,' Beverly said. 'I'd hoped to catch him because there were one or two things I wanted him to bring home, but I can manage.'

'I think she's ever so nice!' the typist said to her friend as they made their way down to the bus stop. 'Wonder what she'd have said if I'd told her *he'd* just left with a smashing American dame!'

'Don't be so nasty!' retorted the other. 'You know he wasn't keen.'

Neither realized how much they had already betrayed.

Jonnie sat beside Elinor in a quiet corner of the bar at the Fifty-One Club. Elinor's martini was nearly finished, but Jonnie's was untouched. She watched him toy with his glass, her eyes hard. 'You're not being very sociable, darling! I'm beginning to feel sorry I looked you up.'

Jonnie looked up at her anxiously. 'Please try to understand, Elinor! It isn't that I'm not glad to see you . . . in a way, I am. It's just that it's easier to forget you when we don't see each other.'

'I do believe you're afraid!' Elinor taunted

201

him. 'For a man of your age, it's really rather absurd, don't you think? Why, in the States a man can take another woman for a drink without his wife flying off the handle in a fit of jealousy. Perhaps she doesn't trust you, darling.'

'Well, you can hardly blame her!' Jonnie was stung to reply on Beverly's behalf. 'Besides, you're right. I don't even know if I can trust myself. You're so damned attractive, Elinor.'

She smiled, a quick, secretive smile. 'Have you thought about me this last month? Or had you forgotten all about me and our times together?'

'How could I forget!' Jonnie burst out. 'I've tried. In a way, I've even settled down again. It's no good, Elinor. I know we can't ever be platonic friends. Maybe it's possible with some women, but not with you. I can't be with you more than a few minutes before I'm wanting you like hell!'

'Darling!' her voice was a soft caress. 'Why torture ourselves this way? I've been miserable, too. It's not as if I ever wanted you to break up your home. I never expected you to do that. I never meant your wife to know and we must have been crazy to let her find out. We must just be more careful in future.'

'There isn't going to be a future!' Jonnie said harshly. 'It's over, Elinor, *it's got to be over.* I'm not the kind of man who can lead a double life and get away with it. Beverly would guess and I'm a rotten liar. I can't, Elinor, and you mustn't try to make me.'

Elinor stubbed out her cigarette and lit another, blowing a cloud of smoke across the table. All around Jonnie was the strong heady smell of her perfume, undimmed by the cigarette smoke, reviving memories of Elinor's creamy white skin, of her smooth bare shoulders in the firelight, of her maddening, tantalizing laugh as she held him tightly and more tightly against her.

'I'm moving house!' Elinor said suddenly. 'I'm selling the cottage and moving into an apartment in town. I thought I might try to find one somewhere in this district—not far from your office. Maybe you could drop in and see me sometimes, Jonnie? We might have lunch together or a quick drink before you catch your train home. I wouldn't ask for anything else, I promise. I'd never try to detain you if you *had* to get home. Beverly'd never find out. If I move away, she'll think it's all over and she'll stop being suspicious. It'll all be so easy.'

The way she put it, it sounded easy, tempting, desirable; and yet in his heart, he didn't want to re-open the affair. Until this evening, he'd reconciled himself to the fact that it *was* all over. He hadn't even expected to see Elinor again. Now, damn her, he wanted to see her; wanted to take what she was offering him. If only he could reconcile his conscience and still the fears that if Beverly found out, she'd never forgive him a second time.

'She was only hurt because she *knew*,' Elinor said, sensing with that extraordinary, witch-like sixth sense of hers Jonnie's hesitation. 'What you don't know can't hurt you. This way, we can all be happy; you, me and your wife, too. And if you ever start to feel she's suspicious, or unhappy, well, we'll just have to stop seeing each other. But it's worth a try, surely?'

She reached out a gloveless hand and gently touched his knee. Jonnie looked up and stared at the face before him. It wasn't a pretty face— not by accepted standards anyway. What was it about this woman that was so devilishly attractive? Why should he still want her? His nights with Beverly had been just as satisfying as his love-making with Elinor, or at least, he'd believed so. What power did this woman possess that she could make him want her against his will? He didn't want to re-open the affair. He didn't want to cheat Beverly. The kind of life Elinor suggested was one he had condemned in other men. And it was dangerous. One slip and Beverly could and *would* divorce him.

'No!' he said wretchedly. 'No, Elinor. Don't ask me. Please believe that if I were free . . . well, you know how it would be then. But I'm not free. I've never been free. We should never have given way in the first place.'

'But we did, darling. What's between us is too strong for us both. I tried to put you out of my mind, really I did. You can't imagine this kind of thing is very satisfying for me? Besides, I could find someone else—there's plenty of other fish in the sea. But I don't want them, Jonnie, not the way I want you, *need* you. Night after night I lie awake thinking about us; of the things we did; the magic we made. There's never been anyone like you in my life before. That's why I'm prepared to take so little, Jonnie. Just a few odd hours. It's not even as if I'm asking for any of your time at home. Beverly would see as much of you as she would otherwise do. You can't throw all this away, Jonnie, life's too short.'

Was Elinor right? Jonnie asked himself. Was there really something special between them that excused them from ordinary conventional behaviour? Elinor wasn't asking much. She didn't want him to bust up his home; she'd even been considering Beverly's side of the picture and making sure that she didn't suffer in any way. He could slip out of the office during the lunch hour; slip away a bit earlier in the evenings. Beverly would never guess—why should she? It was different for her; she was happy with the ordinary domestic life, the kids, and a husband to come home at night. And he would be home as usual. It would only be in office hours that he and Elinor . . .

'Jonnie, don't decide now. Think about it. I

205

don't want to make you do anything you'll be sorry for. I wouldn't have suggested this if I didn't feel so very strongly that it's the solution for all of us. But you have to be sure, too. Otherwise, I could never let you come and see me. I'd rather find someone else—even if I don't, couldn't, love him—to help me forget you.'

No! Jonnie thought with a rush of violent jealousy. No, not that, not another man. Why should another man take what was his? And she belonged to him. They belonged together. He'd been wrong to suppose he'd put her out of his mind; he'd only forced her out. That bond between them was as strong as ever.

'Ring me, tomorrow!' Elinor said. 'From the office. I'll be home all day as I've people coming to see over the cottage. Think about it, honey, and ring me.'

Going home in the train, Jonnie thought. He felt it was wonderful of Elinor to be asking so little, offering so much. There weren't many married men who had the advantage of such understanding, such unselfishness. He'd be mad to refuse, and yet what *would* Beverly think, feel, if she ever knew? She wouldn't know—couldn't know. He could say he'd taken up squash to replace the golf he'd finally given up. At least, he'd written his resignation to the club and hadn't been near the course since that night. He'd post the letter off and in a day or two, he'd tell Beverly he'd decided to play squash with one of the fellows in the office. They might play in the lunch hour or after work. Bev never came to town. She'd never doubt him. Or would she?

He drove home, silent and thoughtful, ill at ease. Their guests had not yet arrived but Beverly was ready dressed looking young and attractive in an olive-green dress that accentuated the colour of her eyes.

'Darling!' she greeted him with a light kiss. 'Whatever happened to you? I thought you'd be on the early train. I rang the office to get you to bring home some cocktail biscuits but the girl said you'd just gone!'

There was no suspicion in her voice. That typist couldn't have mentioned Elinor, unless Beverly was trying to trap him. Maybe it would be better to tell the truth and say he'd run into Elinor, stopped to have a drink with her.

'As a matter of fact, I ran into Elinor. It was quite accidental. I mean, I had no idea . . . She's going, Bev, selling the cottage. She wanted to say goodbye.'

'Going?' Beverly repeated stupidly. 'Back to America?'

'No, I don't think so; she didn't say where. Just that she thought it best to leave here. It's what you wanted, isn't it? Now I can't run into her even accidentally.'

Beverly gave her young husband a curious look. 'Yet you ran into her *accidentally*, in town?'

Jonnie flushed. 'No! Now, look, Beverly, don't start getting ideas. What actually happened was that she came to see me. I didn't invite her; she dropped by the office. It was only to tell me she was leaving and that it was all over. You ought to be glad, not so damned suspicious.'

'I'm sorry!' Beverly said, her hands falling to her sides. Jonnie was right: she *must* trust him. Of course he was hesitant in telling her what had happened. He'd guessed she'd be unpleasant about it, and she had. And it wasn't his fault that woman had called to see him. To make amends, she said quickly:

'Now you won't feel you have to give up your golf, darling. I know what it means to you. You haven't posted your resignation, have you?'

'Well, as a matter of fact, I have. Anyway, I think I should give it up. After all, I don't see much of you and the kids. It means we can have all our weekends together. A fellow in the office was telling me today he plays squash in the lunch hour. I might take that up. I used to play, you know. Much better for me than eating too much in some restaurant. Look, I'd better go and get changed or Sue and Pete will be here before I'm ready.'

He bent to kiss her on the forehead, but she reached up and pulled his face down so that their lips touched. Suddenly, she could detect the faint smell of perfume—not her perfume,

208

but someone else's . . . Elinor's—and she pulled away from Jonnie sharply. He walked away up the stairs and she stood for a moment, watching him go, trying to overcome the inner, nagging suspicion that, despite her desire to trust him, was still torturing her.

Could she trust him? Could she? When was he lying, when telling the truth?

He'd never have told me he'd met Elinor this evening if it had been starting up again, she told herself sharply. He's being completely honest with me. She's going, and that will really be the end of it. I'm going to forget about her and let him forget.

The front-door bell rang suddenly, startling her out of her reverie. She hurried forward to open the door.

CHAPTER ELEVEN

It was nearly Christmas. Soon the term would be over and Nick and Philip home all day for the holidays. Already they were making calendars and colouring Christmas cards, and at this very moment, Julia was sitting on the floor surrounded by yards of paper chains she was making.

Annette was in the kitchen preparing tea and Beverly was playing with the twins in their play-pen in front of the fire.

It was a warm, domestic, happy atmosphere, and yet somehow, she wasn't happy. Her nerves were on edge and she did not know why. Something was wrong, but what? What? Outwardly, everything was so perfectly all right. It was Jonnie, of course, who worried her. But why?

I hate myself! Beverly thought. Jonnie's done everything possible to make amends and to be a good husband; a good father. He'd given up his golf, and true to his word, spent all his weekends at home. Nick and Phil were once more his adoring shadows and Jonnie had immense and quite unusual patience with them. Perhaps that was the trouble; he'd changed. He wasn't a cheerful young boy any more, he was quieter, more thoughtful, more considerate in every way—almost too considerate. It was as if he couldn't forget that he'd hurt her and had to go on proving to her and to himself that he *was* a good husband. Somehow, that in itself made it impossible for her to forget Elinor. If they'd only had a row sometimes, a cross word, a difference of opinion! It would be more natural; more normal. But they didn't. Whatever suggestion she made, Jonnie acquiesced. He was punctilious about little things, like bringing her early morning tea, helping her with the twins, opening doors, carrying trays. He never forgot to kiss her when he came back in the evenings, or when he left in the mornings. And there were presents, far too many—flowers, chocolates, a pair of gloves, something special for dinner.

Even Sue, who only came to the house occasionally, had noticed it and said, laughing: 'I'd call it a guilty conscience, Beverly. Better watch out!'

Of course, Sue who didn't know about that brief affair with Elinor, couldn't have guessed how near the truth her remark had been. But Jonnie couldn't go on like this. Of course, she was happy to have him *want* to make amends in these small ways, but somehow she might have been easier in her mind if he'd chucked something at her one evening and then taken her into his arms and kissed her, shaken her, showed some small sign of passion.

There was that, too. Those brief moments when he had lost himself completely in their love-making, carried her away with him into some new, strange world . . . it was never like that now. He only occasionally made love to her; mostly when she had snuggled up closer to him, wanting affection, some physical sign of love. And then he had been gentle, considerate, kind, but never passionate, never beyond complete control.

If I only knew what was wrong? Beverly thought. Perhaps nothing at all. But I feel I'm always at arm's length; that he is just out of reach. *Why?*

She heard voices at the front door. Nick and

Phil both chattering at once. They weren't supposed to come in that way with their muddy boots. She went to tell them when the door opened inwards and Nick, flushed and excited, said:

'Mum, we've brought Mr Forbes back to tea. He's got something for us. It's all right, isn't it? He can come!'

'Allan!' Beverly said, suddenly terribly glad to see him. They hadn't met since that night and it seemed a world away now. She had glimpsed him across the playing field at school or sometimes shopping in the village, but they hadn't done more than wave to each other and go their different ways.

'How nice. Come in, quickly. It's pouring with rain. But of course, you know that! Boys, take off those boots and ask Annette to give you dry socks. Come in, Allan.'

Julia ran out of the sitting-room to join the boys and for a moment, they were alone together in front of the blazing fire, only the two chubby toddlers staring at them from round, blue eyes.

Allan took Beverly's hands in his and looked down at her, his face still wet with rain, but smiling. 'Let me look at you! Are you well? I get snippets of news of you from the boys, but I had to find out for myself.'

'I'm so glad you came, Allan!' Beverly said. 'I get news of you, too, but it's much nicer to see you in person. Are you well? Are the boys behaving?'

In a moment, all trace of depression had left her and she felt happy, excited, warmed, comforted. It was so nice to see him.

'Sit here and get warm!' she said, pointing to a large wing-chair by the fire. 'You'd better take your shoes off if they're wet. I'll get a pair of Jonnie's slippers for you.'

'I'm not used to being spoilt!' Allan said with a smile. 'And this is so nice and welcoming. What a charming room it is, Beverly, and how those babies have grown! *Look*, it's smiling at me!'

'Not *it*, Allan!' Beverly said, laughing. 'She! That's Melanie, she's always very forward with strange men. This one is Suzanne. She's much shyer.'

'They look alike to me, yet I can see the difference. I think Melanie is most like you. She has your expression, though not your eyes. Beverly, never mind the slippers. Tell me how you are. Happy? All well with your world?'

'Yes, yes, of course!' Beverly said hurriedly, too quickly. She walked away from him to the window and stared out across the rain-swept garden. 'You know Elinor Wilmot left? Jonnie's working hard, of course, but he gave up his golf so we have more time together, really. Allan . . . I never really thanked you for being so good to me that night. You saved my marriage, I think.'

He looked at the slim young back, seeing

213

the slight droop of her shoulders, the delicate back of her neck, the shine of her hair. He knew that it would only be tormenting himself to come here, see her again, yet he had *had* to come, to reassure himself that she was well and happy; that it had all turned out for the best.

Now he was suddenly painfully aware of something new about this girl he loved so dearly. A sadness . . . no, not quite that! A helplessness?

'I'm glad!' he said. 'I'm afraid I didn't do much. Let's not talk about that. Tell me about yourself. What you've been doing. How is your husband? No, you've told me that. Tell me about *you*.'

She turned to him, suddenly smiling. 'There isn't much to tell. I lead a very quiet life, I suppose, though I'm always busy. It's these young horrors.' She pointed to the rosy-cheeked, contented pair in the play-pen. 'I suppose you can't take two more pupils of this age at your school?'

'Not quite yet!' Allan smiled back. 'Besides, what would you do with yourself if they weren't here to keep you occupied?'

'That's just it!' Beverly said in a strange, taut voice. 'I think about that at night, Allan. What will I do when they're all away at school?'

Allan drew out his pipe and slowly, methodically began to fill it. 'I daresay most mothers feel that way,' he said thoughtfully. 'There'll be plenty to do, you'll see. You'll be able to get up to town occasionally, see a matinée, go shopping, get your hair done. I don't know what women do with their days. Get a job, perhaps? What do you want to do?'

Beverly went back to the fire and curled herself on her favourite pouffe, staring into the flames. 'Nothing! I can't think of anything. I think the only ambition I ever had was to raise a family, have a home to care for. I've been so busy doing that ever since I was seventeen, I've never really had time to think about the future.'

'It'll take care of itself!' Allan said comfortably. 'Hullo!' he added as the boys came back into the room, carrying a cardboard shoe-box carefully between them.

'It's a model car but it's all in bits!' Nick said. 'Phil and me thought you could help us put it together. Daddy brought it back last Sunday. It wasn't even our birthday, either. Dad's always bringing us things.'

'You're lucky!' Allan said quietly. 'Don't you think he'd like to help you put it together?'

'Oh, he won't mind if you help,' Nick said. 'Please, Mr Forbes.'

Beverly laughed. 'Unless Mr Forbes has any objection, I think "Uncle Allan" might be more friendly when it is a social visit. Of course, it would still be Mr Forbes at school.'

'That's a grand idea,' said Allan, and

215

although from force of habit, the boys forgot once or twice, they were soon calling him Uncle Allan as easily and naturally as if he had been a real relative.

'You know, you have a wonderful way with children,' Beverly said later, when the boys had joined Julia and the twins in the kitchen for tea with Annette, while they had theirs in front of the fire. 'You only have to be in the house ten minutes before they are all your adoring slaves. Julia positively makes me blush the way she flirts so obviously with you!'

Allan laughed contentedly.

'I think she's a dear little girl. I imagine she must be like you were when you were her age.'

'I was perfectly horrible!' Beverly said, shaking her head. 'My sister was the pretty one of our family and I was madly jealous of her. Mother used to try to make out I had the brains but it never consoled me. I suppose I knew it wasn't true, for one thing and for another, all I wanted was to be ravishingly beautiful!'

Allan looked across the room to where she sat, relaxed, flushed, contented, in front of the warm fire, her empty tea-cup held lightly between small, square, rather boyish hands.

'I suppose I should be gallant and say you are ravishingly beautiful now. But to me, you have something much more worthwhile than mere prettiness. I think you are one of the loveliest women I've ever known.'

216

Allan's tone of voice was so impersonal, despite the intimacy of his words, that Beverly was not quite sure how best to reply to such a remark. Was this Allan's way of telling her he was still in love with her? No! It was just his way of speaking what he felt, without motive.

Without waiting for her to speak, he went on easily: 'You're happy, aren't you, my dear? You are so much more relaxed than when we last met.'

This time his voice did falter and, for a moment, uneasiness lay between them at the memory of their last meeting; of that last embrace.

'I'm afraid I behaved very badly, Allan. You must have thought me an hysterical little fool. Perhaps your ability to understand and deal with small children stood you in good stead with me! I was acting like a child.'

Sensing her discomfort at being reminded of the past, believing that she truly was now reunited with Jonnie and happy with him once again, Allan quickly changed the subject.

'I believe that what you call "dealing" with children successfully, is merely a matter of understanding them. It's so easy to forget how a child feels when it is young. Lots of people think it isn't important, but children do feel things and very deeply, too. Most of their behaviour is a direct result of how they feel— bad behaviour in particular. I don't think any child wants to be bad just for the sake of doing wrong. It's nearly always for one reason or another, to attract attention because they don't have enough love, or something of that sort. Of course, kids are full of mischief and I'm a firm believer in discipline!'

'Did you always want to be a teacher, Allan?'

Her companion nodded. 'Yes, I think I did. It's a very rewarding occupation in so many ways. I know you must understand that. After all, a mother has the same kind of satisfaction in bringing up her children the way she wants them to be. It's a creative way to live. I should hate to deal, say, with accounts or statistics or anything like that. I'm one hundred per cent interested in human nature.'

'It's a curious subject,' Beverly said thoughtfully. 'Human nature, I mean. You may think you know all there is to know about people; then suddenly you find out you don't know them at all. You have to begin all over again, trying to fathom out what is real. Allan, do you suppose men and women are really very different, fundamentally, I mean? Do you think that in some ways, life is more difficult for men? That a woman is more primitive at heart and that for this reason, it's easier for her to be sure of the essentials in her life?'

'Perhaps!' Allan replied quietly, wondering now what was behind Beverly's question. Wasn't she happy after all? Was it a generalization on life, or a question in her

218

mind about that husband of hers? 'Love, home, children; these are all essentials to any woman. But men need to be able to work, too. I think a man's job is very important to him. He must be able to do something and make something of his life beyond emotional satisfaction. Tell me, what does Jonnie actually do?'

'Oh, it's to do with steel exports!' Beverly said vaguely. 'I don't really understand myself what he does. He's a very junior partner in this firm and I believe they are making quite a lot of money now the threat of nationalization seems to have eased off. Jonnie works terribly long hours now. It's often nine, sometimes ten before he gets home. Of course, it's partly his own fault. He doesn't really *have* to stay on at the office after six. But as he says, the work piles up and he daren't let it get ahead of him. He can't relax when he does get back if he hasn't completed everything there is to do. He's hoping for a rise soon, you see, and it'll make a big difference to us financially if they make him a full partner on equal terms.'

'It seems a very long day for him,' Allan said shortly.

'It is!' Beverly said. 'Of course, the train journey doesn't help. It takes him an hour, even when he leaves the office on time, before he's back here. When he's very late leaving he has a bite of supper in town to save me having to cook a meal so late.'

'Don't you ever get out together in the evenings?' Allan asked.

'Not very often!' Beverly said truthfully. 'But we do have the weekends. Now Jonnie doesn't play golf, we have all Saturday and Sunday. I shouldn't complain.'

No! Allan thought. On the strength of it, there is no cause for complaint. A man working hard to get the rise he needs for his family; giving up his golf to be with them weekends. It sounded as if Jonnie were the model husband. But was he? Or was he, Allan, being prejudiced in his mind when he felt rather than thought, that the old tale of 'working late' somehow didn't ring true?

How can I be objective about the man when I'm in love with his wife? Allan thought dejectedly. He despised himself for the trend his thoughts had taken. Besides, he barely knew Jonnie and, had he taken the trouble to get to know him, he might have liked him a great deal better on closer acquaintance. What reason had he to distrust him? Lots of men made mistakes, regretted them, and turned out to be model husbands afterwards, even perhaps the better for that one slip. Why not believe Jonnie was one of them? Beverly trusted him. Or did she? Her voice had been so steady, so emphatic when she spoke of her husband's work. Was it over-emphasized? Was she trying to convince herself as well as him that Jonnie wasn't up to something else?

But what? Elinor Wilmot had left. Everyone knew she'd sold the cottage and disappeared. Back to the States? Gossip did not reveal her whereabouts and Allan certainly had not been sufficiently interested in the woman to make any enquiries. Did Beverly know?

Suddenly hating himself for these thoughts, suspicions, Allan said: 'I'm so happy to know it has all turned out so well for you, Beverly. I thought it would, you know.'

'Yes, you did, Allan. I'm grateful that you made me see sense,' Beverly said eagerly. 'I was so hurt at the time that I just couldn't see Jonnie's good points for the bad ones. But I've grown up since then, Allan. I trust him now and I don't believe he'd ever betray that trust. He really loves us, you know. He spends so much more time with the children; everything's all right between them now. I know Jonnie would never risk losing them or me.'

Yet even as she spoke those words with ringing conviction, some tiny voice, deep buried in her heart, spoke softly to her.

Wouldn't he? Does he really love you? Is everything exactly the same as it was before *her*? You want to trust him, but you don't. Why not? Is it because you feel rather than know that something is wrong, that something is missing?

But nothing was wrong. Jonnie was kind, affectionate, considerate. When they made

221

love—even if it was very seldom these days—he was gentle, tender. What was it, then? Was it her fault? She who had changed? And not Jonnie? Could it be that Allan had somehow made a difference? Was there buried in her mind, a memory of Allan's arms around her, his desperate need of her? Was that it? That Jonnie did not seem to need her now, not the real, essential woman beneath its outer shell. He needed her care of him, of his home, of his children. But did he ever make any demands on her mind, her thoughts, her longing to give of herself? Did he really want her *love*?

'Allan!' she said suddenly. 'Tell me something. When you were married to Louise, what was the most important part of your relationship? What did you miss most when . . . when she died?'

Allan drew out his pipe and began slowly to fill it. 'It's difficult to answer that without a bit of forethought. I missed her presence, of course. The house was suddenly completely empty. I missed all the little things she used to do for me—silly little things like sewing buttons on my shirt and finding my pipe when I'd lost it! But I think more than anything, I missed her company. You see, we used to talk over everything together, not deliberately debating everything that had happened in the day, but it was a kind of sharing of each other's lives. It was the same when we'd been out anywhere together. We always wanted to know

222

what the other thought, felt, about a place, people, situations, life. I think I missed her mind as if I had suddenly lost half my own. Something would happen and I would turn to say 'Louise, do you think—?' and then I would remember that she wasn't there. Each time it happened, it was like her dying all over again. I don't think I've really a very dependent nature. After all, I used to live alone before we were married and I've learned to do so since. But I needed her in so many ways when she was there; her mind, her love, her kindness, her sympathy, her encouragement. Even her criticism. Does that sound very silly?'

'No!' the word was almost a whisper. How could such a declaration of love sound silly? It was what every woman wanted from love—to be needed as a person as well as a woman . . . wife, mistress, friend. It had to be all three to be complete.

'We were very happy!' Allan said quietly. 'I suppose some men might feel it would have been better never to have known that happiness than to have known and lost it. But I'm glad we had those years. Life can be a very long search. Some people never know love. Louise and I thought we had found it in each other and we were happy.'

Because in some odd way he felt so close to Beverly, it did not seem strange talking to her about Louise. It was many years now since he had spoken of his wife to anyone. He had grown so used to being without her until Beverly came into his life, reminding him of what he had lost, of what was good and warm and sweet in a man's life. He'd never thought to meet another woman who could mean to him what Louise had meant. Perhaps Beverly, had she been free, could not have meant exactly the same either. He and Louise were contemporaries, equals. With Beverly, he felt older, wiser, more protective. He wanted so much to be able to take care of her. Louise had never needed that; she was always complete in herself.

It is because there is something *lost* about Beverly, Allan thought. Even now that she is reunited with her husband, she is still somehow lost and alone. Her mouth might smile, but her eyes did not. Only when the children were in the room, noisy, demanding of her time, attention and love, did she become wholly herself. Then all that was warm and generous in her disposition flowed from her, making her a complete woman, wise, maternal, understanding. In those moments, she seemed to the man watching her to be older, wiser than himself.

Allan stayed on till the children's bedtime. When at last he rose to go, it was with reluctance. Outside, the rain fell in sheets and he knew that his fire would be out, that the cottage would seem contrastingly empty and horribly quiet.

Beverly must have thought the same as she helped him into his raincoat, for she said: 'I wish you'd stay to supper, Allan. I hate to think of you having to go home now and cook a meal.'

'Mrs Bates will have left me something prepared to "pop in the oven" as she always says. I've overstayed my welcome as it is.'

'No, no you haven't!' Beverly cried, suddenly unwilling to let him go. 'You'll come again, won't you, Allan? It's so nice for me to have someone to talk to. Promise me you will come. The children love having you here, too.'

'Yes, I'll come again,' Allan said gently. 'It's good of you to put up with me.'

As he walked slowly homewards, he was unaware of the rain as he tried to sort out his impressions and emotions. He was honest enough with himself to admit that going to see Beverly and her children was not a good thing. He knew himself to be falling more and more deeply in love with her. He knew that such a love was bound to be fruitless. Beverly was married and therefore for ever beyond his reach. Even to love her silently and within himself was wrong. Yet he had not the power to keep away from her. He'd tried; these last few months he had thought a thousand times of going to see her, dropping in casually the way he had this afternoon. Each time, he had fought the temptation to see her face, hear her voice, share the same room with her. Now at last, he had weakened, telling himself that he had to know she was all right before he put her completely out of his mind.

What kind of lie was that? Her own letter had told him her marriage was patched up; that all was well. *She* would have come to him if there had been any fresh disaster. No! He had gone because he had wanted so much to see her. He was in need of a love he could never have.

And now he had promised to go back. Something wistful in the tone of her request that he should return, had again weakened him from what he knew to be the right thing to do. He ought to go far away, and forget about her. He ought to ask for a transfer where he would not see her children every day, seeing in Nick's or Philip's innocent young eyes, the reflection of *hers*. But how could he go when she had need of him?

I have no proof she needs me, Allan told himself sternly. I think that because I want it to be so. It would be wrong to let her depend on me, even as a friend. That way love might grow between us and if her marriage failed again, it would be my fault, just as surely as it was Elinor's fault that Jonnie was unfaithful to Beverly. I cannot be responsible for such a thing happening, however remote the chance. I *must* go away.

While this conviction was fresh in his mind and heart, Allan hurried homewards, and before he could change his mind, he sat down at his desk and drafted a letter to the local education authority, requesting a transfer.

Beverly would never know that he was going at his own demand. Better she should look on it as an unfortunate stroke of bad luck.

'I'll see her once more . . . only once more,' he told himself, as he sealed the envelope and stamped it. 'That can and must be our goodbye.'

CHAPTER TWELVE

Jonnie lay on the large divan in Elinor's sitting-room, his jacket discarded, for, despite the near-freezing temperatures outside, Elinor's flat was centrally heated and always seemed to Jonnie like a greenhouse. The dry, airless atmosphere did not suit him and he always had a headache after he had been there a few hours.

It was the only criticism he had of Elinor's apartment. In a very expensive block of flats, it was in every way luxurious and Elinor herself had spared no expense in making it more so. Her own glittering cocktail cabinet stood in one corner of the large living-room; the latest television combined with radio and gramophone in another. There was, of course, a record cabinet and every disc by every new popular singer. Most of all, Elinor liked Eartha Kitt's records. Jonnie did, too, for in many ways, Elinor reminded him of the dusky American singer. Sometimes the two became confused in his mind and when he was making love to Elinor, Eartha's voice rasping yet sultry and provocative in the background, he would wonder just who it was he held in his arms.

Surprisingly, Elinor seemed to be a good cook. Right now she was in the small efficient kitchen 'knocking something up' for their lunch. He was not sufficiently domesticated himself to realize that any exotic meal was easy enough to provide if you had the money. Elinor shopped at Fortnum's and did very little cooking herself.

She only had to open packages and tins and present them prettily on a plate. Her food always seemed so much more appetizing than Beverly's. Jonnie tried not to make comparisons because it always made him feel guilty towards Beverly, who struggled hard to make a tempting meal from the cheaper cuts of meat. Mostly, the food was well cooked, but the menu did not include avocado pears, prawns in aspic, cold partridge and such delicacies. Nor did any meal include the wines Elinor always provided in abundance.

'I wish you'd let me pay something towards all this!' Jonnie had once said. 'I can't let you provide everything.'

'But, honey, why not? I've so much pleasure

doing it—for *you*. Besides, this way we don't either of us need to feel we're taking something that belongs to your family.'

He'd thought at the time how decent it was of Elinor to think that way. She was right, too. He and Beverly had a hard enough time making-do without him drawing a lot more from the bank. All the same, he argued, Elinor should let him take her out sometimes.

'If we go to a restaurant, we lose so much of our time together,' was her reply. He knew what she meant. These lunch hours in her flat meant half an hour to eat, and an hour or more to make love. And Elinor never seemed to have enough of him. It was flattering, Jonnie thought, as he waited for her to reappear with the lunch tray, that, after all these months, she still wanted him as much as ever. Of course, he felt the same way. But she was so exciting, so glamorous, so mysterious, whereas he was such a dull sort of fellow. He couldn't think why she still cared about him so deeply.

He couldn't know that it was his own behaviour that still kept Elinor interested. Never, even at their most intimate moments, could she believe that Jonnie was hers, *all* hers. It was as if he always had one eye to his watch face; was for ever hurrying away from her to the other, greater and more important part of his life in which she had no place.

'I must get back to the office, my sweet,' or

229

'I must rush or I'll miss my train!'

Once or twice she'd tried to persuade him to stay longer, trying every trick she knew to make him forget time, the office, his wife. But he'd only weakened once and then he had been so on edge, he might just as well not have been there for all the attention he paid her.

It maddened, exasperated and intrigued her, this woman who had never yet failed to bring a man to his knees. True, she had been able to establish this part-time relationship with him. He came now as a matter of course, nearly every day, either for lunch or before going home in the evening. But he was never completely, wholly hers, to the point of forgetting his wife. She knew he would unhesitatingly throw her over if he thought for one moment that Beverly might find out. That was behind everything he did or said.

In many ways, Jonnie was far from being her type. He was not really sophisticated at heart although he was fascinated, rather the way any very young man might be, with the sophisticated way of her life, her surroundings. He was not even particularly fun or amusing. But when he made love to her . . . Elinor wanted him and although now she was beginning to have her doubts as to whether she could ever make him leave that dull little wife of his, she was even more determined to have him, at all costs, waiting for her when she beckoned, and not just turning up when he could spare the time.

But she was too clever to make any new moves as yet. She wanted him to take all this, all these meetings, so much for granted that when she suddenly threatened to put an end to their affair, he couldn't face it. Then he'd choose her rather than his family. Meanwhile, he was still far too much on edge to be taking anything for granted. He still looked like a guilty schoolboy when he put his key in the lock; still jumped if the phone rang or the door bell went; still kept sufficient rein on himself to be forever watching that clock.

Later, lunch over and pushed into the kitchen out of sight, she lay in his arms and said tentatively: 'No hope of you staying a whole night sometime, darling? These hours seem to go so quickly.'

Jonnie's body stiffened. 'Oh no, I don't think I could, Elinor. I've never done such a thing and Beverly would be sure to question me. I do so hate these lies I have to tell her.'

'Does she cross-question you a lot?' Elinor asked carefully.

'No! That's just it! I think she trusts me. That's why it seems so awful sometimes— cheating her I mean. I think I'd almost rather she knew.'

Elinor raised her pencilled eyebrows. 'But then you say she'd surely divorce you?'

'Yes! That's why I can't tell her. But I want to, often. I know we ought to stop this, Elinor.

We ought never to have started. Why am I so weak?'

For answer, she bent over and began to kiss him, knowing that for a little while at least, she could still even his conscience, certainly his doubts.

'I can't let you go, I can't!' Jonnie said at last when it was over and they were lying in each other's arms. 'Life without you in it would be empty of all colour, all excitement, all magic. I think you must be a witch, my darling. You've cast a spell on me.'

Elinor leaned across him and kissed him slowly. 'I love you, Jonnie!' she said.

'Do you? I wish I could be sure what love means!' Jonnie said, holding her closer. 'Is it only a transient emotion, Elinor? Once I believed I was as much in love with Beverly as any man could be in love with a woman. There'd never been anyone else and I couldn't believe there ever would be. Now I'm lying here with you, wondering how I lived all those years without you. Is it love we feel? Real love? Or is it just a violent physical attraction?'

'You think too much, honey!' Elinor murmured. 'No one knows what love is. I don't even know if I want that kind of love you read about in books. What we feel for each other is OK by me.'

Jonnie raised himself on one elbow and looked down into those dark unfathomable eyes of the woman whose body he knew so well but whose mind was still a mystery to him.

'But, darling, don't you see that if we don't really love one another, we shouldn't be here together, like this? It's only if it is the real thing that this is excusable.'

'This is real!' Elinor said, running her cool slender hands across his broad shoulders, smiling her enigmatic smile.

It isn't the same for her, Jonnie thought with a sudden despair in his heart. She doesn't have to lie and cheat and deceive anyone. She's free. She has no duty towards Beverly, the children. Naturally, it doesn't worry her as it worries me. If only I didn't hate myself so much every time I see her. Yet I can't live without her, we both know that. At least this way is better than breaking up my home, messing up Beverly's life, the kids . . .

He glanced at his watch. 'I must go soon,' he said sharply. 'We've a board meeting at two-thirty and I daren't be late.'

The usual acute depression at leaving her weighed down his thoughts. He knew he wouldn't be at his best for this meeting. And it was important, too. He had to pull himself together somehow, try to concentrate more on his job, less on Elinor. Old Barkington, the senior partner, had dropped a hint only yesterday about his work.

'Sure you're feeling well? I've been wondering about you these last few months. Nothing wrong at home?'

'No, nothing at all!' Jonnie had replied quickly.

'Well, in that case, I think I ought to warn you that you've made one or two rather bad mistakes lately and this kind of thing can lose us business we need. You know what I'm talking about of course; that contract you drew up and the way you replied to Jenkins' letter. Obviously your mind wasn't on your job in either case. If you want promotion, John, you'll have to learn to be more responsible. I haven't time to check on all you do, you know. And there's one other thing. I know it isn't easy to get lunch in an hour round here and I certainly don't expect you to clock in and out like the typists. But I do think you should start the afternoon before three, and stay after five if there's work to be done.'

'I'm sorry, sir!'

There'd been no excuse; there was none. He knew these lapses had cost him the promotion he'd hoped for for at least another year or more. Old Barkington wasn't being unfair; he'd every right to tell him to pull himself together. You couldn't expect him to make allowances for Elinor.

I ought to stop seeing her! Jonnie told himself as he left the flat. Some men might be able to lead a double life and like it, but for me it's a kind of nightmare. Always wondering if Beverly has noticed something; lipstick on my handkerchief, Elinor's perfume, something!

Maybe she did suspect. She was very quiet these days. There were no arguments, no scenes, no tears. It was as if everything had got a little too much for her, too. Poor Bev! And she tried so hard to make him happy. In a strange kind of way, he was happy with her. The hours they spent together with the children were always satisfying and often great fun. And she was a good mother as well as a good wife. None of this was her fault.

'I'll take her home some liqueur chocolates!' he thought with a lightening of his spirits. 'She loves them and the thought will please her, too.'

He bought a box at the confectioner's outside the office. It didn't occur to him that he might owe Elinor a box of chocolates, too.

*   *   *

'Jonnie! Thank you very much. You know, I haven't finished the last box you brought home yet! But it was nice of you to think of it. I'll put them away for Christmas.'

Beverly picked up her knitting again and tried not to think of Sue.

The results of a guilty conscience. No, that was horrible. Think of something else quickly. Jonnie looked tired, and so much older. Maybe he was working too hard. But he'd said he hadn't a hope of getting a holiday before Christmas. Maybe they could go away at

Easter. Where? With the children? Alone? What would they do alone together for two weeks? What would they talk about? What had they done with themselves before the children had been born? What aeons ago that seemed. They'd been married nearly ten years. Now she was almost twenty-seven and she felt old . . . old. Jonnie would be thirty next birthday.

'What are you making this time?' Jonnie's voice interrupted her thoughts.

'Oh, just a pullover for Phil. He needs another one for school. Jonnie, Nick said there was a rumour going around that Allan Forbes was leaving.'

'Who's he when he's at home?'

'Allan? Darling, Nick's and Phil's teacher. You remember, you met him when—'

'Oh yes, your boy-friend!' Jonnie interrupted with a half-laugh.

Beverly flushed. 'I don't think that's funny or fair,' she said.

'Sorry, Bev! Still, you did like him, didn't you? Can't say I did much.'

'Yes, I liked him. He came over to tea the week before last. He didn't say anything then about leaving.'

'Well, I don't suppose it matters much one way or the other, does it? They'll get another teacher.'

'Yes, but not like Allan. He's wonderful with the children. I hope he doesn't go.'

Something in her voice really caught Jonnie's attention.

'You sound as if you really minded,' he said.

Beverly let her hands fall idle in her lap.

'I do!' she said quietly. 'I know we haven't seen much of him, yet he's been in a way a real friend. I'd be sorry to think of him going away somewhere where we can't ever meet.'

Jonnie studied Beverly's face, his own puzzled.

'Bev, what really went on between you two? I never asked.'

He was surprised by the colour that flooded Beverly's cheeks for an instant.

'Nothing, really! He told me not to be so silly and sent me off home—to you!'

'Did he?' Jonnie said, further surprised. 'I think at the time I was a bit jealous. I had some idea he was in love with you.'

'*You*, jealous *of me*?' Beverly said. 'But, Jonnie, you were mad about Elinor at the time!'

Jonnie shrugged his shoulders. 'All the same, I took a strong dislike to the fellow. Perhaps I was a bit unfair. After all, you say he sent you home. Does that mean you were really going to leave me, Bev?'

'I don't know, Jonnie!' she answered slowly. 'I don't think I'd sorted anything out then. I just wanted someone to tell me what to do.'

'And you haven't regretted it?' Jonnie asked curiously.

237

'Of course not!' Beverly said quickly. 'Nor you, Jonnie?'

'No!' Jonnie said, glad that in this at least he could tell the truth.

Suddenly Beverly smiled. 'You know, we haven't talked this way for ages—about ourselves, I mean. Jonnie, can you tell me now, about Elinor? You don't ever wish you could be with her?'

'No!' Jonnie lied quickly. 'Let's not talk about her, Beverly. I'd rather not.'

'So it still hurts?' Beverly said, as much to herself as to him. 'Yet you weren't in love with her; you said so at the time. Jonnie, you've never been sorry you married me? That we had the children?'

'No, I haven't!' Jonnie said again. 'You know how I feel about them, Bev. And you, too, of course. It's really you who should have regrets. I'm afraid I'm not all you hoped for in a husband. But, Bev, I swear I never mean and never meant to be anything less than perfect. I suppose I'm just weak, or something. I can't think why you don't hate me, really!'

Beverly looked up and met the strange look of appeal with an uneasiness in her heart. 'Hate you! Jonnie, how can you think that? I'll admit I was terribly hurt at the time; any woman would have been. But I wouldn't have cared so much if I hadn't loved you so much. Besides, I don't really blame you, I blame her. She had so much with which to attract a man

238

and she didn't hesitate to try. I think if she could, she'd have taken you away from us. I can understand how at the time she seemed new and exciting and different. But you chose us, Jonnie, and that's all that really matters.'

He wanted then to tell her, to confess to these last months. It was so near the tip of his tongue to do so that silence hung like a thread in the room and but for the sudden whimper from one of the sleeping children, he might have done so, promising to finish with Elinor, this time for always.

But Beverly rose quickly to go upstairs and he was alone with his unspoken confession. In that moment, he hated Elinor, hated the power she had over him, hated her for his own basic weakness. It was Beverly he really loved and really admired, respected, liked. It was Elinor's body he wanted, needed, desired with a passion that seemed to know no abatement. She offered escape from all that was dull and humdrum and ordinary. She offered glamour instead of domesticity. She was the unknown, the quarry he must chase, the mystery, the temptation for a world only half experienced; a world he wanted, enjoyed. That which was evil and bad in her awakened all that was evil and bad in him. He knew it, yet he couldn't break away from it. He was like a man addicted to drugs. Beverly couldn't help him; no one could help him except himself. And he couldn't contemplate any more a life without that heady excitement, devoid of the passion, the colour, the sophistication she had taught him to appreciate.

Perhaps in the New Year, Jonnie thought helplessly. At the end of the year, I'll tell Elinor we've got to stop it. I'll really try to settle down without her. But the knowledge that soon he might have to do without her only increased his desire.

Until Christmas, when he would be home for three days and a weekend, he visited the apartment even more often. Beverly understood that there would be several late nights before the holiday. He had every excuse to catch a late train. Christmas Eve he was in Elinor's arms at six o'clock, a time when Allan called to say goodbye to Beverly.

'Why, Allan! What a wonderful surprise!' Beverly greeted him with genuine warmth. She was tired from all the preparations for the next day and the children were so excited that, even with Annette to help her, it had been a difficult job getting them all settled down for the night.

She led him into the sitting-room, bright with paper chains the children had made, and holly over the pictures and the Christmas tree which stood in one corner.

'How nice it all looks!' Allan said, seeing not so much the detail as the resulting effect of a family's combined efforts to bring out the Christmas seasonal feelings. This was how a home should look at Christmas time. The home-made crib with the Baby in its cradle and the toy farm animals around, lit by a tiny candle, completed the scene.

His own cottage was undecorated, empty, without noise or light or fire. Ever since he had sent in his request for a transfer he had not been able to take any interest in it, knowing he must soon leave.

During a difficult interview with the school governors, he had tried to find adequate reasons for wishing to go, even inventing a sick aunt in Yorkshire. They'd been very unwilling to accede to his wishes and had told him outright that they wanted him to reconsider.

'The fact is, Forbes, we have been thinking of making you headmaster. Jackson retires at the end of the next year and we were all agreed that you'd be the ideal man for the post. I couldn't guarantee this step up if you leave. We'd have no control over you in Yorkshire although we would, of course, give you the best of references. But if you can find a way to sort out your family difficulties, then it would be well worthwhile staying on, Forbes. Think it over.'

The man, meaning well, had refused to take Allan's on-the-spot denial that he would change his mind.

'We'll have another talk after the holidays. Your aunt may have taken a turn for the better by then. Or maybe you can see your way to

241

moving her down to this part of the world. After all, Forbes, your financial position will soon be much improved. I know I ought not to say this, but I can pretty well guarantee you'll get the headmaster's job when he goes.'

Of course he'd been glad to think they *wanted* him as head and thought him capable and fit for the job. It was always satisfying to one's pride to have one's work and efforts appreciated. But the extra money? It wouldn't make much difference when he had only himself to think about. He had no big expenses, no hobbies demanding a lot of money. He'd managed pretty well, even saved a bit. All the same, he would have liked the job; liked to have run the school along his lines, and been in sole charge.

It made the going harder, for go he must. With every day, his thoughts turned more and more to Beverly, to her children, her home. He'd had to come this evening to wish her and the boys a happy Christmas, to bid her a silent farewell. He'd supposed that being Christmas Eve, Jonnie would be at home. He'd hoped the sight of her and Jonnie, close, linked with one another in their home and children, would make him realize how utterly useless such a love must be, now and always. Beverly did not need him and could not possibly do so. There was nothing to keep him here but everything to make him go if he valued peace of mind. Away from her and the boys, he would begin to forget, to find that peace of mind that he had attained with such difficulty after Louise's death.

But Jonnie was not here.

'He said he would almost certainly be late tonight,' Beverly explained as she poured out drinks for them both. 'Actually, I did think he might be on the train getting in at seven. But I suppose he missed it.'

'It's very foggy out,' Allan said, sitting down by the fire and stretching his long legs. 'Maybe the train is held up.'

'It must have come down suddenly,' Beverly replied, going to the window to look out. 'Yes, you're right, Allan. It is thick. I think I'll ring the station to find out if the train is in. You'll excuse me, won't you.'

While she was away, Allan stared into the fire, knowing with a deep sense of pain that the girl he loved was still in love with the man she had married. He knew it was wrong to be jealous of her husband and that he should not allow himself to think of Beverly except as another man's wife. Yet he could not help the emotions she roused in him, even while he hid them firmly in the depths of his being.

'Allan, it seems there's been a hold-up. The stationmaster isn't quite sure what's wrong but he said there'd been an accident further up the line. He might know more in a little while, he said. I hope it wasn't Jonnie's train.'

Her voice was full of anxiety.

'I'm sure it wasn't!' Allan replied in his slow calm voice. 'It's easy enough on a night like this for a truck to get derailed. There's no reason to believe it is anything serious, is there?'

'No, I suppose not!' Beverly said. 'All the same, I'd like to know what has happened. Whenever something is wrong, my mind always goes back to that dreadful Lewisham rail disaster! I suppose I'm morbid or something.'

She laughed uncertainly.

'Well, ring again in fifteen minutes. Meanwhile, tell me what you've been doing since I last saw you.'

'There's nothing to tell really,' Beverly said, relaxing into the chair opposite him. 'Why haven't you come before this, Allan? It's ages since you were last here.'

Immediately she had spoken, she regretted her words. There was a look on Allan's face which betrayed all too easily his real feelings, as he struggled for some excuse.

'I just don't seem to have got around to it,' he faltered. 'Besides, there's a possibility that I might be going away. I wanted to be sure before I told you.'

'Going away? Where?' Beverly asked both questions in one breath.

'To another school. They may be sending me up to Yorkshire.'

'Oh, Allan, no!' Beverly cried, despite

244

herself. 'Not all the way up there. Why, I'd never see you.'

'I know!' Allan said quietly. 'But these postings happen, you know, much the same way as in the Army. I've been here quite a few years, you know.'

Beverly remained silent. Of course, he couldn't know what his words had done to her. Somehow she had never imagined such a thing happening. Allan was there, in the little school at the foot of the hill, or in his cottage. It wasn't that she had seen much of him, just that she'd *known* he was there and that he'd be there if ever she needed a friend.

How selfish I am! she thought suddenly, despising herself. Of course this wasn't much of a job for someone with Allan's gifts. Maybe he was being promoted; she hadn't even asked. He was probably glad to be going; and yet he wasn't. She knew he was not. She knew the real reason he was leaving just as surely as if he had told her. It was the best thing, really, yet she felt utterly miserable, all the joy of Christmas, all pleasure in this unexpected visit, wiped out in a terrible sense of impending loss.

As she could read him, so could he read her. Her face, always mobile, was to him quite transparent. For one brief moment, he was happy because of her sadness. Then he quickly controlled himself, saying: 'You know, it won't make much difference to you, Beverly. Do you realize we've only met half a dozen times?'

'Yes, yes, I know!' Beverly said. 'But it always seems as if we've known each other all our lives.'

You, too, feel that! Allan thought but dared not say. It is the same for me. But I feel that way because I love you. You are not in love with me.

'I know!' he said as lightly as he could. 'There are some people one feels that way about. I think it happens a lot between people who are basically rather alike. There's a familiarity about the way they think, the things they say. It makes you feel you've known them longer than you really have.'

'The boys will be very upset!' Beverly said abruptly. 'I don't know how I'm going to tell them.'

'You mustn't say anything yet,' Allan told her. 'It's far from definite. Anyway, they've left it a bit late now. Term starts in another two weeks. But if I'm to make the move next holidays, well, I'll probably be pretty busy clearing up various odds and ends and there won't be much time for social calls. That's why I came tonight.'

'I wish you hadn't!' Beverly cried impulsively. 'I would rather not have known.'

'Beverly!' The way he spoke her name was like a caress. She heard it and looked up, meeting his gaze and reading in those brown eyes love, compassion, appeal. 'Don't let it bother you. It really won't make much difference. Besides, I'll write and tell you my news and I hope you will write and keep me in touch with the boys. I'd hate to think I'd never know what was happening to them. Little Julia, too. They've been a sort of substitute family, in a way.'

There were tears in her eyes as she turned her head quickly away so that he should not see them. Tears she could not explain except that her own heart was echoing the loneliness, the longing in Allan's, and it hurt.

Why should it? she asked herself, attempting to regain her composure. He's quite right. It can't make any difference to me. I'm only feeling this way because I know *he* doesn't really want to go.

'It'll be a good thing for me,' Allan was saying, trying not to see the bent head, the downward droop of her mouth. 'One is apt to get in a rut in a small country place like this. I'll make new friends, see new places. In many ways, it'll be good.'

'Yes, yes, of course. It was selfish of me to be thinking only of myself,' Beverly said, attempting a smile.

Silence fell, not the gentle quiet silence that sometimes falls between two people who know each other well and have no need for words. But a difficult, strained period of time when the air was charged with all the words that remained unspoken. At last, Allan said:

'You were going to ring the station again. As

soon as you've heard everything is all right, I must go.'

Obediently, Beverly replaced her glass and hurried into the hall. Her mind was not fully occupied with Jonnie, half of it remaining in the room with Allan, when she repeated her request for information.

'You a relative?' the stationmaster was asking her.

'Yes, yes, I am!' Beverly said, suddenly becoming fully conscious of the situation. 'Nothing's wrong, is it? My husband is on that train. At least, I think he might be.'

'I'm very sorry, Madam, but there's been a nasty accident about fifteen miles outside London at the Junction. The six thirty-five ran into the back of a goods train. I'm afraid I can't give you any further information. If your husband was on the train it might be as well to phone the hospitals nearby. I doubt you'll get through to the station itself; they're jammed with callers.'

White-faced, Beverly ran back into the sitting-room, too distraught with anxiety to feel thankful as yet that Allan was there to help and advise her. She stammered out the story.

'Suppose he's on it, Allan. What shall I do? I'm not even sure he caught that train. He may have missed it. Pray God he missed it.'

'The first thing to do is to find out if he *was* on it,' Allan said reasonably. 'Will there be

248

anyone at the office? Maybe someone can tell you what time he left. That would give you some idea.'

'Yes, no . . . there won't be anyone there now, Allan. It's nearly eight o'clock. I don't know who to ring. There's the senior partner; I know his name but not his number.'

'We can find that out!' Allan said calmly. 'I'll ring directory enquiries. He lives in town?'

'Yes, Putney!' Beverly said, suddenly calm now that Allan was in charge. 'He's sure to know when Jonnie left. They were having a conference at four. Jonnie said that might drag on and make him late.'

Allan got through to directory enquiries and, without much difficulty, obtained the home address and telephone number of James Barkington. Another few minutes and he handed the telephone to Beverly.

'He's on the line!' he whispered.

'Mr Barkington? Oh, this is Mrs Colt. I'm so sorry to disturb you but I'm rather worried about Jonnie. There's been a bad smash on our line and Jonnie isn't home. Can you possibly give me some idea when he left the office?'

'Why, yes, Mrs Colt. It was early, being Christmas Eve, you see. All the staff were away by five. We had a drink, just to toast the season, you know, and then we all left together. The typist locked up behind me. It wasn't later than five, I'm sure of that.'

'I see. Thank you!' Beverly said, and after Mr Barkington had made a few reassuring remarks, which she did not really hear, she replaced the receiver, noticing as she did so that her hand was trembling.

'Beverly, what's wrong? What's happened?' Allan asked her, catching her arm to steady her as he led her back into the sitting-room.

'I don't know!' Beverly whispered. 'It doesn't make sense, Allan. Jonnie left at five, certainly not after; Mr Barkington went at the same time, so he's sure of that. It means Jonnie could have caught the five-thirty. Easily. Even if he were held up in the rush hour, he could have caught the five-fifty. Allan, what shall I do now?'

Allan was shaken. Of course, there were a number of things which might have held Jonnie back from catching those two trains. He might have been doing some last-minute shopping. But then, if he said this to Beverly, it would reopen her fears that he was on the six thirty-five.

'He said he felt sure they'd be late. Yet Mr Barkington said he let the whole staff go early because it was Christmas Eve.'

'Maybe they finished earlier than Jonnie anticipated. Beverly, there's no point in sitting here surmising all that might have gone wrong. We must ring the hospitals and try to find out some news.'

'If Jonnie wasn't on the six thirty-five he'd

have been home by now. If he was shopping, he'd surely have telephoned me.'

'Only if he'd heard the news of the train smash. It would have been too late to catch the evening papers. He'd only know about it if he heard it on the radio and he wouldn't be likely to hear a radio in a shop. Besides, we don't even know if the accident has been announced officially.'

'I'm going to ring the hospitals,' Beverly said. And in the next breath: 'But suppose Jonnie is trying to get through to me? No, I'll ring the hospitals. I'd rather do that than sit here waiting.'

With Allan's help, they found the telephone numbers of the five hospitals in and around the locality of the accident. The first two reported numerous casualties received, but Jonnie's name was not among them.

'You mustn't worry,' Allan said as firmly as he could. 'We don't even know for sure he was on the train.'

'But there are so many!' Beverly cried. 'It must have been a terrible accident. Allan, put on the wireless. Something may come through on it. I'll try the next number.'

Allan had barely tuned in to the Home Service before Beverly recalled him quickly to the phone.

'He's there!' she cried. 'At least, they think so. They're checking the names again. Hullo? Yes?'

'We have a Mr Jonathan Colt in casualty now. Aged about thirty to thirty-five, fair hair, blue eyes. Height about six feet, clean shaven.'

'Yes, that's my husband. I'm sure of it! Is he all right? Please tell me.'

'I'm afraid I can't tell you the extent of his injuries at the moment. Can you ring again later?'

'But he's alive?' Beverly cried frantically to the cool measured tones on the other end of the wire.

'Yes, Mrs Colt. Will you call again? I will have more information for you then.'

'Yes, yes, I'll ring again!' Beverly said, replacing the receiver.

'At least we know he's alive,' Allan said. 'Would you like to go to the hospital? Can you leave the children? If so, I'll take you up.'

'Oh, Allan, would you?' Beverly cried gratefully. 'Annette will be all right till the morning. The car's at the station, though.'

'My car is outside your door!' Allan reminded her with a smile. 'Get a coat, Beverly, and if you haven't had anything to eat, then get some sandwiches to eat on the way.'

'I don't want anything to eat,' Beverly began but he interrupted her.

'I do! And whether you want it or not, you'll need it. Five minutes won't make any difference. We can be there in half an hour.'

While she ran upstairs to tell Annette what was happening, Allan paced the sitting-room

252

floor. His mind was deeply troubled, not just by the accident and the possible extent of Colt's injuries, but by the problem of his whereabouts after he'd left the office. With so much else to think about, it seemed to have slipped Beverly's mind for the moment, but at the time she had learned he'd left at five, she'd been shocked and deeply puzzled. Obviously she hadn't expected him to be shopping. Could he have stopped to have a drink with some friends? Hardly, on Christmas Eve, knowing his wife would be waiting for him; things to he done like hanging up the children's stockings, filling them. Where had he been during that hour and a half? With whom? Was it possible the man had been continuing his association with that American woman in town? Was that why he'd had to work so late so often?

It's no way to think of a man who might be dying, Allan told himself sharply. And the last thought in the world he wanted Beverly to have.

They'd both forgotten the fog. The drive was a nightmare crawl. Only Allan's slow, steady voice talking about nothing, everything, anything he could think of, kept Beverly from going out of her mind. It was nearly ten o'clock before they reached the hospital. Even as they arrived, ambulances were drawing up, lined up, waiting to disgorge their burdens.

'It's terrible!' Beverly whispered, holding hard to Allan's hand. 'And it's Christmas Eve, too. Allan, I'm afraid.'

He did not answer her, but led her to Reception where he made enquiries for her.

'He's all right, Beverly. Did you hear me? He's all right. They had to operate, but he's through that. They are ringing through to the ward to ask if you can see him.'

Beverly felt the tears running down her cheeks. Tears of relief, of relief from the tension of these last few hours.

'Don't, darling, please don't!' She heard Allan's voice and felt the strength of his love for her, sustaining her. Somehow the knowledge did not seem important; it was something she had always known, never a burden, always a comfort when she needed him most.

'I always seem to cry when I'm with you!' she said, trying to wipe away the tears with the back of her hand. He did the job for her with a clean white handkerchief. 'I'm so sorry.'

'Don't be. That's what a friend's shoulder should be for—to cry on. Beverly, you can go up. Ward 8. I'll wait for you here. You probably won't be allowed to stay with him long.'

She felt alone, anxious, afraid as she followed the young nurse down the long corridor, smelling of disinfectants and ether, a hospital smell she had always been afraid of. Outside the ward door she hesitated.

'There's nothing to worry about, Mrs Colt.

254

Here, I'll take you in,' the young nurse said, seeing Beverly's hesitation.

She took Beverly over to Jonnie's bed. At first, she thought he was asleep. He lay with his eyes closed, his face chalk-white; only the slight rise and fall of his chest showed he was breathing at all. Her eyes took in the bandages round both arms. Downstairs, she'd been told the injuries were internal. Perhaps they had meant only the serious injuries.

Suddenly, he opened his eyes and recognized her. 'Hullo, Bev. Didn't expect to see you here. They told me you'd phoned. So sorry to drag you out on a night like this.'

She knelt by the bed, regardless of the other patients and nurses in the ward, putting her arms round him gently. 'Darling, of course I had to see you, to see for myself you were all right. What a horrible experience for you.'

'Was pretty grim!' Jonnie said weakly. 'Lucky to come out of it alive. Hundreds killed, I heard them saying so when they dragged me out. Don't let's talk about it.'

'No! *You're* all right and that's all that matters. Darling, does it hurt? They say you had an operation.'

'I'm okay. Hurts a bit when I breathe in too deeply. One of the nurses came along just now and said she'd give me something to help me sleep but I told them not till you'd been. Wanted to talk to you. Bev, I've messed up your Christmas, I'm afraid, and the kids'. So sorry. I always seem to be mucking up your life, don't I?'

'Jonnie, darling, don't. It doesn't matter. Everything is all right so long as you're going to be OK. I was so afraid . . .'

'That I'd die? So was I. Bev, it might have been better in lots of ways if I had.'

'Jonnie!' She stared at him aghast. 'You can't mean that. What would I do without you? And the children? Jonnie, say you didn't mean it!'

He looked at her for a long moment across the white coverlet of his bed. She looked so pretty. Even with her hair blown about and not much powder on her face, she still looked pretty. Funny how long it had been since he'd really looked at her. It was like seeing her for the first time all over again.

'You know, I do love you,' he said. 'I always have. Even if I haven't always seemed to do so, I still love you.'

'Jonnie, I know. You're not to think about anything but getting well. There's nothing to worry about, nothing at all.'

'There is!' Jonnie said the words almost as if he were speaking to himself. 'You don't know, Bev, but there is. I've made such a mess of everything. I never meant it to turn out like this.'

'Like what, Jonnie? What's happened? Tell me what it is that's worrying you.'

'Should have told you,' Jonnie said sleepily.

'Ages ago. I wanted to. Tonight we had an awful scene. I told her it had to be all over because of you. Didn't want to lose you, you see. But she said she'd kill herself if I left her . . . nothing else to live for but me. Funny, I never thought she really loved me until this evening. She suddenly made me see what I'd been doing to her. Ruined her life, too. I'd only thought of you before. I knew then that I didn't love her and never had. She wanted me to leave you, marry her when the divorce came through. But I wouldn't do it. That's when she said she'd put an end to it all. Don't know if she would have done, but I didn't have the nerve to risk it. Had to stay a while longer. That's why I was on the six thirty-five, you see.'

'Jonnie!' She grasped his hands in her own as his eyes closed. He mustn't go to sleep now; not until she was sure he wasn't delirious. But his eyes remained shut and he seemed quite unaware of her existence.

A nurse suddenly appeared at the bedside and seeing her patient asleep, his wife looking as if she might faint at any moment, she said briskly:

'Time you left, Mrs Colt. There's nothing to be upset about, you know. He's sleeping because he had an injection just before you came up.'

'But he said—' Beverly began when the girl interrupted her.

'No, he didn't want it until after he'd seen

257

you. Said he couldn't rest until he had. But we gave it to him all the same. He thought it was penicillin.'

'Then he didn't know what he was saying just now?'

'Well, I can't be sure about that, but he would have been quite conscious until a moment or two before he dropped off. Come, Mrs Colt. Let me see if I can get you a cup of tea; you look all in.'

'No, no, I'm all right!' Beverly said. 'Besides, there's someone waiting for me downstairs. Thank you, Nurse.'

'You can come in again in the morning,' the nurse said. 'Doctor or Matron will be able to see you then. As you can understand, they're frantically busy just now. Cases are still coming in all the time. You must be thankful your husband is going to be all right.'

'Yes, yes, I am!' Beverly said with an effort. 'Thank you, Nurse. Good night!'

Somehow, she found her way back along the corridors.

Allan was waiting where she had left him. As she approached him, he jumped up and went forward to meet her.

'Beverly, you look ghastly. He *is* all right?'

'Yes, he's asleep. Allan, take me away from here quickly. Let's go somewhere, have a drink or something. I want to think.'

He knew then that something was terribly wrong. Mistakenly, he imagined it must be

258

with Jonnie; that he might have lost a leg, an arm? Be injured about the face? Yet the hall porter had assured him that there were only internal injuries and a few cuts and bruises. Why was Beverly so shaken?

He waited until they were seated in a nearby restaurant, until Beverly had taken at least two sips of the large brandy he had ordered for her. Then he said quietly:

'You must tell me what is worrying you, Beverly. Unless you do, I can't help you.'

'No one can help me!' Beverly said. And then: 'I suppose you might as well know. It's Jonnie. He's been seeing Elinor again. I don't know how often but there must have been other times before this evening. That's why he was on that train. He'd been with her. It's probably been going on all along, ever since she left home. Oh, Allan, it's horrible, horrible.'

Allan drew in his breath. With every nerve in his body, he wanted to say to her: 'Leave him, come away with me. I love you . . . I love you so much. I'd die for you. Give me a chance; let me show you what love really is.'

But he remained silent, trying to say only what was best for the woman he loved so dearly.

'What made him tell you now?' he asked at last.

'I don't know; I just don't know. I think it was on his mind, on his conscience. It had all

259

got too much for him. He hadn't meant it to be more than an affair. When he tried to break away—for good, he said—she threatened to kill herself.'

'But she'd never do a thing like that,' Allan said, astounded. 'She isn't the type.'

'No! But Jonnie believed her. He probably wanted to. I expect it appealed to his ego. No, that isn't true. I think he was badly shaken. He'd thought he could have his cake and eat it. Silly Jonnie! Surely he must have known that with a woman like that he couldn't come out the winner.'

'I'm glad you can feel sorry for him!' Allan said quietly and truthfully. 'I think it sounds as if he needs your help and understanding, Beverly. I'm sure he must love you and trust you. Otherwise he would never have told you, no matter how wrong things have gone.'

'Trust me? Takes my love and my forgiveness for granted, you mean,' Beverly said bitterly. 'I forgave him once. Why not again? Oh yes, he loves me. If you can call what he feels love. It isn't my idea, Allan.'

'Nor is it mine!' Allan agreed softly. 'But it is wrong to judge other people by one's own standards. Obviously this woman had him under her thumb. He's weak, but that doesn't mean he loved her or that he had stopped caring about you.'

'How can you be so damned righteous about him?' Beverly burst out, hysteria mounting in her. 'I don't understand you, Allan. I don't understand anything any more.'

'Darling!' The endearment calmed her instantly. 'Darling,' he said again. 'Don't you see that it is because I love you so much that I have to think this way about him? It would be so terribly easy to say all kinds of things about him. That way would serve my ends, for then you might turn against him, divorce him, maybe even marry me. It's because of that, I have to make you see the best in him. I think you're still in love with him, and if you ever leave him, Beverly, it cannot be because of something I said to you.'

She suddenly took both his hands in her own and clung to them tightly. 'Allan, I'm sorry. Forgive me. I ought not to have made you talk this way. I knew you loved me, although I sometimes found it difficult to believe. I think I was afraid even to think about it because of what it might mean—to us. I needed you so badly, Allan. So I buried my head in the sand and pretended you were just a good friend. But deep down I knew. Now you are going away, and I can speak the truth to you. I'm Jonnie's wife; I hate him for what he has done to me, and yet I know I couldn't ever leave him. He is weak. He's like a small boy who can't resist the forbidden sweet, even though he knows he'll end up being punished for it. What would happen to him if I leave him? He'd get trapped by someone like Elinor

Wilmot and go from bad to worse. I think I know now what my life with him will be like; this kind of betrayal over and over again. But he'd never leave me. I think he needs me, Allan, far more than you do. But if that isn't so—'

She broke off, uncertainly, but the man beside her finished it for her. 'If ever it gets too much for you, Beverly, you *know* I'll be waiting for you.'

'It's so unfair!' Beverly cried with a childish bitterness. 'You deserve so much more, Allan. Life has treated you so badly.'

'Don't pity me, darling!' Allan said gently. 'Besides, it isn't true. Life gave me Louise to love and then you. I know I can never have you, but it means something to me that you are in the world, too, perhaps even thinking of me sometimes.'

'Oh, Allan!' Beverly whispered, her heart so filled with pain and sadness that it was almost too much to bear. 'I think I feel that way, too. Just to know you are there; that you love me. I suppose I should not feel this way but the thought is so wonderfully comforting. I know I ought to tell you to forget me, find someone else. You should be married, Allan, and have children. It isn't too late. I would hate myself so if I were responsible for keeping you from such happiness.'

'Dearest Beverly, surely you know that no one else would do for me? Believe me, I don't want to get married, have children, just to ward off loneliness. I have lived and can live alone and be happy. That is true, you know. You see, my work is so much amongst others. I don't have a great deal of time to think about myself. I shan't be unhappy.'

And I? Beverly asked herself. Can I ever be happy again? What kind of future can there be for Jonnie and me? I can't love him or respect him, ever again. Has it always been like this, only I unaware of the truth? Has Jonnie always been weak? Must he always want what is forbidden? Perhaps that is *why* he married me; because my mother was so set against it.

But she knew that wasn't altogether true. They had been deeply in love in the beginning. They had discovered love together. They'd been so very young, so full of ideals and confidence.

Beverly realized with a sense of shock that if she were willing to forgive a second time; to forbear from reproaching him; to give him affection and a happy home, then their marriage could still go on. Perhaps love could no longer exist, but she could never be indifferent to Jonnie's well-being. She had lived with him, cared for him, considered him too long. She could not put him out of her life as if he had never existed.

'I must stay with him!' She spoke her thoughts aloud. 'I don't altogether understand why, Allan. I'd be justified this time in leaving him and going away with you. I think that is what I *want* to do. I could feel safe with you, certain about the future. This way there is no security.'

'Marriage means more than a few words spoken in church and a piece of paper saying it is legally done. You make vows, promises before God. That is why you cannot cast off those promises, darling. I wouldn't ask you to. Jonnie's failure to keep his vows doesn't excuse you from breaking your own. You'll find happiness in deciding this way, I'm sure of it. If you came to me, you'd feel guilty all your life.'

'You always understand!' Beverly said, with an immense gratitude in her heart for that understanding.

'That is because I love you!' Allan replied matter-of-factly. 'I think that helps me to know you, perhaps better than you know yourself. Beverly, had you thought what you want to do about the immediate future? This is Christmas Eve. Tomorrow you will want to be with the children.'

'Christmas!' Beverly echoed. 'I'd forgotten. I told Jonnie I'd go in and see him in the morning. What shall I do? Will Jonnie understand, or will he think I've chosen to be with the children because of what he told me tonight?'

'Can't you write him a letter, explaining?'

'I'm not sure he would understand.' She

paused, uncertain where her duty lay.

'Why not come home, spend the morning with the children, have lunch and then come back up here?' Allan suggested. 'I'm quite free tomorrow. If you like, I'd go in and spend the afternoon with them so they aren't disappointed. Annette could manage the twins.'

'Yes, yes, she could!' Beverly cried gratefully. 'Will you really do that, Allan? I'd be so grateful. And the children wouldn't mind my going if they knew you were going to stay with them. They all love you. You must come to lunch, too. I'm going to ring up the hospital now; ask the Ward Sister to tell Jonnie I won't be in until the afternoon.'

As soon as she had done so, Allan drove her home, stopping at the station so that she could pick up her own car. It was dark and deserted. No trains were running although the fog had cleared and the night was cold and starry. As Beverly stood by her own car to bid Allan good night, their breath was like smoke on the cold air.

'You'd better go, Beverly. You're shivering,' Allan said considerately, opening the car door for her.

'Yes!' she agreed, but did not move. 'But first I want to thank you, for so much, Allan. I don't know how I'd have got through this night without your help.'

Impulsively, she stood on tip-toe and lightly

265

kissed his cheek.

Every nerve in his body jerked with the swift rising desire to return her kiss; to hold her in his arms, show her with deeds, not words, how great was his love for her. She looked so young, so helpless, with her face turned in gratitude to his, her beautiful green eyes bewildered, as if life was proving too hard a task for her.

She couldn't know how provocative was that softly parted mouth, the gentle slope of her shoulders beneath the warm coat, the cloud of dark hair touched now with crystals of dew.

'I'm no better than Jonnie!' Allan told himself fiercely. 'I love her, I want her, and she's another man's wife. I dare not touch her, or I'll never let her go.'

'Good night!' he said harshly, abruptly, and turning on his heel, walked the few steps to his own car and hurriedly climbed in.

She stood a moment longer, staring after him, feeling already a sense of loss, loneliness at his going. Then, her heart beating in sudden knowledge, she guessed why he had gone so quickly from her.

Don't leave me! The words formed on her lips, an unbidden inarticulate cry from her heart. But they stayed unspoken, only half thought. And she, too, turned and climbed into her own car.

They drove off into the night, one behind the other until the road divided and each turned opposite ways. Only their thoughts remained together, each concerned with the other until, exhausted, they found release from torment in sleep.

*   *   *

Jonnie gave his wife a sheepish smile. He was sitting up in bed, more colour in his cheeks. He had seemed genuinely very pleased to see her.

'Jolly decent of you to come, Bev. Seeing it's Christmas and everything.'

Beverly deliberately ignored the last words. 'It's quite all right, Jonnie. I left Allan Forbes with the children and they didn't mind a bit. They sent their love and were, of course, thrilled to death to hear about the train accident.'

'Ghoulish little horrors!' Jonnie said, grinning. 'I suppose they were even glad I was in it! Were they pleased with their presents? What about you, Bev? Did you like my present to you?'

'I didn't open it!' Beverly said quietly. She hadn't wanted to. Any present from Jonnie would have seemed like a bartering; a bribe. But seeing the hurt disappointment on his face, she added: 'I thought I'd wait till you were home to see me open it. I've brought these things up for you.'

Jonnie took the parcels with enthusiasm and

tore off the paper wrappings as eagerly as Nick or Phil or Julia had done that morning. He commented on everything.

'Super!' he said when he had opened Beverly's present to him—a set of carpenter's tools he had been coveting for some time in a local ironmonger's window. 'Just what I wanted. You spoil me, Bev.'

She didn't answer. She felt tired and on edge and this visit to Jonnie had been far more of an effort than he knew. But he seemed on top of the world. It was hard to believe that he'd had quite a serious operation only a few hours ago.

'Tough! That's me!' he told her. 'The pretty little Irish night nurse said I was delirious last night and tried to kiss her—' He broke off, suddenly anxious in case Beverly should take this too seriously. But when she did not comment, he went on: 'I wish you'd find out how long I've got to stay here, Bev. I'm fed up with it already and I can't get the Doc to tell me anything. He just says "We'll see!" and that's that.'

'I'll try and find out. I expect they will want to know at the office when to expect you back. Mr Barkington phoned this morning and I told him you were here. He asked me to send his best wishes.'

'Oh, thanks!' Jonnie said. 'By the way, Bev, I wonder if you'd be a real sport and do something for me. I don't really like asking this, but obviously they won't let me near a phone for a while. Could you make a phone call for me?'

Beverly felt the colour rush to her cheeks. From the hesitant way Jonnie was asking her, she was in little doubt that it was Elinor he wanted her to ring up. How could he ask such a thing?

Seeing the flushed face and downcast eyes, Jonnie went on quickly:

'I know it's a beastly thing to ask you, Bev, but I thought if you did, you could tell her then that I meant what I said last night; that it was all over, I mean. I think she might believe it, coming from you. Then if she gets hysterical again, you'll know better than me how to deal with it.'

He behaves as if I were his mother, helping him out of a scrape! Beverly thought with astonishment. He doesn't realize what he is asking me to do.

'All right!' she said weakly. 'Give me the number and I'll ring on my way out.'

'You are a good sport, Bev,' Jonnie said thankfully. 'I can always count on you. I know I don't deserve it. I've behaved rottenly to you and I wouldn't blame you a bit if you said you'd had enough of it. Believe me, darling, I despise myself. If she hadn't come to my office, I'd never have got in touch with her. You do believe that, don't you?'

'Yes! I believe she made the first move. But

269

that doesn't exonerate you, Jonnie. You could have said "no".'

Jonnie scowled. 'It's all very well, Bev, but you don't know Elinor as well as I do. She just doesn't take "no" for an answer. Oh, I know I'm weak. But I never meant you to be hurt, Bev. There were lots of times I *tried* to break away. But it's really finished now. You do believe me?'

'I want to believe you!' Beverly said truthfully. 'I know you meant it to be the end, but you promised me it was all over before, when all the time—'

'No, it wasn't like that, Bev. I really did tell her it was all over. Then she came to see me at the office and it began again. Bev, you won't let it make any difference, will you? You don't want to divorce me?'

'No, I don't want a divorce!' It was all she could say with truth. It was bound, after all, to make a difference. It was Jonnie himself who had changed, at least in her eyes. He'd shown himself for exactly what he was, a Peter Pan, the little boy who would never grow up, on whom she could never depend. He was resilient, just as children are resilient. He'd forget about all this as soon as he knew she'd forgiven him. Things like unfaithfulness and lies and deceit were not important; his code was different from hers. He could even ask her to telephone Elinor for him. That more than anything showed her how incapable Jonnie was of understanding what Elinor had done with their lives. Any scheming woman could do as she pleased with Jonnie; he was weak, weak.

'Bev, you don't mind about ringing her. I can't help feeling responsible. Suppose she has done something awful. Last night was horrible; there was a ghastly scene. It was all so *unlike* her.'

'I don't doubt it!' Beverly said wryly. 'She put on a very good act, Jonnie, and you fell for it.'

'You mean, you think she was pretending to be suicidal?' Jonnie asked, visibly brightening. 'Gosh, I hope you're right, Bev. It isn't that I'd really care—at least, not much—about her, but I kept thinking of what the scandal would be like. It would be so awful for you and the children and at the office.'

Even in love you are selfish, half-hearted, Beverly thought. I'd have respected you more, Jonnie, if you'd really loved her. Then there might have been some excuse. Aloud, she said: 'Let's not talk about her any more, Jonnie. It's over and I want to—to forget. Tell me, how are you feeling? Does it hurt much? Did the doctor tell you what was wrong?'

'It isn't too bad,' Jonnie said, cheerful again now he could forget about Elinor. 'Bit of a mess inside, Doc said, but nothing he hasn't been able to put right. I was lucky. There were at least five other people in my carriage and three anyway were dead. I could see that

271

before I was dragged out.'

'It must have been horrible!' Beverly said shuddering. 'The papers are full of it and the radio, too. It's ruined so many families' Christmas. Somehow it's all the worse because of that.'

'I hate having to be away from you all too,' Jonnie said truthfully. 'I did want to see Nick's and Phil's faces when they opened the Hornby. I wanted to help them set up the track, too. I suppose Forbes is doing it for them.'

'Yes!' Beverly replied. After all, it wouldn't hurt Jonnie to be hurt just a little himself.

'Bev, I know you like the fellow. When I get home, would it make you happy if I try to make friends with him?'

Jonnie and Allan friends. No, it wasn't very possible even if Allan had been staying on. They were too unalike.

'Allan's going away; it's almost definite. I don't suppose we'll see much of him after these holidays are over.'

Hearing the sadness in her voice when she spoke of Forbes' departure, Jonnie took a closer look at his young wife.

'Bev, you're not in love with him, are you? Oh, I know I couldn't blame you if you were, after the way I've behaved. But I'd hate to think that you and—'

'No!' Beverly broke in sharply. 'There's nothing between us, Jonnie. We're just good friends. Now about tomorrow . . .' Quickly she changed the subject: 'Mother can't get down immediately so I won't be up for a couple of days. Once she arrives, well, I'll be in every day to visit you. Anything you want when I next come?'

'I don't think so,' Jonnie said. 'A few decent books, that's all. And look, darling, if it's difficult for you to trail up here every day, well, I won't expect to see you. I don't deserve it. You've been absolutely topping about everything and I'd like to make amends. I'll be all right. I'll be home anyway in a week with any luck, you'll see.'

But it was a month before Jonnie finally came home. He was very changed. Gone were the bright smile and the cheerful optimism. He was thin, irritable and very weak.

'I'm fed up with feeling lousy!' he said violently soon after his return. 'Those damned doctors don't know half as much as they pretend. X-ray after X-ray until I felt like a half-cooked goose. And still they don't seem to have got me fit.'

Beverly looked at him anxiously. 'You're sure you *should* be home, Jonnie?'

'Darn right, I'm sure. If I'd stayed another day in that place, I'd have gone crazy. Oh, they didn't want to let me out. But I'd had enough. Old Doc Massie knows as much as the whole bunch of them, specialists included. He'll get me fit. I told them so, too.'

'What is wrong with him?' Beverly asked

273

their family doctor, the kindly man who had brought all her children into the world. 'He seems to have got worse instead of better.'

'I had a full report from the hospital, Beverly. I'm afraid much of it is Jonnie's own fault. He's a hopeless patient. Men of his temperament often are, you know. About ten days after the operation, he got out of bed and had a haemorrhage. He wouldn't let them tell you, but I think you ought to know what we're up against. Of course, that set him back another few weeks. Instead of learning his lesson, he fretted and champed at the bit, driving everyone silly with his requests to come home. Well, you must have heard him yourself on visiting days. Then finally, he discharged himself. Of course, he isn't right yet. You can't have your insides knocked about like that and not feel the consequences. He'll be OK if he'd only rest, take things easy. You've got to help me, Beverly. Find some occupation for him he can do sitting down; anything to keep him off his feet.'

It wasn't easy. Jonnie seemed to a take a childish pleasure in getting up the moment her back was turned. When she caught him out, he would grin and tell her not to fuss. She had to restrain herself from a constant nagging to take care, take care. It became so that he regarded her in the same light as he had the hospital authorities.

'The trouble with you, Bev, is that you enjoy

274

keeping me chained to the apron strings. I suppose so long as I can't get out of the house, you feel you can trust me!'

'Jonnie!' Such a thought had not crossed her mind. Deep down, she did not think Jonnie meant it. There were many other hurtful things he said which she did not think he meant. But they lay in the air between them.

He was irritable with the children, too, shouting at them to keep quiet because his head hurt; the next minute telling them not to look like a bunch of stuffed sheep and to wake up and *do* something. They didn't know where they were with him and it became Beverly's especial task to try and protect them from their father's bad moods.

She felt desperately alone and over-burdened. Sue came in when she could but there was another baby on the way and Beverly did not feel she could worry the girl with her problems. Allan was still at the school, but he had not come to see them since Christmas. Knowing why, Beverly could not turn to him for the comfort, advice, friendship she knew would be hers for the asking.

But for Jonnie's 'good' days, she felt she might have been unable to bear it. But there were days when he was the old Jonnie, affectionate, grateful, understanding, apologetic. Then she would come close to loving him again. Pity for him was always uppermost in her feelings for him. He was often in pain and the days went by without any visible signs of his making any progress. Jonnie could never be patient and she knew how hard it was for him to sit still, day after day, week after week.

Mr Barkington had been extremely kind, keeping Jonnie on full pay so that they should not have any financial worries to add to their difficulties. Once he came to see Jonnie, making a special trip down from town. Jonnie had been surly and, afterwards, at his worst.

'Just wanted to make sure I wasn't faking!' he sneered at Beverly. 'Don't give me that "How kind of him!" any more. I know his sort.'

Because he was so restless in bed at night, Beverly had moved their double bed into the spare room and replaced it with twin beds. It had, in fact, been Jonnie's suggestion. But he seemed to have forgotten that. One night when neither was asleep, he said:

'Don't think I don't know why you won't share my bed any more. It isn't because of Elinor . . . oh no! It's because you're in love with Forbes!'

'Jonnie!' Beverly sat up in bed, holding the sheet against her throat. 'That's a lie and you know it. It was your idea, you know it was.'

Jonnie ignored this. 'Don't think I haven't noticed you mooning about the house with a face as long as a yard. You're thinking about him all the time, aren't you?'

'No!' The denial rose swiftly to her lips. 'If I have been looking unhappy, it is only because

276

I've been so worried about you. You're my husband, Jonnie. I want you to get well, to be fit and happy again.'

'If I only knew what was wrong!' Jonnie burst out, suddenly despairing and wretched.

In a moment, Beverly was out of her own bed, sitting on the edge of Jonnie's, stroking the hair from his forehead. Appalled, she felt his shoulders shaking and knew that he was crying.

'Darling, don't, don't!' she begged. 'You're going to be all right. Dr Massie said you could begin to walk around a bit next week. Be patient, darling. I know it isn't easy, but you're getting better. He promised me you were.'

'It's been three months, Bev . . . a quarter of a year.' Suddenly his arms were round her and she felt his cheek, wet against her own.

'You've been so wonderful to me. I wish I didn't hate myself so much. No, don't shake your head. Don't you think I've had a lot of time to think things over? Day after day I've had hours and hours to think about the mess I've made of your life and mine. Do you think Elinor would have cared for me the way you have? Nursed me, put up with my rotten temper and grumbling? No, she'd have left me to get on with it. No man ever had a better wife, Bev. I know that now.'

Those few moments Beverly clung to long afterwards. They made it all worthwhile, the hurt, the humiliation, the loneliness, the bitterness, the tiredness. She was glad at last with her whole heart that she hadn't divorced him. Jonnie needed her and, for as long as he wanted her, she was his wife.

* * *

'Back to work next week,' Jonnie said cheerfully as he walked through the French windows into the garden and stood for a moment, watching Phil bowl to Nicky at the far end of the lawn. Summer had come and there were delphiniums, lupins, pinks in full bloom all along the border. The birds were singing their usual mad chorus and there was real warmth in the sun for the first time this year.

'It'll be difficult sitting down at an office desk after so long,' Beverly said, smiling.

'Oh well, do me good really. I'm getting fat and lazy,' Jonnie said, his arm round Beverly's shoulders. 'Besides, I do owe it to old Barkington, don't I? Six months on full pay. Pretty decent of him.'

'Let's sit down for a bit!' Beverly said, pointing to the iron bench beneath the copper beech. 'It's so nice and warm.'

Obediently, Jonnie sat down beside her. He was watching the boys.

'Nick shows promise,' he said contentedly. 'I must give him some practice this summer; make a really good cricketer out of him. And

278

you know, Bev, I've quite changed my opinion of Phil. I used to think he was growing up a bit of a sissy, but this morning, he was up the top of that apple tree like a cat—far higher than Nick went. Where are the girls?'

'Out for a walk with Annette,' Beverly said, closing her eyes to the warm sunshine, feeling relaxed and happy.

Suddenly Jonnie bent and kissed her on the mouth—a lover's kiss which brought the colour into Beverly's cheeks.

'Pretty girl!' he said, smiling. 'Prettiest and nicest girl in the world. I love you next best to Julia and those fat little scamps. We've been lucky, haven't we, Bev? With our kids, especially.'

He leant back, reaching up his arms to stretch them above his head in lazy contentment. Quite suddenly, he gave a little gasp and his arms swung down to clasp his stomach.

'Oh, God!' he whispered. 'Something snapped, I'm sure of it. Ring the doc, Bev!'

White-faced, Beverly tore indoors to the telephone. Within five minutes, she was racing back across the lawn, her heart beating with an appalling fear. Jonnie was slumped across the garden seat so that she could not see his face.

Kneeling beside him, she lifted his head and looked into his eyes.

'Jonnie! Jonnie!' Frantically, she slapped his cheek—anything to make him move, look at her properly, tell her where it hurt. Down at the far end of the lawn, the boys played on with their game of cricket, unaware.

'Jonnie!' But she knew then, quite suddenly, that it wasn't any good calling him. He wouldn't answer her, now or ever. He was dead.

'You're out!'

'I'm not!'

'You were. It was l.b.w.'

'It wasn't . . . oh, all right. I quite like bowling anyway. I'll soon bowl you out.'

'You won't!'

'Bet I will!'

'Beverly! Come, my dear. You must help me to get him indoors before the children notice.'

'Doc! Doc, he's dead! Jonnie's dead. Why? Why?'

'Never mind now. Help me to get him in. Do you understand? You must help me get him to bed before Nick and Phil find out.'

'Yes, yes, I'll help!' Beverly said.

They carried him to his room and Beverly slumped into the chair beside his bed, holding his hand. Doc was downstairs on the phone. Presently Annette came in with a cup of tea.

'The doctor says you must come down now, Madame.'

'No, I must stay with him. He needs me. He's always hated being alone.'

Presently there was another voice—Allan's.

'Beverly? Come away, darling. Please.'

It was a kind, gentle voice.

'But, Allan, I can't. He needs me.'

'No, not any more. Come with me.'

'Why?' Beverly asked as she allowed him to lead her away. 'I must know, Allan. He was so well, so happy, so pleased to be alive. Why? I have to know why?'

When she woke up from the stiff sleeping draught Dr Massie had given her, Allan was there beside the bed. For a moment, she could not understand what he was doing there or why she was in the spare room. She knew only that she was terribly glad to see him. Then slowly, sickeningly, memory returned. With it came tears of shock, unbelief, grief.

He held her tightly in his arms, rocking her to and fro like a child. He had been appalled at the change in her since he had last seen her at Christmas. She had lost at least a stone in weight and although she was not yet thirty, there were lines round her eyes, grooved into her forehead. These six months had taken their toll. Downstairs, while she slept, the doctor had told him something about her life these last months. Only in the last two weeks had Jonnie begun to behave like a rational human being. Up till then, he had made life pretty much of a hell for Beverly and the children. She'd never complained, but none knew better than Dr Massie what kind of patient Jonnie had been. Beverly was physically as well as mentally completely exhausted.

'I've been expecting a nervous breakdown any day,' the doctor said. 'How she kept going, I don't know. I'm afraid this shock will just about finish her. Try to make it easy for her when she comes round.'

It was Annette, surprisingly, who had told Dr Massie to send for Allan. Returning from her walk, she had taken the news of Jonnie's death with her usual calm acceptance. She answered Dr Massie's questions quietly and told him that she thought Madame might prefer to have her good friend Mr Forbes to assist her in this difficult time.

'Very nice man!' Annette said in her halting English. 'Madame tell me very good man, very kind.'

'Yes, of course. He's the schoolmaster who teaches Nick and Phil, doesn't he?' agreed Dr Massie.

When Forbes arrived, the doctor had given him a brief account of what had transpired. 'We must send for her mother, of course, but I know she lives in town and it will take a little while before she arrives. Meanwhile, I have a lot to see to. Can you stay with Mrs Colt? She can't be left alone.'

'Of course I'll stay,' Allan said at once. He was deeply shocked by the news. It wasn't as if Jonnie had been ill. Only yesterday Nick had told him his father was returning to work after the weekend. Now he was dead.

'Allan, what can have happened? It's unbelievable. He was telling me how fond of us all he was, and then, suddenly, he gasped and by the time I came back from the telephone he was dead.'

'We don't know why, Beverly. But they'll find out. Try to be happy about the way he went, suddenly, and when, as you say, he was so happy. That's a good way to die if die you must. He couldn't have suffered or known what was happening.'

But he knew his words were of little comfort in this hour of shock and horror. He let her cry, holding her in his arms, feeling the deepest love and tenderness for her, thanking God that *he* had been called in to help when she most needed him.

Within an hour, she was asleep once more and he went quickly downstairs to telephone Beverly's mother. Having done this, he went into the sitting-room where Annette was reading a story to the children as if this was a quite ordinary day. They would have to be told soon. Jonnie's body would be taken to the hospital for a post mortem; the ambulance would call; the phone would be ringing. Already they had sensed something had happened for the boys jumped up and ran to him as he stood in the doorway.

'Where's Mum?' Nick asked. 'Isn't she well?'

'Is something the matter with Daddy again?'

Phil asked. 'Why was Dr Massie here?'

Perhaps it would be best to wait and let Beverly's mother tell them, yet somehow he felt that he might be able to do it better, less emotionally.

He sat down and, taking Julia on his lap, he said, 'I'm going to tell you a story.'

'Oh good!' said Nick, curling up at Allan's feet. 'Indians?'

'No! It's about a king and queen and their five children.'

'Go on and begin!' ordered Julia from the safe circle of Allan's arms.

'Well, this king and queen lived very happily. They had five children, two princes and three princesses. They loved their children very much. One day, the king became ill. Of course, the queen was very worried about him because she loved him very much and she knew the king hated being ill. She nursed him herself and the five children were as good as they could possibly be to make things easier for the household.'

'But the king got better, didn't he?' Nick broke in, somehow sensing something familiar about this tale although he could not recall Allan having told it before.

'Yes, Nick. The king got better and the queen and her children were very glad. But although the king looked better and felt better and everyone *thought* he was quite well, deep down inside he wasn't. One day, he went into

284

the garden with the queen and they sat down on a seat in the sunshine. The king was very happy, because he didn't know he wasn't really well after all. He could see the two little princes playing together and he thought proudly how big they had grown and what fine sensible boys they were. Then he fell asleep. When the queen tried to wake the king, she found she could not do so. She called the doctor and he told her that the king would never wake up again. You see, he'd gone to live in another Kingdom where people are always well and always happy, and he liked it so much, he decided to stay.'

'But what about the queen and the five children?' Phil asked in a small querulous voice.

'Well, of course they were very sad. But the queen had the two brave princes and the oldest of the princesses to comfort her. The princes said they would take care of her and fight all her enemies. So she was not quite alone. And the five children had the beautiful queen to love them and take care of them, so they were not alone either. And as they all knew that the king would be very very happy in this new Kingdom, they tried not to be sad because he had gone away.'

'I don't think I like that story!' Julia said, holding tight to Allan's neck with two chubby arms. 'It's sad.'

'I don't like you!' Nick said suddenly. 'I

285

think you're silly!' He turned, scowling, and ran out of the room.

Phil looked at Allan apprehensively. 'Aren't you going to punish him, Mr Forbes, for being rude?'

'No!' said Allan. 'You see, he didn't mean to be rude. He wanted to hurt me because I had had to hurt him. Nick guessed who the king and the queen really were.'

'Well, I guessed *that!*' said Phil uneasily. 'It's Mummy and Daddy. But it isn't true, is it? I mean, Daddy's not really gone away.'

'Yes, yes, he has!' Allan said very gently.

'*You're* not going, too, are you?' Phil said, suddenly afraid.

'No, I'm not going, Phil. I'll be here whenever you or Nick or Julia or Mummy need me.'

'Oh well, that's all right then,' Phil said, comforted.

'Do you love me, Uncle Allan?' Julia asked, half asleep.

'Yes!' said Allan. 'I do.'

'Will you marry me when I'm big enough?'

'No! You're a princess and you have to marry a nice young prince.'

'All right!' agreed Julia. 'But you've got to be the king.'

'I hope so!' Allan barely breathed the words as he laid his cheek against the child's soft hair. 'I hope so, Julia, with all my heart.'

We hope you have enjoyed this Large Print book. Other Chivers Press or Thorndike Press Large Print books are available at your library or directly from the publishers.

For more information about current and forthcoming titles, please call or write, without obligation, to:

Chivers Large Print
published by BBC Audiobooks Ltd
St James House, The Square
Lower Bristol Road
Bath BA2 3BH
UK
email: bbcaudiobooks@bbc.co.uk
www.bbcaudiobooks.co.uk

OR

Thorndike Press
295 Kennedy Memorial Drive
Waterville
Maine 04901
USA
www.gale.com/thorndike
www.gale.com/wheeler

All our Large Print titles are designed for easy reading, and all our books are made to last.